This is a work of fiction. Names, characters, places, locations and others are products of the authors imagination or are used fictitiously and are not to be construed as real. Any resemblance to actual events, locals, organizations or persons, living or dead is entirely coincidental.

The Gifted

A Berkley Book / published by
arrangement with the author

All Rights Reserved

Copyright © 2024 by Bruce Michael Osborn

No part of this book shall be used or reproduced in any manner whatsoever without written permission, except in the case of brief quotations embodied in critical articles and/or reviews.

The Berkley Publishing Group, a division
Of Penguin Putnam Inc.

ISBN: 9798332995606

Acknowledgment

A special thank you to Teri J. Shusterman without whose continued support, instruction in life, and friendship this work would not have been possible.

Additional consideration is given to Catherine (Renee) Peterson whose unfailing pursuit of original thought prompted this work.

Preface

Mr. and Mrs. Tetherspoon, of such a place now so-called Badminton, found themselves in an unusual situation. They were deep, you see, into the process of determining something rather important, and in doing so, they may have wondered off course, just a fraction leaving those imposed upon to wonder what it might be that the Tetherspoons were setting about to do.

To the Tetherspoons' mind, their behaviors were of course nothing so mysterious or socially awkward that one would expect them to be no less prone than others to declare that they were but simple, proper folk.

Yet, to their neighbors, who held fast to the notion that moving about beyond ones' socially accepted limits of habitation might not indeed be considered proper. To them, the Tetherspoons posed somewhat of a nuisance.

The Tetherspoons were, of course, nothing of the sort.

Proper, that is.

But the introduction of the Tetherspoons is meant for another time. We have important details to discuss at length, so I find it best that we begin.

Off we go, then, into the tale of a most unusual and precocious child with the rudely given name of Elzibeth. A name not found to be as polite or kind as others such as Elizabeth, Liz, Lisa or Liza. But Elzibeth.

No pretense was taken in the naming of young Elzibeth. Her name, of course, was given in keeping with the traditions of the Order, who roundly appreciated and accepted such a name, for it is considered by those in the know to be as unusual as the little girl for which it was deemed appropriate.

Nonetheless, here we stand with young Elzibeth seeking to determine of which and where she belonged, which puzzled her as she was yet unsure as to whether she belonged at all.

You see, finding oneself is not so much an understanding of self, as it is a gift. Yet, no such understanding bothers to include the soul. It is the soul of the one to whom special gifts are granted that such ferocity of predisposition resides.

We begin our introduction of young Miss Elzibeth at the address of one Finias Shoop, who resides presently, though quite temporarily, within the confines of 1/2 Humbleton Place.

You see, Finias, it was decided, is to take on the task of the keeper of young Elzibeth. Not a small task, but one in concert with his nature, for Finias is a kind man at heart, and after some debate, it has become evident to the members of the High Council that the trouble brewing ahead was of a kind not to be fought as a battle but to be won through a spirit of decency of the heart... and ferocity of the soul.

Finias was soon to be paid a visit by two of the most unusual of people. Tetherspoon would be a name he would not forget.

Contents

Acknowledgement i
Preface ii
Chapter 1 1
Chapter 2 4
Chapter 3 8
Chapter 4 12
Chapter 5 20
Chapter 6 23
Chapter 7 29
Chapter 8 35
Chapter 9 41
Chapter 10 48
Chapter 11 53
Chapter 12 56
Chapter 13 58
Chapter 14 66
Chapter 15 70
Chapter 16 76
Chapter 17 82
Chapter 18 92
Chapter 19 99
Chapter 20 102
Chapter 21 105
Chapter 22 112
Chapter 23 116
Chapter 24 121

Chapter 25 131
Chapter 26 135
Chapter 27 141
Chapter 28 150
Chapter 29 158
Chapter 30 160
Chapter 31 166
Chapter 32 169
Chapter 33 172
Chapter 34 174
Chapter 35 181
Chapter 36 185
Chapter 37 192
Chapter 38 194
Chapter 39 195
Chapter 40 199
Chapter 41 208
Chapter 42 214
Chapter 43 220
Chapter 44 225
Chapter 45 232
Chapter 46 240
Chapter 47 244
Chapter 48 250
Chapter 49 257
Chapter 50 261
Chapter 51 269

Chapter 52 275

Chapter 53 278

Chapter 54 281

Chapter 56 284

Chapter 57 289

Chapter 58 293

Chapter 59 296

Chapter 1

A slight knock at the door of Finias Shoop's humble home bothered him awake. It was late, and in keeping with his nightly ritual of a small imbibe prior to sleep, he had dozed in front of a warming fire in the comfort of his home while settled into his favorite chair.

Sensing nothing amiss, he settled back into his chair and was drifting off to sleep when, again, came the same faint knock.

The knock, or so he thought, was so light that it seemed as if it were from a child. A small hand or a neighborly trick of which he was not certain. Internally, he questioned the need to answer, when again came the same faint knock.

Curios now, he moved to the door with caution and shouted, "I'll know if this is a trick, you little hooligans. Please leave me be."

The response was the same faint knock. "Blimey, what business is this?" he spoke to himself under his breath.

Now at the door, he opened it just a crack to peer outside.

Suddenly, a small shoe shot forward and became wedged between the door and frame. White with pink laces and the outline of a Nike swoosh. Taken aback, Finias could only watch as the little foot began easing itself further into his home, accompanied by a tiny hand now firmly established on the door's leading edge.

"Mr. Smoosh, is that you?"

"Smoosh? What? Wait, what? Who are you, and why are you here?" Finias asked, startled.

The door pushed open a bit, and Finias stood aghast, for standing in the door's frame was a child of no more than six years of age.

Rubbing his eyes as if to clear the remains of the toot he had toddled into his tea, he again looked down and said, "What?"

"Okay, so we've established all that who and what stuff," Elzibeth said. "Now, are you going to let me in or not?"

Elzibeth moved purposefully through. She stood before Finias and offered a small hand.

"My name is Elzibeth Mankin, and I'm your charge. And please don't begin with 'Who,' 'Wait,' or 'What?' It's late for me to be up, and I'm beat. And frankly, if I may say so, it's kind of annoying," she said.

Finias began to say just those things, then caught himself. He stood for a moment, unsure of what to do next, as he took in the sight of this adorable child with an oddly strange name. Sensing something beyond his immediate understanding, he asked, "My charge, you say?"

"Yes, I'm your charge, and I would appreciate your shaking my hand in response."

"Oh, yes, of course, indeed," Finias said, taking her tiny hand in his. "Would it be too much trouble for me to ask what this is all about?"

"Not at all," Elzibeth said. "In the morning. Right now, I'm tired, and as your charge, I hope that you find it suitable that I stay here until such time."

Finias, having been caught off guard and who hadn't quite cleared the nap from his head, said, "I, I've not made arrangements for a charge."

"I don't think you have to make arrangements for a charge. Do you?" She asked, turning her face up to Finias with a questioning look.

Finias began stammering again while looking around as if lost in a dream. "I, I, don't really know. It seems like the right thing to do, one would think, but then again, you did come unexpectedly." Finias had said this out loud but meant mostly to question himself.

"If, um, it would be suitable for a 'charge', the, um, sofa by the fire is quite comfortable."

"That will do. Good night, mister Sloop," Elzibeth said.

And just like that, Elzibeth made her way to the sofa, and to Finias's somewhat surprise, she looked soon to be fast asleep.

"It's Shoop," began Finias. "Oh, never mind. Here, this should do nicely," he said as he covered her with the blanket from his chair. Settle in for now, but be aware that come tomorrow I will be in need of additional information," Finias said, by way of goodnight.

Elzibeth turned her small head from the back of the sofa and, with one eye open, gave Finias a look. "Of course," came her reply as if expected, causing Finias to turn slightly and glance back at her as he began ascending the stairs.

"Well, goodnight then to you, Miss Charge."

Chapter 2

During the night, Finias's sleep was restless, as his dreams, it seemed, were not of his making, as they involved a somewhat overly determined little girl dressing him down as Mr. Smoop, or Floop, or something, and her pushing her way into his home.

Finias moved to the closet then came about in a suit of comfortable clothing, and headed downstairs to fix himself breakfast. "Maybe a healthy helping of bangers and mash," he thought. "Yes, something stout to begin the day after a bit of an anxious night."

Moving into the hall toward the stairs, he became aware of the faint smell of sausage.

"Must be my imagination," he mumbled as he made his way down the remaining steps.

As he did so, the living room came into view, and as he looked to the sitting area, he noticed that his quilt had been moved from his chair to the sofa.

"Odd," he believed. "Surely, I would not have fallen asleep downstairs." "No matter," thought Finias, "I'll just fold her away and be on with breakfast."

Hearing his footsteps coming close, Elzibeth gave a good morning greeting of "Hey, Mr. Goop. How do you like your eggs?"

"Oy, what? Who is there? Show yourself, or I will call the authorities!" Finias shouted.

"I don't think the authorities will be much interested in how you like your eggs, Mr. Bloop," Elzibeth said, with a smile.

As if in slow motion, the prior night's events began to crystallize in Finia's mind. The knock, the shoe, the hand, and the push of the door. A little girl giving him the business and, frankly, bossing him into a place on his sofa. The quilt, the fire, the foot in the door, the hand, the pink laces with a Nike swoosh. It was all coming back to him now, and he wasn't sure how to proceed other than to...well, proceed.

Settling into a cautious rhythm, Finias carefully placed one foot after the other as he made his way down the last few steps, then into the kitchen.

There, on a step stool, was an improbable little girl stirring eggs on the stove. She wore jeans and a white top, and yes, there they were—white tennies with pink laces.

Finias stopped in his tracks as he took in the scene.

Sensing he was near, Elzibeth turned and said, "I hope you like scrambled because I just made a mess of trying to fry these things off a step stool."

Stupefied does not begin to address the state of mind of Finias Shoop at that moment. He took a careful step forward and said aloud, "You're real."

"Real ain't the word for it, Mr. Stoop. I don't know what I am yet, and that is what I am here to find out."

"To find out, you say?" Suddenly, Finias understood. Astonished, he was not sure how to continue. There were procedures in place through the Order for such things, and nothing had been brought to his attention. This was highly unusual, and Finias, being a cautious man, was unsure of just how to, well, proceed.

Under the current circumstances, Finias, having been found to be caught off guard by this... little girl, decided to question carefully.

"So, um, Elzibeth, is it? Would it be too bold of me to ask if you believe that you are something other than what you are not? You understand my meaning, of course." Finias said, though obviously still confused by the events of the morning.

Elzibeth, now with humor on her face, turned and said, "No, Mr. Droop, being something other than what I'm not would be just being what I am, right? If you are asking if I am one of the chosen, I suppose so. I don't really know. If you mean that I can do things with my mind that others my age can't seem to or want to, I guess that would be accurate."

Finias was stunned by this admission. That this little girl standing on a step stool in his kitchen might well be the "Chosen One."

Not knowing what to say, or more precisely, what not to say, he simply went on, "Accurate, you say. A fine vocabulary for someone so young. Would you mind if I asked you your age?"

"Of course not silly. I'm six and a half. I mean, it's not like you are asking someone old enough to not want to answer."

"Yes, no, of course not... I mean. You are correct," Finias said.

"Mr. Poop, can I ask you something?"

"Only if I can ask you something when you finish."

"Deal. Okay, so here I am standing on this stool messing up these eggs, and I'm wondering why you are just standing there rather than helping?"

"My standing here? Oh, yes, of course. How shall I assist?" Finias said.

"Grab me that platter over there," directed Elzibeth.

Finias handed her the platter.

"Now, take the sausages warming in the oven and plate them, please."

Finias did as instructed and instinctively knew to set them on the counter next to Elzibeth so that she could add the eggs.

"Put the platter on the table there and add some plates and stuff, and let's set down to eat," Elzibeth said, in a manner belying her age.

Finias did so, but not before asking, "Coffee, tea, or, perhaps, chocolate milk?"

"Is that the question you were holding in reserve to ask me, Mr. Croup?" Elzibeth said.

"It's... Look, no. My question is, why have you not once called me by my proper name? It's Shoop, by the way," Finias said.

"I know... It was just more fun to watch you get all clenched up when I called you Mr. Poop," Elzibeth said, smiling.

Chapter 3

After breakfast, Finias cleared the table and made do with the dishes. When finished, he found Elzibeth standing in front of the fire, seemingly entrenched in either its warmth or some other detail of which Finias was unsure.

Not knowing what enthralled her so, Finias came around and found himself a place in his chair and said, "Elzibeth, would you do me the courtesy of telling me what is on your mind? Not long-term, in a moment for that. I just can't help but wonder what might be on the mind of a child your age having come to my door; having made us breakfast, which was delicious by the way, having slept on my couch, and now you are either curious about the flames and how they dance or something I've not yet thought."

Finias was sure the answer was to be in the order of "What now? How do we move forward from here? Where is my family? Why am I alone, at six years of age, in a strange man's home, searching for life's answers? Or why me?" Something to that effect. The answer she gave was so unexpected that Finias could not help but wonder.

"What holds up your mantel piece?" she asked.

"My what?" asked Finias louder than was necessary, having been caught off guard by the strange question.

"Please, not that again. You know, the 'what' thing," Elzibeth said.

"Sorry. No. So, yes, the mantel. What do you suppose?" Finias said.

"Magic of some sort," answered Elzibeth.

"Magic, you say," Finias said, feeling again the strange pangs of doubt as to how to continue. "You know, there is no such thing as magic. But, if there were, how do you suppose magic would come into play with something as unassuming as a mantel piece?"

"First, I don't know that at all, and second, it's really simple. There is no visible means of support. Something that large can't just hang out in space, so it must be magic," Elzibeth said, proudly turning to smile up at Finias.

The mantel itself, eight feet of hardwood white oak, three inches thick, long as a ladder, and more than a foot deep, appeared to simply cantilever straight away from the wall.

"Well, young lady, I'm afraid you are both right and wrong," Finias said. "The mantel itself is held in place by physical forces you cannot see. The magic behind it is sitting in this chair."

"I thought you said there is no such thing as magic," came her reply.

"Well, magic was just a poor choice of words on my part. What I meant was that there is a bit of deception involved with the craftsmanship."

"Show me," came her reply.

"I'm afraid that would not be possible without dismantling it in its entirety," Finias said, slightly alarmed.

Suddenly, as Finias watched in horror, it was as if the entire process of its placement was being reversed. The surrounding wall began to fade away as if a dream played back, and slowly, the substructure was revealed and the horizontal to vertical attachments exposed. One by one, the bolted segments hidden behind the wall detached themselves, and the mantel was laid on the floor.

Finias was both beside himself at the prospect of the destruction of something he had so carefully crafted and enthralled by the beauty of its deconstruction. The entire process seemed ethereal, ghostly, and supernatural, yet he was unafraid because it was at that moment that he knew the reality of his Charge.

"So, I don't suppose you could put that back?" The question came as one might ask a neighbor if they could borrow a cup of sugar.

Elzibeth turned and looked at Finias with tears in her eyes. She stood rooted to her spot, a tiny little girl whose life had been upended, and she began to sob.

"I'm sorry," she cried. "I didn't mean to do it. I just thought, and it came apart. I'm so sorry."

Then tiny Elzibeth ran from the room and through the front door.

Finias lept from his chair and followed.

"Elzibeth, come back. It's no big deal. Come on. Come back, and you and I will put it back together. Then you can see the truly magical part. With me."

Finias was sure he would catch her within a few yards of his home, but as he left the porch, she was nowhere to be seen.

Suddenly, the sky, which had mostly cleared overnight, began to cloud over. A swirling black mist swept the street, and abruptly, Finias could see only a few feet in front of him. It was impossible to know in which direction Elzibeth might have run, just as it was impossible to know in which direction he was facing. It was as if the world itself was lost to him as he drowned in the sea of fog.

Panic set in, and he raced forward, screaming at the top of his lungs. Knowing now that this was not a storm, he gave chase into the darkness that surrounded him, only to run smack into his mailbox, knocking him to the ground. Though painful, this at least gave him a landmark and a sense of where the street ahead would lay. He continued his pursuit into nothingness, his hopes fading with each anxious stride as he ran blindly into oblivion.

Chapter 4

As if awakening from a dream, Finias suddenly found himself at home in his chair in front of his fireplace. Outside, the black fog had lifted, yet he remained damp with its dew. He had no recollection of events after entering the fog other than calling for Elzibeth, and now he found himself seated comfortably at home facing two unfamiliar faces.

Seated across from him on his sofa was an attractive couple, with Elzibeth sandwiched between them, seemingly at ease in a very odd and somewhat uncomfortable situation.

"So, hello," began the chap to Elzibeth's right.

"Hello," Finias said, somewhat dumbfounded by the recent turn of events.

He could think of nothing to offset the oddity of the moment, so he simply said, "Um, so, I suppose the three of you are from the Order."

"Yes, very astute of you, young man," said the chap with a smile.

"Then, to what do I owe my discomfort with your sitting on my sofa?" Finias said.

"Yes, right. I suppose it is best that we get along with things straight away. My name is Theodore Tetherspoon, and this is my wife, Teri. You, of course, have met this little darling, Elzibeth."

"It would seem to me that Elzibeth was sent here to meet me," Finias said.

"That is correct, and the point is well made. Would you mind if I had a look around before we go too far into this? It might save us a little time and a spot of trouble," Theodore said.

"Look around at what? The big hole in my wall? My mantel lying on the floor. What is it you intend to be doing here, if I may be so bold as to ask, Mister, what is it...Tetherball?"

"Hah, that's a good one, but no. It's Tetherspoon. Teri and I are here to see to it that you might make an appropriate surrogate for our little Elzibeth."

Finias, now confused, was forced to ask the obvious. "Is Elzibeth your daughter?"

"That's correct," Theodore said.

Finias had been too upset, what with his eggs being scrambled, not fried, bangers but no mash, and his mantel creation departed to see the logic in what had transpired.

"Surrogate, you say," was all he could think of as he stared at the floor in contemplation of what this might mean.

"Her Keeper, to be more accurate," Theodore said.

"Her Keeper?"

"That is correct."

"I have more questions regarding that, but first, if I may be so bold as to ask, do you know the meaning of that awful black fog? It simply appeared the moment Elzibeth left the premises," Finias said.

"Yes, well, it's a bit complicated, and better answers are yet to come. I will tell you this for now. There are dark forces at work. Very dark forces indeed, and they will stop at nothing in their quest for power. Young Elzibeth maintains a special set of gifts that, as of yet, no others are known to possess. These gifts are a threat to that power, so once Elzibeth left the premises, her departure from a protected structure signaled both Teri and I, and unfortunately, the darker side of gifted folk, that she was unprotected. You see, they wish to put an end to those special gifts, if you get my meaning. So, good for us for being Johnny on the spot, then, don't you think?" finished Theodore.

Elzibeth, still seated on the couch and having listened to this, seemed very much at peace with things, considering she had recently run out the door crying. She looked, in fact, entirely normal, all things considered.

After overhearing the conversation between her father and Finias, she offered, "I'm sorry about your mantel piece, Mr. Shoop. If I thought hard enough, I think I could put it back."

And that was all. There was no mention of the dark side wishing to obliterate her and her special gifts.

Finias could not help but smile at the child. There was something oddly adult about her, and yet, there was a hint that underneath her mature manner, there was a playfulness waiting to break free from what was expected of her.

"Don't worry about the mantel, Elzibeth," Finias said. "I assume that at the conclusion of this little meeting, the two of us shall be spending quite a bit of time together doing such things, gifted or not, in the near future."

"Terrific old chap," Theodore said, to nobody's consideration. All the attention of the remaining parties seemed to be focused on the floor.

"So, anyway, off we go then," Theodore said, who then stood and turned as if to leave before Finias had a chance to bring home the point that he didn't know exactly what it was that he was to do, for how long, and for goodness' sake, most importantly, why him.

"Wait just a bloody moment, Mr. Threshold."

"It's Tetherspoon."

"Whatever. Look, I need some answers. Like, what kind of name is Tetherspoon anyway? I thought Elzibeth's last name was Mankin," Finias said.

"That would be correct, sir. Tetherspoon is simply a moniker adopted in a time of need for Teri and I. You see, in the Order, it is often necessary in the realm of gifted people to simply disappear and reestablish. Common fare for a gifted folk, is it not Mr. Shoop?" Theodore said.

Finias looked Theodore square in the eye and said, "I wouldn't know, now would I? It seems that your beloved Order has overlooked my progress these last few years."

"Is that so, you say? Well, I shall have to have a look into that. It wouldn't be right to have our gifted daughter, so impressed with you by the way, protected by someone with no gifted abilities," Theodore said.

"Yes, you do that," Finias said, with obvious disdain, having been overlooked in the granting of gifted powers.

"Do me a favor, old man, and hand me that dish towel by the sink. It seems that I have a bit of dew left across my collar after having chased young Elzibeth, and yourself, I might add, into that dreadful black fog," Theodore said.

"Sure," Finias said, having followed Theodore as they moved to the kitchen.

Finias then turned from the sink, towel in hand, and projected in his mind's eye it shooting vigorously toward this strange man's handsome face. And to his surprise, that is indeed what happened.

Theodore appeared not to have paid attention and was, in fact, looking at the pair on the couch when the cloth sailed toward him. Without notice and without looking, he simply plucked it from the air, and having completed the task of wiping down his collar, he asked, "Teri, do either you or Elzibeth require a cloth?"

Finias was stunned. Did what just happened truly happen? Had he made the cloth sail simply by thinking it so?

"Very well then, did you have anything else to consider, Mr. Shoop, before my wife and I depart your humble home?" Theodore said.

"Yes, I have many things to consider. The first being, How did I do that?" Finias said.

"Yes, about that. Good show, my man. And a fair question. You see, when you answered the door last night and gave comfort to our little girl, it was deemed by the Order that you were sufficiently self-aware to now become. So, I suppose congratulations are in order from the Order so to speak," Theodore said.

Not knowing quite how to respond, Finias simply said, "Well, um, thanks, I guess."

"Now, Mr. Shoop, for a bit of instruction. You and Elzibeth will be leaving this home, displaced mantel and all, at 12:00 p.m. sharp, as you are expected at your new quarters in Briarwood. You may want to begin packing shortly, as you and our dear Elzibeth shall be transported there immediately on the strike. You wouldn't want to be caught in your skivvies now, would you?" joked Theodore. All answers to further questions or matters will be handled at the appropriate time. Now, we truly must be going. We will be in to check on the two of you from time to time, so fret not."

And with that, Teri and Theodore disappeared.

"But wait!" Finias shouted, but it was of no use, as the pair had simply vanished.

Elzibeth, apparently taking things in stride as if this were an everyday occurrence, said without concern, "You might want to get a move on Mr. Plop. It's quarter till."

"Please just call me Finias. Not Mr. Smoop or Mr. Plop. Just Finias."

"Very well, then, Finias. Times a wastin," Elzibeth said, pointing at the clock.

Finias was not sure what to do next. How does one pack an entire house in fifteen minutes? The obvious answer is that one cannot. So, he simply went upstairs, pulled an old trunk from the cupboard, and began shoveling in whatever came to mind.

Elzibeth, for her part, thought they were short on time, so she decided to lend a hand.

Suddenly, in the middle of the sitting room, a great chest appeared, and all the things necessary for Mr. Shoop to feel comfortable in what was to be their new home disappeared from sight and found their place in the depths of the chest.

Finias, having reached for his shaving kit, found that it was now gone from his hand, as he had suddenly noticed everything else in his room.

"What in goodness blazes is going on here?" he shouted to no one.

Elzibeth, having heard him, said, "Don't worry, Mr. Snoop, it's all down here."

"Finias, just call me Finias. Merlin's beard," Finias mumbled.

Finias descended the stairs to find that his old trunk had been transformed into a giant chest, with Elzibeth standing by, smiling as if to say, "See, that wasn't so hard."

"So, I suppose that if you could conjure a giant chest within which contains all my worldly possessions, it would be fair to say that you might give me some insight into the whereabouts of this Briarwood?" Finias said.

"It's in Briarwood, silly," Elzibeth said.

"Is that a place or a location?" asked Finias.

"It's both. You sure ask a lot of strange questions, Mr. Shoop," Elzibeth said.

"Please, just Finias."

"Very well. Finias. I had supposed you would be up to speed on such things," Elzibeth said.

"Well, you supposed wrong. I'm not up to speed on anything at the moment, so it seems. Tell me, young lady, as you have the upper hand here, would it be fair to suggest that this... this circumstance was not a surprise to you?" Finias said.

"Of course not. Mum and dad have been researching others as a suitable Keeper for me for a rather long time and have been annoying the heck out of the neighbors."

"Yes, well. That goes without saying. Not that I find your mum and dad annoying, per se. Rather, they are a bit intrusive."

"Yeah, I guess that's part of their job, from what little I hear. I do know that they have been here on several occasions, observing you once you were decided. Dad thought it best to suggest we 'take a look around' to see if things were fit as a way of not letting on, but yeah, the truth, Mr. Shoop, is that this circumstance, I think you called it, has been in the makings for quite some time," Elzibeth deadpanned.

"They've been observing me?"

And with that, the clock over what had been Finias's mantel piece struck twelve, and the two of them found themselves standing in the vast expanse of what he would come to know as The Grand Entrance of Briarwood.

Chapter 5

The space itself was impressive in its simplicity. The curvilinear shape of the room was imprinted with the texture of the formwork used during placement of the now exposed architectural concrete, and the natural gray color was in nice contrast to the highly polished black marble floor with flecks of grey, white, and sand. The ceiling was of clear glass, which arched from the exterior walls to form a flat center circle etched with the Briarwood logo, and the vast expanse of curved wall was unadorned except for tables set about in four locations containing varying maps with instructions for their use related to the complex layout of the diverse wings of the facility.

Looking around, Finias saw not much else other than an inlay of stainless-steel lettering embedded in the floor, which announced, "Welcome to Briarwood" in large, two-foot letters.

"Merlin's beard," thought Finias, hopefully not aloud. "What have we here?"

"What we have here, Mr. Shoop, is Briarwood."

Finias turned to see a most attractive young woman approach wearing a tight-fitting V-neck bandage-style dress in black with bottom fringe trim and a black garnet necklace, which gave her an elegant but youthful look. She was not overly tall at 5'-6" or so, but she imposed a rather striking presence, he thought as he spied her shapely legs and impressive figure.

Finias guessed her age to be in her early twenties. She had beyond-shoulder-length blonde hair, which she had pinned back, green eyes, and, to Finias, a rather uncommon allure.

Finias found her to be quite stunning.

"So, this is Briarwood," he heard himself say, this time out loud for all rather than to himself. Amazing. Oh, and please, I suppose introductions are in order. I'm…"

"Yes, Mr. Finias Shoop," she said. "And this young lady I know to be Elzibeth."

Again, with her beautiful smile, she approached Finias, hand extended, and said, "Hi, I'm Francine Mankin, Elizabeth's sister."

"Is that so?" Finias said, taking her hand. "Very nice to meet you. I certainly see the resemblance; you both being quite beautiful, if you don't mind me saying so."

"Not at all, Francine said, and it's very nice to meet you as well," came her response, as if such compliments frequently came her way.

"Before I show you to your quarters, I must ask if you have any particular questions. It is my preference to answer while Elzibeth is with us, as I would want any answers I should give to be heard by all so there may be no misunderstanding," Francine said.

"Why exactly am I here?" Finias said, beginning straight away.

"For protection, Mr. Shoop. Yes, for protection. For your wisdom, your courage, and your kind heart. And to be strong for those who cannot be strong for themselves."

"But I am none of those things. I am a simple carpenter. A pretty good one at that, but at my base, I am a modest man," Finias said.

"Exactly."

"Wait...What?" Finias said. Elzibeth rolled her eyes at this but decided it was best to let it go. "What do you mean by exactly?"

"Just that. It is the heart of the man that makes him a man. You see, you had been chosen prior to Elzibeth joining us here in her first year at Briarwood to be her mentor and her protector. Not for using the powers you now possess, but for your need not to use them. Your heart, Finias, and the strength and goodness within. That is what brought you here."

Chapter 6

Briarwood, as it turned out, endured as a modern architectural marvel. Born of concrete and steel, it held fast to the rising cliffs of an island surrounded by a mile of ocean to the nearest land mass.

Majestic in both art and form, it was obvious to those in the know that this was not a building built by the hands of men. The location itself, isolated from the mainland, and the shear audacity of its construction would indicate that it required help from otherworldly sources.

Francine had explained that The Grand Entrance served as a kind of hub for the spokes of the facility, with the varying floors and associated rooms moving about and around the Grand Entrance on an axis not unlike a Rubik's Cube; and that he should not be surprised to look out his window in the morning towards the East, then, depending on positional changes to his wing, he may in the evening find himself to be looking North, South or West.

After Francine had shown him to his door, Finias stood looking at the tranquility of the ocean from the floor to the ceiling glass panes of his new room. The water, so richly blue, seemed at peace with nature, the tides rising and falling ever so softly, then coming to rest in graceful plumes of white mist at the base of the cliffs below.

Taking a moment to adjust to his surroundings, Finias began by moving to the bar, setting off some ways to the right of his door, and pouring himself a drink.

Having done so, he couldn't help but notice the large television mounted to the wall over the bar and thought it to be a rather nice setup for having guests and watching a sporting event.

Finias took his drink with him as he went about the business of unpacking.

With his personal belongings put away, he took some time to move about his suite, which he found to be rather extravagant.

Nothing less than a large home. At some 000 sq. ft., he found it to be ridiculously large and, to his taste, overdone. He discovered, though, to his liking that one of the areas contained a Jacuzzi bath, a shower with multiple spray heads whose doors closed to also become a steam chamber.

Through a series of doors down a long hall, he came upon a computer room, a full though small workout room, a fully functioning classroom for what he was not yet sure, a movie room with seating for eight, a basketball court, and a two-lane bowling alley.

Finias had made his way back to the bar to freshen his drink when a chime sounded from somewhere he did not know. Suddenly, his television came to life to announce the presence of Francine, standing just outside his entry door.

"Stunning, absolutely stunning you are, Ms. Francine," Finias said aloud to the image on the screen.

"Why, thank you very much, Mr. Shoop. How very kind," Francine said, from the confines of the television.

"Oh my," Finias said. "I meant to have kept that to myself. I was unaware that, you know, I could be heard. Please do not be offended by my careless remarks."

"Not at all," Francine said. "Frankly, I am quite flattered and am admittedly enjoying your discomfort immensely."

Finias could see from the image on the screen that she was smiling brightly and looking as if she were indeed enjoying his charming clumsiness.

Now, if you don't mind, I would be appreciative if you would allow me to please speak with you directly."

"Oh, of course. How silly of me! Do come in," Finias said.

And with that, she did.

Francine had changed clothes and was now dressed casually in jeans and a light blue chambray shirt worn in with a tan belt and backless tan open-toe shoes.

Finias's first impression was that the people at Levi Strauss must have used her as a model to mold her jeans, as they fit her fine shape and narrow hips perfectly.

Having stepped through the door, she closed it quietly behind her and turned to face Finias. His heart racing just a bit, he offered her a drink, which she politely declined, and the two of them moved to the seating area set just off the kitchen.

"I've come to see how you are getting along in your new surroundings. Have we failed to address any particular need you may have?"

"Not at all," Finias said. "Everything is quite lovely. In fact, it is a bit overwhelming. I want for nothing, I assure you."

"Then we have done our job in that regard. Excellent, yes, most excellent," she said.

Francine was looking about the place with an air of congratulatory self-satisfaction. But not in a smug off-putting way. Finias got the impression from watching her that it was more of a sense of proud but quiet relief. One is never exactly sure how their efforts may be evaluated, and learning that such efforts are appreciated and not scorned brings about a bit of joyous internal celebration.

It was at this precise moment that Teri and Theodore appeared, seated at the table, having seemingly teleported directly into his suite from God knows where. Finias, being caught entirely off guard, fell over backward in his chair and, in doing so, managed to kick Theodore in the shin.

"Ow, that hurt," Theodore said. "What on earth has gotten into you? Have you not been witness to an exigent arrival before? Here, let me help you up."

And with that, Theodore gave his head a slight nod, and Finias found himself sitting upright in his chair as if a moment ago.

Francine stood to greet her parents. "Mum, Dad. So good to see you."

They were in the middle of exchanging hugs and kisses when Finias said, "Exigent? That means some type of emergency, or something, does it not?"

"Well, yes. Though there are times when it could be just a need, necessity, or something else, but let's not dwell on semantics," Theodore said. "Teri, how is it that you would explain our sudden need to be here?"

"Oh, that nasty old Thaime Pregmierar has returned and is up to his dirty tricks again. Word has it that he has been lobbying the members of the Order to grant him a seat at the head of the table of old. And when I say 'lobbying' I use that term loosely. Coercion seems to be a better fit," Teri said.

"Thaime? My understanding was that he had been shunned and was no longer of the gifted world, much less in a position to sway the headminsters of the Order," Francine said. "When did you hear of this news?"

"About a minute before we arrived, my dear," Theodore said.

"Thaime? Who is this Thaime?" Finias said.

"A most evil sort," Teri began. "Has the smile of a shark if sharks could smile. He seems to take pleasure in the pain of others and delights in death when it happens. It is rumored that he has gathered together a rather large following of miscreants who share his enthusiasm for the dark side of things and that his legions are being exploited by some in the non-gifted community for less than the greater good, if you understand my meaning."

"Actually, no, I'm not entirely sure that I do," Finias said.

Having addressed Teri directly, he suddenly noticed just how much she looked like Francine. Or how it is that Francine resembles Teri, he thought.

"Well, these are delicate matters, and I should preface what I'm about to tell you with the fact that most of what I understand about such things is simply hearsay," Theodore began. "There may be nothing to it at all other than that I have heard similar stories from multiple sources around these parts whose paths could not have crossed. That being said, and with that understanding, it seems that our bad actor Thaime has indeed been a bad boy. You see, there are certain factions within the non-gifted community who make their living off the backs of others. Gangsters, mobsters, drug lords, and other old-fashioned names come to mind. So, it seems that our boy Thaime has been doing a good bit of the so-called "wet work" for these organizations."

"Wet work?" Finias said.

"It's a term used by to indicate that blood will be shed," Teri explained. "You see, subbing out this type of work to gifted folk who, as you know, have a certain way of making the circumstances and scenes of such crimes appear to be either of a natural cause or of a nature that makes them unsolvable. Thaime has found this to be advantageous to the criminal element."

"In short, he's a murdering bloke for hire, and his desire to take a seat among the Headministers is his power play into the eventual full-scale involvement of gifted people everywhere in his schemes," Theodore said.

The mood around the table had grown solemn after such talk, replacing the previous lighthearted discussion between Finias and Francine with a darkness matched only by the fading twilight.

The evening had settled in among the four seemingly unannounced, and after much thought and further discussion, it was decided it was time to share this new information with the headmaster of Briarwood so that he may decide the best course of action.

'Before we go, Theodore, it has been some time since our last meal, and I could stand a spot of wine as well to settle my nerves after all this terrible talk," Teri said.

"Yes, splendid idea. What say you, Finias? Francine?"

"Absolutely," Finias said.

"Brilliant," added Francine.

"Then off we go, shall we?" Teri said.

Chapter 7

Upon their arrival at the Grand Entrance, Francine led the four to the farthest wall, if you could call it that, the entrance being round. Nonetheless, the farthest point from which they had entered and pressed a button on a large control panel marked simply "Dining."

Finias could hear a "whirring" noise, not unlike an elevator, and after a moment, two huge doors, large enough for a family of elephants to have walked through, appeared where moments ago a natural gray concrete wall had been.

The massive wall slid open with a faint "whoosh" exposing a hall of enormous proportion.

Four long tables of glistening black granite and stainless steel ran from front to back of the hall, two to either side of a wide center aisle, with a large open-air kitchen at the far end.

The walls were of unadorned white marble, laced with streaks of gray and crimson. The ceiling was of vaulted glass open to the late evening sky, and the floor was simple concrete stained dark with a massive circular-shaped Briarwood crest in the middle aisle with a band of meaning around its edge that Finias found odd. "Serve to protect, protect to ensure, ensure to the end; to the end we shall serve."

Finias read the inscription aloud as they passed, then added, "A bit corny, don't you think?"

"Finias! Bite your tongue," Teri said somewhat harshly. "Though it's true that some think Briarwood unusual, it is historic and considered by many as a place of freedom and honor for all, and I would suggest you be respectful of your surroundings and choose your words more carefully.

Yikes, Finias thought. So Francien's mother has a sharp tongue and is quick with a word. He wondered to himself for a moment if being so direct might turn out to be hereditary.

Shaking the idea of Francine turning out to be a giant pain in the behind, he then offered a quick "Yes, mam," thinking of nothing else to say. "I meant no disrespect. Just thinking out loud really, which often gets me in trouble."

"You are not in trouble, dear boy," Teri said. "I'm simply suggesting that you be more mindful of your words while here, especially when you are in the company of people you barely know."

"Yes, of course," Finias said, embarrassed, then, to quickly change the subject, added, "I see none in the kitchen, and as I fancy myself a bit of a cook if you'll allow me, I would be pleased to whip something up."

"No, no," Teri said with a chuckle. "Let us all find a seat, and the wait staff will be along shortly."

As the four made their way down the aisle, Finias found a place for the four, and they sat down in comfortable, high-backed black chairs. After a moment, two waiters in tuxedos appeared, one on either side of the table. They were elegant in every way and manner, and after securing orders from the four, they floated gracefully out of the room.

Finias turned to Francine and said, "You notice how they float and not simply walk? Is that supposed to be part of the charm or just to freak people out?"

"I don't know," Francine said. "I hadn't really given it much thought until now. I have seen them walk when we have state dinners and the like, with non-gifted people in attendance. Maybe floating ensures that they don't trip on a shoelace or something and dump a load of food in your lap."

Finias laughed, which, in turn, made the others laugh as well. It was good to see Francine laugh, thought Finias. Her expression appeared to soften from the concerns of the day and relax into the face of the lovely young woman that she was.

Finias, though not sure of Francine's age, thought again of how youthful she appeared and placed her a few years younger than himself, having just turned 23. He found himself drawn to her, and to his surprise, he was ever hopeful that there might be some attraction to him on her part. But he knew one could never be sure. For the moment, anyway. For his part, he did know his attraction to her might be a bit obvious, and he reminded himself to take care as to his behavior.

The food arrived with a flourish, and the waiters, most professional, stood at the ready for a nod to begin, which Theodore gave with a smile. The pair then carved and served roast duck tableside along with a parsnip puree with figs, caramelized baby carrots, creamed spinach, and asparagus sautéed in a compound butter of garlic and thyme, accompanied by bottles of fine wine carefully selected, of course, by Theodore.

Upon serving portions from two of the ducks to each guest, the waiters placed the remains into what Finias didn't know were duck presses.

Once the carcasses were placed in their respective chambers, the waiters each began to turn a threaded wheel on top of each of the two large brass devices, pressing the juices from the remains, which were collected and whisked into a fine sauce the likes of which none at the table had ever experienced.

Between bites, Francine again thought of just how handsome she found Finias to be. Tall with a swimmer's body, he had the roughhewn hands of a stone mason, yet she found his movements to be deliberate and precise. His bright blue eyes seemed to be constantly on the move, taking in everything yet giving nothing away. To Francine, his face appeared always relaxed, even when she knew him to be tense, such as when they first met, yet like his eyes, gave nothing away.

"Who are you really, Finias Shoop?" she wondered to herself.

Theodore had been going on about the duck press, finding such a simple thing to be extraordinary.

"A fine contraption that is, my man," Theodore offered. "Yes, a very fine contraption indeed."

"Thank you, sir. Will that be all?"

"I suspect I might want a spot of dessert later if it wouldn't be too much trouble," Teri said.

"Not at all, mam. We shall be at your service for the remainder of your meal. Just give this bell a tinkle when ready." And with that, a crystal bell appeared next to Teri's plate.

"Splendid, simply splendid," Teri said.

And with that, the waiters floated gracefully away.

At almost the same time, the doors to the Great Dining Hall slid open, and a raucous group of young girls made their way down the center aisle, laughing and giggling as they went.

"Hey, there's Mr. Shoop," noted Elzibeth out loud. Waving her arms, she shouted, "Hey Shoop, over here."

Finias laughed and waved them over. "Yes, I both see and hear you. Come sit down and have a bite with us, won't you?"

Elzibeth and her band of merry young ladies skipped and giggled their way down the long center aisle until they reached the others.

"Hello, mum, hello, dad," Elzibeth said in greeting.

"Hello dear," Teri said.

"Come hear my sweet child and give the old man a hug, will you?" Theodore said.

And that she did.

There were hugs and kisses all around, then more hugs. Elzibeth introduced her friends, then went around to the other side of the table and sat down next to Finias.

"Whatcha eatin there, Shoop?" Elzibeth asked.

"Roast duck with a delicate sauce made from the birds cooked blood and the juice of their bones squeezed from the remains of their carcass," answered Finias in a pleasant voice, as if suggesting delicious pie and ice cream.

Elzibeth's face scrunched up, and she made a gagging noise. "Gross."

"No, it's actually quite good. Here, have a taste," Finias offered.

"No way, Jose. That's disgusting," Elzibeth said. "I'd rather eat a dead bird's toenails."

"I don't think birds, either dead or alive, have toenails," Finias said.

"Okay, then…. How about?" Elzibeth began.

"I get the point," Finias interrupted, wrapping his large hands around her and giving her a hug.

Everyone laughed at this exchange.

"Mr. Waiter, instead of that duck thing, I think I will go with a cheeseburger and fries. Maybe a chocolate shake as well," Elzibeth said.

The rest of her entourage joined in with, "Me too, and strawberry for me, please."

A waiter had appeared seemingly out of nowhere and, without writing anything down, took the individual orders, including a chocolate souffle for Teri, then floated off to fulfill their requests.

Soon the wait staff floated back in with shakes, burgers, fries, and desert, and the girls settled into the rhythm of youthful conversation between bites.

Finias couldn't help but notice how pleasant it was to both see and hear the laughter of all and the sentiment of the prior hugs and kisses. The evening rolled into night, and through the high windows on either side of the Great Dining Hall and the open ceiling above, Finias could see the bright, cool light of the moon and various faded stars. He could not remember feeling so relaxed and reveling in the comfort of his company. It was a fine, heady feeling. One he would need to remember during the trying times ahead.

Chapter 8

Once dinner was finished and the dishes cleared, Finias turned to Francine and, with some hesitation, asked, "It's quite lovely out tonight, would you do me the honor of showing me the grounds?"

"I would love to, but I believe we have an appointment with the headmaster," she said with a sly smile.

"Oh, yes indeed. Pity. It is such a lovely night. Some other time, perhaps?"

"Perhaps," she said, with that same sly smile.

Finias swooned at the thought of her walking with him and found himself utterly disappointed that this would not be the case.

Francine, for her part, thought that she would have indeed enjoyed going for a walk with Finias, yet she found that it was almost as much fun to flirt and then pull back a bit just to watch him squirm a little. She also thought that it was going to be great fun playing such games with a man she was attracted to while fulfilling her duties to Briarwood.

Theodore stood and, addressing the group, suggested that the girls be off to bed as it was getting late and that the others should join him in a visit to the headmaster's quarters.

With much coaxing and more than a bit of fuss, the girls made their way out of the dining hall and off to their rooms.

From inside the Grand Entrance, Francine pressed a button on a wall panel labeled "Headmaster," and they waited as they could hear the shifting of the building with various rooms exchanging places until an opening appeared to the entrance of the hallway leading to the headmasters' quarters. Once there, Francine gave the entry door a good rap, and from within, a voice instructed them to please come in.

"What on earth?" Finias said under his breath as they entered.

The headmaster's quarters were, to put it kindly, a bit haphazard and utterly incongruous with the ultra-modern quarters Finias inhabited.

Finias found upon entering ancient antiquities placed about in no particular order. Odd but pleasant-looking art adorned the walls at varying heights and intervals, with no apparent thought given to their placement. All the furnishings seemed to Finias to be overly large, including the desk of the man they came to see. The headmaster was seated at an enormous birch wood desk with ornately carved legs in front of a massive floor-to-ceiling glass wall behind him.

Headmaster Calderón stood and greeted his guests. "Theodore, Teri, how good to see you. Ah, and the lovely Francine. Please, please, do come in."

Finias found Calderón to be tall and strikingly handsome and noticed that he moved with uncommon grace as he came around from behind the mammoth desk. Finias guessed his age to be in the early fifties, with a slight graying around the temples and a bit of peppering on top. He was trim and wore his three-piece suit well, and Finias noticed his eyes had a piercing quality containing a depth of both intelligence and humility. An unusual combination, he thought.

Calderón came about to formally greet his guests and shook hands quite vigorously with Theodore, then did what Finias thought to be, a kind of ridiculous European air kiss thing to both cheeks of Teri and Francine.

"And who might this young man be? No wait, let me take a guess. Finias Shoop, I believe."

"Yes, sir, it's a it's a pleasure to meet you," Finias said.

"No, most assuredly, the pleasure is all mine," Calderón said as he gave Finias the same aggressive handshake. "I'm afraid there may not be much pleasure in this little venture for you, my boy, but we will make every effort to offset any efforts by those seeking to do you harm."

Finias was a bit dumbfounded by this and was not sure how to respond. A red flag had been raised, and he now had many questions, but the timing for these didn't feel right to express at the moment, so he felt it best just to be quiet for the time being.

"Well, please come and sit, and we shall have a chat," Calderón suggested.

He motioned the group to a set of large, high-backed chairs covered in some type of rather off-putting brocade.

"Before we begin, might I offer each of you a beverage? I have a very fine brandy that I have been saving for just such an occasion," proffered Calderón.

"None for me, thanks," Francine said.

"I think I too shall pass," Teri said. "We just came from a most exquisite dinner, and with desert, I'm afraid I've already overdone things."

"Nonsense," Theodore said. "With your fine figure, you can choose to indulge a bit, my dear."

"How sweet. Thank you, darling, but no, I truly believe that I shall pass," Teri said.

"Well then, how about you two gents?" Calderón asked.

Both Finias and Theodore were pleased with the offer of brandy, and after having poured their drinks into large globe-shaped snifters, they settled in to discuss the events of the day.

"So, Theodore, tell us a story," Calderón said.

Theodore began by relating an article he had read two days ago about a hillside mansion that was blown to pieces in an exclusive neighborhood outside of Burlington. He went on to say that the article made mention that the home was owned by the son of notorious mob boss Franky (Francis) Marcon.

"Anthony Marcon, his son, Anthony Junior, and his pregnant wife Sharron were lost in the blast, as was their dog Debutante," Theodore added before pausing, thus allowing the information to sink in as to how terrible an outcome the loss of life is simply for the sake of the advancement of the criminal agenda.

Theodore took note that Finias seemed moved by this story, as he had folded his hands in his lap and released a heavy sigh during its telling.

Calderón remained passive, his face and his body language as unmoving as his will, for Theodore knew that regardless of the depth or lack of it, it was not in Calderon's nature to allow such depravity to go unattended. Teri and Francine had both raised a hand to cover their mouths in horror.

Calderón was the first to speak after the completion of this tale, and the question that came to his mind was the most obvious.

"These types of stories come about all too often these days, I'm afraid, my dear Theodore. What troubles you so much about this particular one?"

Theodore began by suggesting that by all accounts from local and government officials, this type of action against a heavily fortified compound was nearly impossible without the use of heavy equipment, tanks, helicopters, or the like, along with maybe twenty-five to thirty very highly skilled operatives, all with the advanced technological advantages they maintain.

"There were no witnesses to any such hardware moving on the roads or in the air." He continued.

"Keep in mind now that this has the appearance of a mob hit," Theodore said. "The problem, as I see it, is that even the most sophisticated criminal elements known do not come close to having the type of skill, advanced knowledge to plan, or the equipment required to pull off such a job. So, that brings us to who? The government? Obviously not. Their job is to capture and put people away, not blow them up. So, the question then becomes, to what level, if any, was the involvement from the dark side of those gifted?"

"Troubling times are ahead, I'm afraid," Calderón said. "Something wicked this way comes, I believe the saying goes. The more explosive the situation, so to speak, the more explosive the response, and the more explosive the outcome for many, including the innocent. The possibility that gifted people are involved brings new dangers to us. This cannot go on, but I am at a loss as to how to move forward. Any suggestions from either of you two fine gentlemen or you two lovely ladies would be most appreciated, keeping in mind that my highest priority is the safety and security of all who reside within the confines of this establishment."

"Yes, of course, the protection of students and staff is paramount," Finias said. "But if we are in any way threatened, as gifted people, I think we fight fire with fire. Take the fight to whoever did this and punch them in the mouth."

Oh please, thought Francine. Just like a man to go off halfcocked like that. Silly. Unless, of course, he was doing this to impress me. That's an interesting thing to consider, she mused.

"Spoken like a true twenty-something," Calderón said. "And please do not be offended by my remark. I was simply harkening back to my youth, when I too was so passionate. But passion alone does not always lead to positive outcomes, and I would caution against moving too quickly in a direction whose map has yet to be deciphered."

"I have a question," Francine said. "Maybe I'm confused, but why would Briarwood need additional protection? Surely the mob or whoever has no business with us."

"Ah, but there is the rub," Theodore said. "Though it's true we do not go off frivolously meddling in criminal business, if there are factions of the gifted world working in concert with such groups, they would be aware that we gifted folk would be the only ones who could stand in their way if we chose to get involved. In short, we are an unknown threat, and it has been my experience that they prefer to leave nothing to chance.

"The pathology of the people who did this speaks of pure evil and hatred," Teri said. "I know myself to be biased in this regard, but I think we would be remiss not to consider the possibility that Thaime was somehow involved."

"Agreed," offered Francine. "But I would suggest that we let the authorities come to some conclusion before we go too far with this information."

"A fair statement and one I tend to agree with," Calderón said. "Though I may add that I see no ill effects from bringing this matter before the council of old simply to let them know of our concern for the safety of Briarwood and to ask that additional protections be provided to the grounds here. I myself happen to know a couple of protective spells that I could conjure up that are real doosies, but they would need council approval as they could be quite lethal to intruders or anyone who simply happened to blunder by."

Chapter 9

The morning unfolded into streams of sunlight cascading through the glass wall of Finias's room. He rose to see herring gulls floating on tufts of wind before crashing into the surf below, then surfacing with food for the day.

The thought of food caused his stomach to rumble, and he thought fondly of the sound of sizzling bacon and the smell of freshly brewed coffee.

Not wanting to dine alone, Finias placed a quick call to the room of Francine and found that he was more than disappointed when she did not answer. Not to be dissuaded, he quickly showered and dressed before heading out to the dining hall for breakfast.

Finias had no more than finished tying his laces when the television announced the arrival of Elzibeth.

"Hey Finias, you in there," came both the image and voice of little Elzibeth from the television.

"Yes, good morning. The door is always open to you, Miss Elzibeth. Please do come in," he answered.

The suite's door popped open, and Elzibeth came bounding inside.

"Wanna grab some breakfast?" she offered.

"Certainly, but wouldn't you be more comfortable having breakfast with your friends?" he asked.

"Half of them are not even awake yet, and half of the other half haven't dressed, and the rest went back to bed," she said.

"I see. Well, it's you and me, then. We must hurry though, as I understand the kitchen to be running low on their fine maple syrup," Finias teased.

"Yeah, well, I bet they're not out of ice cream, and that's just as good," Elzibeth countered.

"Hmmm...I may just have to test that theory," Finias said, with a smile.

"Come on, then. Let's get a move on there, Shoop," Elzibeth said.

And off they went.

Though still early, upon their entrance, Finias and Elzibeth found the great dining hall to be more than half full.

The room was filled with the aroma of breakfast, the sounds of cutlery on porcelain, and the hum of random chatter. Waiters, seemingly by the dozens, floated about with individual trays of breakfast items to serve those who stopped them for a second, helping along their circuitous routes. Others floated back and forth, taking orders while avoiding the constant flow of traffic coming and going in and out of the hall.

After a breakfast of waffles and ice cream, Finias was not sure what to do. He had not been given an agenda for the day, and though he had a classroom in his quarters, he had no curriculum and no instructions on how to host class or what subject a humble carpenter was to teach. So he did the only thing he could think of and asked Elzibeth if she would like to do a bit of exploring.

"You bet," she said. "I know this place like the back of my hand. What say we take a tour of the grounds first? Then we can come back inside, and I'll take you through the building when the weather gets warm."

"Perfect. I had tried to get Francine to walk the grounds with me last night, but that didn't work out so well," Finias said.

"Yeah, I bet you tried," Elzibeth said.

"What on earth do you mean by that?"

"You know."

"No, I'm afraid I don't. What are you getting at?"

"Oh, come off it, Shoop. I see the way you practically drool on your shoes when you look at her."

"What? Wait, what? I have never once drooled on my shoes."

"You really need to get over that stammer of yours. It's not very becoming," Elzibeth said. "Besides, she is a beautiful woman. More than one of the guys around here has been caught in soggy shoes."

"You are something else, you know that." Finias said. "How old did you say you were again?"

Elzibeth gave him a sideways glance, and Finias was sure that she had rolled her eyes.

"Come on," Elzibeth said. "The backside of Briarwood is anchored to the cliffs, but if you are up for a bit of a hike, we can circle around to the top of the island to its expansive plateau."

"Expansive plateau, you say? You truly are a precocious little thing, aren't you?" Finias said as they exited the dining hall into the main entry and marched right out of the front door.

"Why, there is a road leading to the mainland," Finias said. "I don't recall that being there when we arrived yesterday."

"It's always there." Elzibeth said. "It must be in use today, as it is usually kept invisible. You know, to keep away unwanted visitors."

"Hey, you wanna walk over to the mainland?" she suggested. "It's only a little more than a mile, and the view of the water along the way is quite nice."

"Are we allowed?" Finias said.

"Beats me. I'm the chargee. So that makes you what? The charger? Anyway, I'm in your care, so right or wrong, I'm in the clear," Elzibeth said.

"Good grief," Finias said. "Very well. I say we go for it."

"Now you're talkin," Elzibeth said, and they set off.

The road itself was more of a parkway. There were two overly wide lanes each way, with a median wide enough for a coach to move through. On either side of the median were landscaped planters with large umbrella trees that grew together in the middle, providing a canopy of shade to those who walked beneath. Sunlight filtered through the branches as the leaves created a sparkling display of light that shimmied across the meandering walk below.

A three-foot-high columned barrier of ornate white iron posts and rails separated the road sections from the median, and beautiful rosebushes, having grown together between the huge trees, created a mosaic of red, yellow, orange, pink, and white hedgerows. Baroque-style streetlamps with hanging baskets of colored flowers dotted either side, as did benches of similar fashion for those who chose to rest along the way.

"My, this is simply stunning," Finias said.

"Not bad, right?" answered Elzibeth.

"You've walked down here before, then I take it?" Finias said.

"Yeah, but not far. Just far enough to get the flavor of things," Elzibeth said.

The two continued in silence, enjoying the view of the ocean as the relentless tides continued to push wave after wave to the shore beyond. A school of dolphins breached the water to their left, and Elzibeth squealed with delight. The walk was pleasant, and Finias enjoyed the sensation of the physical activity and the smell of the fresh ocean air.

It seemed not long when they came to the end of the road, which flared as it crossed the sand below, and they were welcomed with a large stone arch spanning its width with an inlaid message of "Welcome to Brighton Beach."

Below the arch, Finias pointed to a sign hanging from its center that read, "Home of the World's Finest Chocolate, Candy, and Nuts."

"Chocolate, candy, and nuts? Three of my favorite things," Finias said. "Good call, kid."

"I'm not much for nuts, but chocolate and candy sound pretty good," Elzibeth said.

"Then I suggest we go find some," Finias said.

And off they went. The seaside town had the quaint feel of most seaside towns. Humble shanties open to the front selling various wares was the norm, with an occasional roadside stand selling popcorn balls, hot dogs, cotton candy, and the like. Between buildings were several entrances to the beach where artists performed their works on canvas or instrument with an occasional mime milling about pretending to be stuck in a box and such.

Elzibeth came upon a man with the improbable task of stacking smooth, curved rocks. He had accumulated a small tower about two feet high, and Elzibeth was taken with the task.

"Hey Finias, check this out," Elzibeth said while tugging on Finias's elbow. "Do you think it's magic?"

"Oh no, not this again," Finias said. "I still cry myself to sleep at night over the loss of my poor mantel piece."

"Oh, stop being so dramatic," Elzibeth said. "I said I was sorry, and you said you could fix it."

"I know. I was being dramatic for effect so as to rub it in a little," Finias said.

Elzibeth turned her face up, smiled at him, and said, "Oh, you. And don't worry, I'm not going to wreck his pile of rocks. I was just curious, is all."

The man continued the delicate task of rock stacking as the two watched for a bit, but when it took nearly twenty minutes for the man to place the next rock, the novelty had worn off, and Finias and Elzibeth moved silently away, as it would seem a whisper of their movement might bring the whole thing crashing down.

Finias and Elzibeth moved on down the coastal way, stopping occasionally at one or two of the many shops as they went. At one such place, Elzibeth was taken with a pair of pink sunglasses, which Finias was happy to purchase for her. They were a bit large for her small features, yet they looked adorable nonetheless.

Moving on, they then happened upon Elliot's Home of Chocolate Delights and Other Candied Confections and went happily inside. The depth of the place emerged as a much larger market than one would expect from its narrow frontage.

Elzibeth was thrilled, of course, and moved about in childlike wonder as only children can. She made her way past the peanut pops and nuts of all sorts to what caught her eye the most: foot-long, brightly colored lollipops twisted onto wooden sticks, set into a magical display of fairies and unicorns in similar colors. To a child, they were something to behold, and Finias knew without asking that he would buy one for Elzibeth and each of her friends.

They left the candy shop with a bag full of pops and made their way across the street at the light and began to backtrack toward the sea to land bridge, which had brought them there.

Finias, having had more than his share of coffee that morning, said, "I need to stop and use the facilities somewhere along the way." They came upon Bob's Baked Goods and Crab Shack, which Finias found to be an odd combination, but there was no sign dissuading non-customers from using the facilities, so he decided it was as good of a place as any for a quick stop.

He took Elzibeth aside, explained the situation, and asked that she wait on the bench outside and that he would only be a moment away.

Elzibeth sat down and couldn't resist opening her bag and taking out one of the pops. She carefully unwrapped just a slight portion of one end but resisted the temptation. It just seemed too pretty to simply eat, so she wrapped it back up but held fast to it, admiring its many colors in the sunlight.

Finias, for his part, had finished his business, carefully washed his hands, and made his way to the front of the restaurant. Suddenly, the entire place grew dark, and a terrible black fog descended through the street, growing denser by the second.

"Oh, my good God," Finias said aloud as he sprinted out the door and into the blackness beyond.

"Elzibeth!" he shouted. "Elzibeth, where are you?" Oh, dear God, no, please no, he thought as he went about searching aimlessly for Elzibeth while continuously shouting her name.

After what seemed like an eternity, a feeling of intense dread washed over Finias to the point of shear paralysis. "Oh my God, oh my God," he kept repeating. "What have I done?" This he said over and over as he stumbled about in the darkness.

Chapter 10

Finias understood he must act quickly but was unsure of what to do next. The fog was thick and choking, and he knew not where he was in relation to anything.

He continued to move along the walk, bumping into a no-parking sign, a mailbox, and a phone booth before eventually tripping over a fire hydrant and landing hard in the gutter.

"Blasted fog," he said aloud.

As if in answer, a gust of wind moved down the street, seemingly pushing the fog away as if a giant broom were pushing debris.

Finias stood, gathering his bearings, and turned toward where he knew the road to be. He knew now that he had gifted powers, so he thought to himself that there must be a way to teleport back to Briarwood, he just had no idea how. He could give it a try, he supposed, but thought better of it, picturing himself scattered across half the town.

He knew of no other way. He had to get back to Briarwood and alert the others, so he took off on a dead run toward the road that had brought them there.

Adrenaline pushed him, and though breathless, he pressed on. The panic he felt had not only not subsided, but it seemed to grow within him as he knew that with each stride that he took, another second ticked by as the capturers held Elzibeth.

It seemed a lifetime before he reached the Briarwood entrance, and he sprinted through the doors at full speed, yelling for help to no one while seeking out the room of Francine from the room selection panel in the strange round entrance.

He found it and pressed the button continuously until a set of doors appeared and opened with a whoosh.

He soon found himself outside the door to Francine's quarters, and he began to pound on the door furiously.

"Francine, Francine, are you in there?" he screamed. "Oh, please, please be there, Francine."

As if in answer to his pleas, the door was flung open, and Francine, appearing somewhat shocked, said, "Goodness gracious. What has gotten into you?"

"Elzibeth, he said, between gasps for air. I've lost her. She was…taken. Black fog. Bad guys. I ran as fast as I could."

"It's OK. It's OK. Come in and catch your breath," Francine said.

As Finias walked through the door, he found Theodore and Teri sitting on a black leather sofa to his right. Between them sat Elzibeth.

"Dear God, child. Thank you, Lord, above, for keeping her safe," Finias said as he ran to her, plucked her from the couch, and hugged her with all his might.

"Ugh… You're hurting me," Elzibeth said. "Put me down. Francine was right, what has gotten into you, Shoop?"

"What has gotten into me? Dear lord. You disappeared and scared the life out of me," Finias said, still panting from the effort he had expended.

"How on earth did you wind up back here?" Finias nearly shouted. "One minute you were there, and the next you were gone. The fog. That horrible black fog. I thought for sure that you had been taken."

"I was," Elzibeth said.

"You were?" Finias said, now completely stunned. "I'm afraid I don't understand. How did you end up here? And what happened to your captors?"

"It was just the one guy. He was a bit of a lummox, so I whacked him in his fat face with my bag of suckers," she said. "I had started to unwrap one, so I still had it in my hand. When he flinched from getting whacked, I stuck the stick end in his eye. Went down like a bag of sand."

"My goodness, child, how incredibly brave of you! And resourceful, I might add," Finias said.

"I thought the saying was "went down like a sack of potatoes," Theodore said, out of nowhere and somewhat lamely.

"We were at the beach, dad," Elzibeth said. "Sand seemed an apt equivalence."

"Ah yes, so, well done then," Theodore said.

"Equivalence?" Theodore, tell me truthfully. How old is she? She speaks in a manner finer than I," Finias said, with a bit of a smile.

"The ripe old age of six, my good man," Theodore said.

"Six and a half," corrected Elzibeth.

"Ah, yes," Theodore said. "I remember those heady days when I too would count years in fractions."

"So, you are okay then?" Finias said.

"Of course, why wouldn't I be?" Elzibeth said.

"You were kidnapped for goodness' sake," Finias said.

"Not the first time," Elzibeth said. "It's no big deal."

"No big deal," said a stunned Finias. "Good gravy. I was scared out of my mind."

"Here, have a seat," offered Francine. "I'll pour you a brandy, and we can settle down and discuss both what happened and a few ground rules for you to follow to avoid... further occurrence, shall we?"

"Yes, fine," Finias said. "It would be less bother if you simply skipped the glass and brought me the bottle."

"You'll have a glass," Francine said. "And, if you don't lose Elzibeth again by the time you've finished, I'll pour you another."

Francine moved away to get Finias his drink, smiling over her shoulder as she went.

"Very funny," Finias said. "By the way, I'm still not clear as to how Elzibeth got back here ahead of me."

"Mum and dad picked me up. You see, when I am outside of normal protections, they are alerted right away. You remember the black fog at your house? Well, same thing," Elzibeth said.

"And what are normal protections?" Finias asked.

"Well, when you are near Elzibeth, the dark side cannot either see or sense her," Theodore said. "Of course, if she remains here on the grounds of Briarwood, the grounds themselves offer similar protection. It's not until you move away from her, or she distances herself from you or a protected structure, that the dark side is able to sense that she is vulnerable."

"So, what is it with that black fog?" Finias said. "These people who are constantly after Elzibeth must be from the dark side of the gifted community, right?"

"Hard to tell, really," Theodore said. "What we call black fog could be a combination of smoke bombs and some liquid agent I'm unaware of. It's just too early to tell. The one thing that is apparent to me is that whoever is doing this understands the potential threat Elzibeth poses, and they want her taken out of the picture."

Chapter 11

The meeting was not the first at the location, though it had been some time since the small army of men had met. The stench of diesel fuel and engine oil hung in the air, as did a musty smell from the rotting timbers of the old structure.

The men stood as there were no seats around a makeshift table barely large enough for the thirty of them to see if they stood two deep. On the table was a rather detailed scale model of what appeared to be a mansion and surrounding complex of some sort.

At first glance, the model appeared similar to a 3D version of a PowerPoint presentation. Directional arrows, bubble diagrams, explanations of equipment and apparatus, and instructions as to how to move forward were precisely marked at each of the individual checkpoints of Marcon's mansion.

There was no roof to the structure of the model, exposing the third level. The second and smaller third levels were adjacent to each other each other and contained similar markings.

Each room of the model had been labeled and marked with directional arrows and instructions as to what was to be done, with individual steps on how to carry out the tasks.

Larger individual areas were coded in color to indicate which team was responsible for a particular task to be carried out. Areas of the compound, such as separate floors, were of different colors, as were the equipment area, gas, electric, and water lines, as well as a separate cabana. Areas such as the tennis and basketball courts, parking lot, and gymnasium were simply white, indicating that they were non-target.

Initially, the overall plan was discussed as a group, with the specific color-coded teams taking their turns to go over their responsibilities in detail. After each team had a chance to review the model, they met in separate areas of the structure and outlined detailed responsibilities according to each man's particular talent or ability.

Leaders were designated, sub-vocal audio gear was checked, and call signs were practiced, as were hand signals in the event of audio failure.

White boards were used to take ideas as to the equipment needed by each man for each specific task. One by one, the men detailed their needs, and to each of their surprise, their requests were granted regardless of how extravagant or, in some cases, a bit over the top for what was required.

As this became evident, the men began to modify their requests, and again, one by one, they took their turns outlining particular needs or desires until each was satisfied.

The men were each measured and fitted for tactical clothing and protective gear, then given physical exams and drug screens.

Once each team had decided each man's specific role, they took their place at the model and performed a mock walk-through of expected events one by one. When each team had done this, they did it again, and again, and again.

As the men continued to prepare, the man known only as "The Major" silently slipped away to what had been the back office of the auto shop operation in the '40s. Waiting for him was Thaime Pregmierar. How he managed to appear out of thin air was a mystery to the Major, who, in all honesty, could care less about Thaime's oddities as long as he and his men were well-supplied and well-paid for the misadventures that had taken place and those that were about to begin.

"Are we set for tonight?" Thaime asked without preamble.

"As set as we can be. We know the layout, the manpower on-site, and the utility structure. We expect to blow the main gate at 03:00. From there, once the guards are removed, it will be a simple matter to storm the castle, so to speak, take Marcon hostage, and set charges in the designated locations provided so generously and quite conveniently by you, Thaime. What is your stake in all this? What do you intend to gain?"

"That is none of your concern, Major, and I suggest you disregard your idle curiosity about me and focus on the task at hand."

"We'll do our part. Just make sure the crypto deposit hits my account before my tires hit the pavement on the way home. If not, I'll be delivering Marcon back to his nest with my men as his new guard, and I don't expect he will react too kindly to me telling him about your part in his abduction."

"I don't threaten, Major; you must know that by now. I am a businessman, though, with an understanding of your request and will do my part to make sure this operation goes as I have planned. Is that clear enough for you, Major?"

"Crystal, though I'm sure you meant to say, as we have planned."

"We'll see," was all he said.

Chapter 12

At 03:05, a call came into headquarters at the old abandoned building and was immediately picked up by the Major.

"What is it?" he asked, clearly annoyed at receiving a call so early in the operation.

"We need air support," came the hysterical reply. "We are being overrun by God knows how many men, if they are men at all. They don't seem to be using conventional weapons but instead are firing strikes of lightning or flame or something. It's a massacre."

"Calm down, son," came the reply from the Major as he looked at the terrified face of the young man before him on the video call.

"Calm down? Christ, sir, they are everywhere. This isn't at all as we had planned and prepared for. We need help and immediate air support... sir."

"Listen, son, you hold tight there. Find a safe place but keep this line active if at all possible. I'll get on the horn and get help on the way."

The Major walked out of the small office and punched the table holding the model of the objective. Never in his thirty-plus years as a field spook and mercenary had he failed a mission, and he wasn't about to start now.

Retrieving his cell phone from his field jacket pocket, he called Thaime.

"Thaime, what in the name of all that is holy is going on with this little operation of yours? My man in the field relayed that things are not really going according to your wonderful plan as you said they would."

"That is where you are wrong, Major," Thaime said. "They are going exactly as I had planned."

"What are you talking about?" the Major practically screamed into the phone. But before he had finished, he heard the distinct sound of gunfire and the screams of dying men in the background. It was then that he knew he had been double-crossed. And for the first time that he could remember, he felt afraid.

Chapter 13

Finias, Francine and Elzibeth were seated in the Great Dining Hall, about to order lunch. Theodore and Teri were off doing whatever it is they do, and what appeared to be the balance of the attendees and staff of Briarwood filled most of the remaining seats. Elzibeth's friends had stopped by to see if she wanted to join them at their portion of the stadium-length table, but Francine waved them off.

"I'm sorry girls, the three of us have had a rather rough go of it this morning, so we are going to enjoy each other's company for lunch today," Francine said, giving them her most polite smile. "She won't be long, I promise."

The girls looked disappointed and possibly prepared to argue, but when Francine's smile morphed into a stern look, they thought better of it and went off to find their seats.

A waiter came floating by, seemingly out of nowhere, to instruct the three of them on the day's lunch menu.

"Madame Francine, Elzibeth, and your gentleman friend," began the waiter.

"Finias Shoop," Finias said, by way of introduction. "You can call me Finias."

"Very well then, Finias, and ladies, today's lunch preparations begin with a superb lentil soup with mint, sautéed onions, and diced heirloom tomato. We suggest following that with a crown of lamb with mint pesto, chive-buttered fingerling potatoes, roasted beets, and a crisp Little Gem Caesar salad.

"My goodness," Francine said. "That sounds wonderful, and that is what I shall have."

"Make it two," Finias said, "though I think Francine and I shall split the crown of lamb if that is fine with you, Francine?"

"Yes, that will be quite alright, I do like to keep a watch on my girlish figure," Francine said.

"As well as I," Finias said, aloud with what he suddenly hoped had been a silent thought.

"Why, Finias, you do speak your mind, don't you?" Francine said.

"Not always on purpose," Finias said, somewhat embarrassed. "And forgive me, but I do find you to be quite lovely, and with that being so, I find it hard to varnish my opinion of you."

"I'm flattered, so there is nothing to forgive. Thank you for noticing," Francine said while smiling deep within.

"Thank you for allowing me to notice," Finias said, with a smile of his own.

"Good grief, I hate to break up this little love fest, but I'll have a grilled cheese, fries, and a Coke, please, Mr. Waiter," Elzibeth said.

Finias and Francine exchanged embarrassed looks.

"Elzibeth, you can't live on grilled cheese and hamburgers. Francine said. "You need to expand your culinary palate."

"Why?" Elzibeth asked.

"I don't know," Francine said, somewhat flustered. "You're just supposed to, that's all."

"Compelling argument," Finias said. "Have you ever thought of becoming an attorney?"

"Listen, mister, who can't look after a little girl for more than five minutes," began Francine, showing for the first time her rather quick and biting temper. "It's my job to make sure Elzibeth receives a proper upbringing while mum and dad are out doing business for the Order. If you have an issue with that, I suggest you take it up with the I don't give a damn about your opinion club."

"Whoa, whoa, whoa, where did that come from?" Finias said. "I was just joking around. Do forgive me."

Elzibeth put her hand on Francine's arm and said, "It's okay, sis. I don't like it when you're mad, so I think I'll go ahead and have that soup for lent with the mint and things."

Francine put her face in her hands and rested her elbows on the table for a moment. After a while, she said, "You are just too much, you know that, Elzibeth? I do love you, so, no, go ahead with that grilled cheese. You have plenty of time to develop your palate. And, by the way young lady, its lentil soup, not soup for lent."

Finias and Francine both had a small laugh at this, and the waiter drifted off with their order.

"Look, Finias. I'm sorry about that," Francine began. "The pressure of the day with Elzibeth showing up with a tale of being kidnapped and you nowhere to be found just got to me a little bit."

"Missed me, did you?" teased Finias.

"Don't be cute," snapped Francine. "This is serious business. She may be too young to understand this, but Elzibeth's survival means our survival. All of us. Do you understand that?"

"I believe I do, yes." Finias said.

"Good," Francine said. "From this point in time forward, if the two of you leave the protections of the grounds, she is not to leave your sight. Not for a second, understand?"

"Yes, not for a second." Finias said.

"And that means that if you have to go potty, or God forbid, the other thing, you are to either hold it, make it in your pants, or take her with you to the loo, understood?"

"Again, yes. I see your point, angry as it might seem." Finias said.

"Good," Francine said. "But I reiterate in case you have a short attention span. Not for a second shall she leave your sight, for if they, whoever they are, take her from you again, I will see to it that you spend the next twenty years making snow cones in the arctic. Understood?"

"Understood."

After what seemed to be just a hair's breadth in time, their food arrived in the customary manner, and the three of them settled in to eat.

The food, as always, was of the highest caliber and was enjoyed immensely. Elzibeth ordered a second grilled cheese and Coke, but after a few bites, she announced that she had indeed had enough.

When finished, the waiter came by and whisked away the dishes, and Francine politely asked Elzibeth to go find her friends so that she and Finias could talk in private.

"Does that mean you want me to leave so you can do mushy stuff with ole Shoop here?" Elzibeth said.

"Goodness gracious, no," Francine said. "There is no mushy stuff going on between Finias and me."

"I don't know," Elzibeth said. "You might want to check his shoes."

"Elzibeth, that is quite enough," Finias said.

"What on earth do you mean, check his shoes?" Francine said.

Finias's face turned redder than his lunchtime beets, and he said, "Never mind," a little too loudly. "Just a little joke between the two of us, isn't that right, Elzibeth?"

"Huh? Oh sure, just a joke," Elzibeth said, with a most mischievous smile.

"Elzibeth, this is strictly business between Finias and I. You can stay, of course, if you like, you already know what we are going to talk about. I just thought it would be more fun for you to join with your friends. After all, you've had a most unusual morning, and I'm sure they would enjoy hearing all about it."

"Oh yeah," Elzibeth said. "This is going to be great fun. See you later."

And off she went.

Finias and Francine sat there, not saying anything for a moment. They both seemed lost in their own thoughts when Calderón happened by. He sat down next to Francine without saying a word. A waiter came floating by, said good day to Headmaster Calderón, and took his order of coffee light with one Equal, a sprinkle of nutmeg, and a touch of vanilla. He added a blueberry muffin at the last moment, and the waiter made off to fill his request.

Finias was the first to speak, feeling possibly that Calderón's arrival was not mere happenstance. He wasn't nervous about relating his failure to guard Elzibeth while she was in his care, but he was embarrassed, and Calderón's silence spoke volumes about his feelings on the matter.

"Headmaster," Finias said.

"Finias."

"I guess you've heard about what happened this morning," Finias said.

"I have," Calderón said.

"And I suspect you are not happy about it," Finias said.

"I am not."

"Did Francine provide you with any of the details?" Finias said.

"No, I've not spoken with Francine about this as of yet, so it is my good fortune that she is here now," Calderón said. "Theodore and Teri stopped by on their way to... well, it's not important where they were off to. They gave me their version in a general sense. Do you suppose you could be so kind as to tell me what you know in detail? It would be most helpful to me to decide how best to deal with this situation."

Suddenly, Finias could taste mint pesto, and the crown of lamb in his stomach was doing flip-flops. The word "situation" made his heart drop for Francine, who, maybe unwittingly, had given him a sense of false hope that perhaps he was going to skate by with the slap on the wrist he had received from her. Now it looked like he was about to get paddled backside by a wooden board named Calderón.

"Sure" was all Finias could manage before the waiter arrived with Calderón's food, granting him a temporary reprieve.

"Headmaster, let me begin by saying just how sorry I am about this whole mess," Finias began.

Calderón interrupted. "Sorry is a most adroit word, isn't it?" He began. "Its overuse seems universal, and its suggested meaning truly covers much ground. The word "sorry," it seems, provides endless protections, from something as simple as a polite response for stepping on the back of someone's shoe to losing the most precious asset this world has ever known while on an ill-advised adventure into Brighton Beach. Yes, a very nimble word indeed."

Finias was now tasting beets as he looked at the headmaster straight on.

"I see your point," was all Finias could manage while attempting to keep his lunch in place.

"The beginning is usually the best place to start, don't you think?" suggested Calderón. "Why don't you try starting there?"

"Yes, of course," Finias said.

And that is precisely what he did.

After hearing the full tale, Calderón was quiet for a moment, digesting his thoughts along with his coffee and muffin, Finias supposed. After a while, he let out a heavy sigh and said, "I believe we have failed this young man, my dear Francine."

"What?" Francine and Finias said it in unison.

"Yes, we have failed him," continued Calderón. "We took it for granted, given his helpful and pleasant nature, that maybe he was more prepared for this task than he truly is. We failed to provide proper instruction as to the limits of protection either he or Briarwood provide, and he has not been properly trained in the use of his considerable gifts."

"Sir, I beg your pardon, but Finias took it upon himself to leave the grounds without permission, which I would have certainly denied if he had come to me before making such a stupid decision," countered Francine.

"I see you have thrown me under the bus and stepped on the gas," Finias said.

"And what do you mean by that?" Francine said, her voice rising more than an octave.

"Oh, you know exactly what I mean," Finias said, obviously flustered. "Why don't you put that thing in reverse and back over me?"

"How dare you?" Francine shrieked, then stood as if to leave.

"Do take your seat, Francine," Calderón said. "I'm not quite through with the two of you."

"I'll not sit here and have him insinuate that I'm running over him with some kind of bus to save my own skin."

"I'm sure that Finias is terribly regretful of his remarks and feels shame for having voiced them. Am I not right, Finias?" Calderón said.

"I am both adroit and nimble about my remarks," was all he said, refusing to say he was sorry.

"Well, there it is," began Calderón. "A most terrible apology to be sure, but I myself would like to put this bit of nasty business behind us."

"I have a few ideas on how best to advance from here," he said. "But I thought I would begin by taking suggestions from the two of you first before making my final determination."

"If the Wizard of Oz is still available, we could ask him if he could find Finias a brain," Francine said, obviously still stung by the bus remark.

"Now, Francine, that is not a very practical suggestion," Calderón said. "That movie is several decades old, and I'm sure the wizard is no longer with us."

It was obvious that Calderón was trying not to laugh.

"Or we could send him off to Cotillion to teach him respect, manners, and charm," offered Francine, now smiling.

"Or detective school so that he might learn the many not-so-difficult ways to keep track of a little girl," Calderón said as he began to chuckle.

"Okay, you two, that's enough," Finias said, but even he could not help but smile.

"I must be going, but I would like to leave the two of you with this," Calderón said. "Anger can lead to wounds that cannot be healed. Do not allow this incident to cut any deeper, as I see something special about you two. Allow our laughter to act as a salve, as you'll find it to be the greatest medicine of all."

Chapter 14

Before departing the Great Dining Hall, the three of them stood in close conference and concluded that training Finias in the use of his gifted powers would be most helpful.

"More so than charm school?" Francine offered.

"Ha, ha," Finias said.

Calderón suggested at first that Theodore be the instructor, then thought better of it. Theodore's talents leaned more toward coercion than instruction. He then proposed Professor Raphael, Keeper of the Hidden Secrets of the Gifted.

"Professor Raphael would be a fine choice, sir," Francine said. "But if I may be so bold, I would suggest that Elzibeth also join in this training. I believe we discussed her possibly beginning such activities last summer prior to her first year, but she was considered too young. It became painfully obvious this morning that her particular situation suggests that some instruction would be beneficial."

"And you do not feel that Professor Raphael is up to the task of instructing Elzibeth?" Calderón said.

"It's not that, sir," Francine said. "It's just that his level of mastery is terribly sophisticated, which Elzibeth may find to be intimidating. If she is going to do this at her age, I want this to be a positive experience for her. I would want her to feel that every failure was actually a success if you gather my meaning, Headmaster."

"Yes, I see," Calderón said. "The instructor must demonstrate unfailing confidence in every failure and celebrate every success so that Elzibeth does not lose her will to participate but instead gains enthusiasm for the process. Very astute of you, Francine. Very astute. Now I don't suppose you have an alternative instructor in mind."

"I do," Francine said.

"Yes, I thought you might," Calderón said. "And when do you propose to begin?"

"With your blessing, as soon as possible, sir," Francine said.

"Very well then. It seems your mind is made up," Calderón said. "And having had the pleasure of knowing you all these years, I know it will not be up to me to change it. So please, do carry on. I will expect to have a report on the progress of both on my desk before dinner each day. Preferably an hour or so before so that my reading will not interfere with my plans to feast in the Great Dining Hall."

Francine led Finias back to her quarters and picked up the phone to have Elzibeth paged. It wasn't long before Elzibeth came through the door with a wry smile on her face.

"So, you actually made it into her room, aye Shoop. Pretty slick," Elzibeth said.

"Elzibeth!" Francine said, somewhat shocked. "I'll have no more of that kind of talk. Do you understand?"

"I was just teasing ole Shoop here a little. He's still in the drooling on his shoes stage, so I knew nothing was going on," Elzibeth said.

"What is all this nonsense about shoes and drool?" Francine said.

"Oh, it's nothing. Finias here just has the hots for you, but I mean, what guy wouldn't, am I right, Finias?" Elzibeth said.

"I think I'm going to faint," Finias said.

"Is this true?" Francine said, looking directly at Finias.

"Well," Finias began. "I mean, look at you. You're amazing in every way except maybe warmth and charm."

"Is that so?" Francine said. "How's this for warmth and charm?" and she bounced Finias's head off the ceiling.

He settled on the floor in a heap and stayed there, rubbing his head.

"You are a sweet little thing, aren't you?" Finias said.

"Well, you asked for it. I'm very... what did you say... both adroit and nimble about that?" Francine said.

"Might I suggest that we get on with the business that we came here to attend to before my concussion takes hold and I'm unable to concentrate?" Finias said

"Elzibeth was right, you are a bit of a drama queen," Francine said.

"Drama queen," Finias said, surprised. "Did you really say that about me, Elzibeth? I'm hurt by that."

"See sis, there it is," Elzibeth said.

"Yes, quite obvious now that you mention it," Francine said.

"If you two are finished, I think I'm going to go look for a bit of rope, a chandelier, and a wobbly stool," Finias said.

"Sad that he makes it so easy, isn't it, sis?" Elzibeth said.

"Yes, quite sad," Francine said, as the two of them chortled under their breath.

"Well, now that I have been completely emasculated, shall we get on with business?" Finias said.

"Yes, of course," Francine said. "Elizabeth, it has been decided that since Finias is incapable of looking after you for no more than two minutes."

"Five," interrupted Finias.

"Yes, for no more than five minutes, that, though you are quite young, it would be most beneficial for you to receive instruction into the fine art of your great gifts," Francine said.

"Awesome," Elzibeth said.

Chapter 15

The three met outside on the island plateau early, around 7:30 the following morning. The weather was clear with only a slight breeze, and the smell of moist grass and sea hung in the air. Gulls could be heard going about their business from somewhere behind the cliffs, along with the crash of an occasional wave, as hawks circled lazily overhead, taking advantage of a thermal which kept the birds spiraling above as they searched for prey. In the distance, airline vapor trails crisscrossed the sky, and as he watched them dissipate, Finias under his breath wished all safe passage.

Finias noticed too that the plateau itself was of such expanse that if one were not to look toward the mainland, they would not know they were on an island at all.

Francine arrived dressed head to toe in authentic military camouflage, complete with combat boots. Her hair had been pulled through the opening in the back of her camo hat into what Finias thought to be a rather sexy ponytail.

"Hiding from the hawks overhead?" Finias said, referencing her outfit as Francine approached.

"Hiding from you, actually, Mr. Drools on his shoes. Yes, Elzibeth told me all about your little joke," Francine said.

"It was her joke, and I told her straight away that I've never once drooled on my shoes," Finias said.

Finias felt rather silly after saying this but held a stern face to offset his embarrassment.

"Let's get on with this," Elzibeth said. "The sun is hurting my eyes."

"What happened to your sunglasses?" Finias asked.

"I lost them when I smacked that fat lummox in the face with my bag of suckers," Elzibeth said.

"I shall have to see if I can remedy that, being as it is my fault you had to smack anyone in the face with a bag of suckers," Finias said.

"Really?" Elzibeth said. "That would be awesome. I really liked them. Thanks, Shoop. You're alright. Soggy shoes and all."

"Good grief," Finias said. "Are you never to let that go?"

"Nope," Elzibeth said.

The day's lesson began rather simply. Francine began by providing insight into the physical components of their gifts.

"So, the thing you have to understand about being gifted is that we cannot create something out of nothing," Francine said. "For instance, if I am unarmed and in need of a weapon, I could not simply make one appear. It is the same principle with money, food, etc."

"Then how does Briarwood exist?" Finias asked. "Surely it must cost a fortune to keep the place running, and the food—the food is of the highest quality."

"Huh, for someone looking for help from a Wizard in the brain department, that is actually a cogent and reasonable question," Francine said. "The answer is that we can manipulate physical objects and forces which already exist. Our funding comes from several sources, the main being mining. The Order maintains several of the world's largest gold, diamond, and copper reserves through ownership of hundreds of mines, along with bauxite for aluminum and others. You see, it is a simpler matter to extract such things from the ground by manipulation of our gifts than it is to do all that terrible strip mining. As for the food, the chef buys local produce and livestock from a select group, and they simply take a truck across the bridge to go pick it up. Probably why the bridge was visible the day you lost Elzibeth. The balance of things like personal care products, or say canned goods, it's mostly Walmart, Costco, or Food 4 Less."

Now it was Finias's turn to say, "Huh."

"Ah, there is that sharp intellect of yours," Francine said.

"It may be just me, but I'm sensing a bit of hostility here," Finias said.

"Could we please get this over with?" Elzibeth said. "I don't know if it's the sun or you two fighting, but I'm getting a headache."

"Yes, of course," Francine said. "For today, I thought we would start with a protective measure that is both simple and effective. A fireball."

"Cool," Elzibeth said.

"Finias, I want you to look straight away toward the tree line and picture in your mind a fireball resting in your hand," Francine said. "Do you have that?"

"I do," Finias said.

"Now, I want you to picture it just sitting there. It might be moving about a bit, but that is okay. Just pent-up energy," Francine said. "We okay so far?"

"Yes," was all he could muster without breaking his concentration.

"Now you see that tree off to your left? The one with the broken limb?"

"I do."

"Now I want you to project in your mind the fireball leaving your hand and striking that tree. Can you do that?"

"I can," Finias said.

"Then fire when ready."

Suddenly, a fireball appeared in Finias's hand, roughly the size of a grapefruit, and after a moment, it shot forth about twelve feet, landed in the soggy grass, and flamed out into a puff of smoke.

"Splendid," Francine said. "You are one crackerjack defender of our young Elzibeth with such a gift. Tell me, were you born with this talent, or has it simply developed over time?"

"Very funny," was all Finias could muster as both Francine and Elzibeth laughed.

"Okay, Elzibeth, you up for this?" Francine said.

"Heck yeah," Elzibeth said. "This is awesome."

"Okay, do you remember the instructions I gave to Finias?" Francine said.

"Sure do," Elzibeth said.

"Okay, when you are ready, give it a go," Francine said.

And that she did. After a moment's hesitation as Elizbeth's face registered extreme concentration, an enormous fireball, the size of a beach ball, emerged from her now outstretched hand and flew the hundred or so yards across the plateau, obliterating the target tree and three others behind it.

"Goodness gracious," Finias said.

"My word," Francine said.

"Holy cow," Elzibeth said.

The three of them stood in stunned silence for a moment before Finias shouted, "Elzibeth, that was amazing. Good show, kiddo."

"Yes, that was quite something. Well done, Elzibeth," Francine said. "But honey, if I could make a suggestion, it doesn't take a sledgehammer to kill an ant. Do you see my meaning?"

"Yeah, but you have to admit, that was pretty cool," Elzibeth said.

"Yes, very," Francine said. "Let's try not to use that one to show off to your friends, okay?"

"Really?" Elzibeth pleaded. "Not even once?"

"Not even once," Francine said. "I need to be clear on this. If you feel you cannot resist, let me know, and we can gather your friends out here for a show. But you cannot let on as to how you know how to do that. We wouldn't want the other six-year-olds running about setting each other on fire now, would we? Is it a deal?"

"You bet it's a deal. Thanks, sis," Elzibeth said.

"Well, Finias, what say you give it another go?" Francine said.

And so it went. Elzibeth was successful in her second attempt to blow up only one tree, and after several attempts, Finias managed to bounce a fireball short into the trunk of a closer tree, causing no damage.

The rest of the week was spent in a similar fashion, with Elzibeth teleporting all over the place, and Francine running about piecing Finias back together. They learned how to manipulate time and space and to rearrange the physical aspects of matter.

Elzibeth was clearly beyond her age in such things, mastering all in short order. Finias struggled but after a period, began slowly coming around. Francine was unsure as to why he was having difficulties. He just didn't seem to want to change the physical properties of objects and was hesitant to blow things up. In confidence, he told Francine that he just couldn't bring himself to blow up such a majestic tree, and for her part, Francine understood why. It was the reason he was at Briarwood in the first place. His heart.

Chapter 16

Francine stopped by the headmaster's office to drop off a copy of Finias's and Elizbeth's progress reports for the day when she found her mum and dad in conference with Calderón.

"Well, hello," she said upon entering.

"Hello dear," Teri said.

"Good to see you, Francine," Theodore said.

"Please, do come in," Calderón said. "Perfect timing really. Would you be so kind as to give Finias a ring and ask him to join us?"

"Of course. Here, I've brought today's progress reports for you."

"Ah, very good. Please just set them on the credenza there, and I'll get to them a bit later," Calderón said. "It seems that we have very pressing matters at hand that need our immediate attention."

Francine went to the phone and had the operator put out a page to Finias requesting his immediate presence in the headmaster's office.

Finias arrived shortly, gave greetings to all, then settled into one of the oversized chairs directly across from Francine.

"Well, these little get-togethers of ours are becoming quite commonplace," Calderón began. "It may get to the point where I have to keep Theodore and Teri here in the classroom rather than roaming the world so that all the bad news they continue to surprise me with simply goes unnoticed, and we go about our merry way in ignorant bliss."

Theodore and Teri looked taken aback by this bit of news, which did not go unnoticed by the others.

"I jest, of course. You two do fine work in the care and protection of this facility, and I and all the staff and students are grateful for it," Calderón said.

Teri gave an audible sigh of relief. "Oh, good heavens, you frightened me half to death."

"I've heard rumors, but I didn't really want to believe that our classrooms were that frightening," Calderón said.

"Excuse me," Teri said. "I'm afraid I don't understand."

"I apologize," Calderón said. "I was making an off-hand joke about the students being so difficult in the classroom that they're frightening. Oftentimes, my humor is lost even on me. I'm guilty of using it to offset the bad humor I feel when I receive terrible news. Please forgive me."

"Oh, yes, of course," Teri said. "Went right over my head I'm afraid. Anxiety tends to step on my funny bone."

"Yes, I suppose that is true for all of us," Calderón said. "So, getting back to the business at hand, I now introduce our soothsayer, Theodore."

"Soothsayer, yes, I did get that one," Teri said. "Wasn't particularly funny, but I did understand where you were trying to go with it."

Everyone chuckled a bit at this, and it seemed to break up the tension within the group. It had been a stressful time for all lately, and it seemed a little levity always helped to heal things.

Theodore stood to address the group in a more formal manner, but truth be told, he felt the need to move around a bit while he spoke to avoid fidgeting in his chair. He had been terribly tense these past weeks, and he knew the strain was beginning to show.

"Is anyone familiar with the name Tomas Huerta?" Theodore asked.

The room was quiet with various horizontal shakes of the head.

"Cartel boss, drug kingpin, murdering drug smuggler, and all-around bad guy?"

More silence and shakes of the head.

"I thought not. Well, he was decapitated during a birthday celebration for his eldest son in front of a large gathering last evening."

"Good lord," Francine said.

"My word," Calderon said.

"Holy crap," Finias said.

"Yes indeed, to all that," Teri said.

Theodore continued, ignoring the comments. "Huerta's property, if you can imagine, is surrounded on all sides by sheer cliffs. Picture a large, oval-shaped bowl with vertical cliffs along the back and sides. At the bottom of the bowl is a large lake, and Huerta's residence is backed up against the tallest side. On the far end away from the residence is an opening as the two sides taper down to the mouth of a small flow of water which feeds the lake. The only way to Huerta's property is by air, water, or to rappel down the cliffs. Witness statements suggest that a kind of wet black smoke filled the bowl for an extended period and a number of men with guns took control of the compound, killing all of the guards and personal protection for Huerta. That there were any witnesses left alive is a blessing in itself, but I suspect that was done on purpose so that the message of Huerta's demise and the method in which it was carried out would send a signal to others in the underworld business that there is a new sheriff in town, that no one is safe, and whoever or whatever it is means to take over the entire criminal enterprise. Huerta, from what I have been told, was brought out in front of those in attendance, handcuffed to a chair. A gentleman with a machete stood alongside and told the onlookers that this was a message to all that would stand in the way of progress in the new underworld. Whatever that means. Anyway, you know the outcome. The black smoke faded and when clear, the perpetrators were gone."

The silence in the room was deafening. They all looked around at each other, but it was as if no one could find the words to express their thoughts.

Finias was the first to speak.

"I guess what I'm confused about is why should we care? I mean, the guy was a drug-dealing scumbag. Doesn't seem to be much of a loss if you ask me."

"True," Theodore said. "I doubt I will lose much sleep over this. The problem I see is that Huerta's main rival is Francis Marcon. Now, four things come to mind with this. First, could it have been Huerta that ordered the hit on Marcon's son? And if so, did he have the means to do so, and if not, who did he hire? Second, why Marcon's son and not Marcon himself? Clearly, if they could get to the kid as well fortified as his compound was, they could get to Marcon. Third, if Huerta didn't order the hit on Marcon's son, who did? Was it Marcon himself? And fourth, if not Marcon, who is this new Sheriff in town that hit Huerta?"

"Why would you suspect Marcon of hitting his own son?" Francine said.

"A male's intuition I suppose. Anthony. Why Anthony? Why not Francis?" Theodore said.

"Well, Francis is kind of a dorky name," Finias said.

"Good God, Finias," Francine began, "Have you never kept a single stupid thought to yourself? What he is getting at is there is a tradition among certain families to pass down the name of the father. Could it be that Marcon had known that Anthony wasn't his son, and with that, no longer wanted to share the wealth and power?"

"But what would that have to do with the hit on Huerta?" Teri said.

"Nothing, I don't think," Francine said.

Seated frozen and staring about a foot above everyone's head, Francine finally said, "Wait... think about it. In order for Marcon to become the new Sheriff in town, he would need to re-establish his power base in his son's territory, and he would need to eliminate Huerta as his competition."

"Precisely my thought, Francine," Theodore said.

"Well, it sounds like we have much to consider," Calderón said. "The least not being, what role do we play in putting an end to this nonsense in order to protect ourselves from becoming targets."

"I don't see that we need to play any role," Finias said. "I mean, we're not The Avengers."

"Says Mr. Let's punch them in the mouth. What happened to that? No longer so eager for a fight?" Francine said.

"I just don't see the need for us getting involved until we are forced to do so," Finias said. "Let these guys duke it out. Maybe in the end, they will have all killed each other; then we can live peacefully, happily ever after."

"What troubles me," Teri said, "is what if it's not Marcon. Could it be someone from our side using his gifted powers to become the new Sheriff in town?"

"Thaime," Francine said.

"You think?" Finias said, sarcastically.

"Well, we know you don't, so I'll step in here and say it's possible," Francine said.

"Would the two of you please cut out this bickering," Teri said. "It's most unbecoming. Here, why don't the two of you stand up, give each other a hug, and tell each other you are sorry for whatever is eating at the two of you. Come now, I won't take no for an answer."

And with that the two of them stood. The pair locked eyes and moved slowly toward each other, each one looking wary.

Francine was the first to make a move, stepping closer and saying, "I'm sorry that you are such a knucklehead."

"And I'm sorry that, though quite lovey, you are such an outwardly angry young lady."

And with that, they both stepped forward and embraced.

"Now see, isn't that nice," Teri said.

"Yes, I'm about to tear up," Theodore said.

"As touching as a poisonous thorn," Calderón said.

Chapter 17

Finias was currently camped out on the basketball court in his suite, shooting hoops and staying loose. Class sessions were out for the summer, and while he found being cooped up in the confines of Briarwood to be oppressive; the physical activity released some of the pent-up energy he was feeling. Having taken a shot and missed, the ball bouncing off the rim and shooting off to the right, Finias chased it down and set up for another try.

He was about to let go of his shot when the backboards at both ends of the court came to life, and the handsome face of the Briarwood receptionist filled their expanse.

"Good morning, Finias."

"Good morning, Mary," Finias said.

Finias had met Mary only once. He guessed her age to be sixty-ish, and his understanding was that she had been at Briarwood for over forty years.

"Good thing I wasn't in my underpants," Finias said. "Or worse."

"At my age, I could use a little worse," Mary said.

The two of them chuckled at this.

"And what might I do for you this fine day?" Finias said.

"Finias, this is most unusual," Mary said. "But there is a member of the Order here to see you."

"Swell," Finias said. "I could use a little company. Maybe shoot a few hoops."

"No, I don't think you understand," Mary said. "It is one of the Headminsters."

"A member of the High Council is here to see me?" Finias said. "Why on earth would they want to see me?"

"I have no earthly idea. For a member of the High Council to ask to see anyone other than the headmaster himself is most unusual," Mary said. "Why they would ask to see you of all people is beyond me."

"Well, that was insulting, but okay," Finias said. "Send him in."

"It's a she," Mary said.

"Even better."

The television over the bar announced her arrival, and Finias was surprised to see that she was quite attractive. He had pictured her as more of the grumpy school librarian type. Old dusty sweater, hair in a bun, face like a fingerprint.

Before the woman outside could press the intercom, Finias announced, "Please, do come in."

"Oh my," she said as she pushed her way through the door. "You scared the dickens out of me. How did you know I was outside your door?"

Finias pointed to the television which maintained a view of the outer hallway.

"Trust me," he said. "I've been surprised by that myself."

Finias moved forward to greet her.

"Finias Shoop at your service."

"Lindsey Sterling. It is a pleasure to meet you. I've heard so much about you from Calderón during our monthly joint sessions."

"The pleasure is all mine," Finias said. "Might it be too much for me to say that you are...well, not what I was expecting."

"And what were you expecting?" said Lindsey.

"Not someone who looks like you. I am most pleasantly surprised," Finias said.

"Why thank you," said Lindsey. "How charming."

"And sincere," Finias said. "You are indeed very, um, surprising."

"Why Finias, are you hitting on me?" asked Lindsey, as she tilted her head slightly and smiled.

"No, no. Of course not. If I were hitting on you, you would feel uncomfortable and a little sorry for me," Finias said. "I apologize, my mouth often runs ahead of my brain."

"You're cute," said Lindsey.

"I'm surprised Calderón has mentioned me at all. Something about him makes me feel small, as if I'm always about to be in trouble to some degree."

Lindsey laughed, and Finias got the feeling that this meeting might not be so bad after all.

"Trust me, when Calderón addresses the council with his mind set on something, we all feel as if we are about to be in trouble to some degree."

It was Finias's turn to laugh, and he felt comfortable enough to offer Lindsey a drink.

"It's a bit early, but I suppose if you had champagne with a splash of orange juice, I wouldn't complain bitterly," said Lindsey.

While tending to their drinks, Finias couldn't help but notice that she was indeed attractive. Lindsey Sterling was tall, at 5'-9," and the four-inch heels she was wearing put her at nearly eye level with Finias. She was dressed casually in jeans, a tan, grey, white, and black horizontal striped cotton shirt worn long under a mid-thigh heather-colored basket weave cardigan worn open, which Finias thought gave her a rather alluring look.

Her hair was jet black and cut short around the back and sides. The top was longish with short wispy bangs above the eyebrows that gave her a sexy appeal. She was trim with long legs and a nice figure with wide-set brown eyes, a perfect nose, and a full, sensual mouth.

"Here you go," Finias said, handing Lindsey her drink.

"Salute."

"Salute."

"So, shall we have a seat?" Finias said.

"Yes, let's do. I can't stay long. Which is probably a good thing for my reputation. If I stayed too long here with a handsome young man such as yourself, people may begin to talk," said Lindsey, touching his arm lightly as they sat together on the couch.

"Handsome?" Finias said.

"Indeed, you are."

"Well thank you, um, you have a pretty nice lady setup going on there yourself," Finias said.

Lindsey laughed and said, "you might want to work on that."

"I don't get out much," Finias said.

"Let's remedy that," said Lindsey. "Meet me tonight at Akitas, 7:00 sharp. It's a seafood and sushi restaurant about four miles southeast of Brighton. Any cabbie will know where to find it. It's quite popular. We have important things to discuss lest you get the idea that this is anything other than business."

"No, of course not," Finias said, then asked. "I'll need to take a cab?"

"Of course, you can't simply plop yourself tableside. Someone might choke on an edamame."

"Look, I have to ask, if this business is so important, why not talk with Theodore? Or Teri?"

"Theodore poses a threat to my safety. The people he asks questions of are not overly fond of him nosing around in their business, and the potential of his being seen in my presence would put me in jeopardy. Teri is predisposed to place blame for all this nonsense on Thaime, which frankly, I too believe to be more likely than not. But I need someone with an open mind."

"Okay, I suppose. I mean, I don't know what I have to offer, but I know there have been some strange goings-on that I would like to discuss. And I suppose that you have heard tell about the troubles with Elzibeth lately and that I had been a part of that. So, I understand that you might want to hear what took place firsthand. I hope you weren't offended. I had to ask you understand," Finias said.

"I do," said Lindsey.

"Will you be so kind as to provide me a hint of what we are to discuss," Finias said.

"And lessen the suspense? I think not," said Lindsey with her most charming smile. "Anticipation is half the fun, don't you think?"

"Then I shall be fully anticipated when I arrive," Finias said.

"And I certainly hope before we finish," said Lindsey, giving him a devilish smile. "I would love to stay to discuss your full anticipation at…length," said Lindsey, eyeing him up and down. "But I really must be going."

"Shall I see you to the door," Finias said.

"I would be disappointed if you didn't."

As they were making their way through the Grand Entrance, a section of curved wall opened to their left, and Francine stepped through from wherever it was that she had been.

Their eyes met and locked for a moment, and Finias took the opportunity to place his hand at the small of Lindsey's back as he ushered her through the front door.

The two said goodbye after confirming their plans for the evening, and Lindsey was shuttled away in an awaiting limousine; her chauffeur having been standing ready at the door awaiting her return.

Finias noticed a bulge under the chauffeur's coat, which he assumed to be a firearm. Not common apparel for gifted folk he thought. And why would she need a driver at all? Why, if she so chose, she could have teleported straight away into Briarwood.

Strange he thought, then simply dismissed the whole notion. She was a member of the high council, and it was probably required of her to fit in somewhat with the non-gifted community.

When Finias returned to his suite, he noticed that he had a message at the ready, so he picked up the phone and retrieved it. It was Francine. "Call me," was all it said, and so he did.

"Francine, Finias."

"So, who's your lady friend?" Francine said.

"Wouldn't you like to know?" Finias said, and she hung up.

Finias dialed her number again, and after a number of rings, the call went straight to voicemail.

"Oh, for goodness sake," he said out loud.

Finias headed out the door to find Francine and made his way into the Grand Entrance where he met her hurriedly coming his way.

"How dare you?" Francine said, at the top of her voice.

"How dare I what?" Finias said.

"How dare you bring your lady friend here then flaunt her in front of me," Francine said.

"What? Wait a second. What?" Stumbled Finias.

"You are the Keeper of a child. Your charge and a very special one at that. You dishonor her by dishonoring yourself in this way," Francine said.

"In what way? What are you talking about? And, Keeper, yes, I do remember now that's what it's called. Elzibeth thought that since she was the Chargee that I would be her Charger or something like that," Finias said.

"What on earth are you talking about?" Francine continued to rage.

"What?" Finias said. "I forgot about the Keeper thing is all."

"Ugh, you are unbearable," she said, as she stormed off to the room selection panel and pressed several buttons in succession then stood waiting for a door to open somewhere along the vast expanse of curved concrete wall.

Finias walked up behind her and said, "having to wait for the building to shift around is a bit of a nuisance when you are trying to storm off isn't it."

Francine turned around with her head down and tears in her eyes. Finias was taken aback by this as Francine seemed to have folded into herself. Up to this moment, she had seemed to him to be so strong and had demonstrated nothing but self-confidence to the point that he wished to be much like her, except maybe lacking a bit of her temper.

Taking her into his arms, he hugged her and held her close. He kissed the top of her head as she wept, and being unsure of what to do next, he simply continued to hold her gently as one might hold an injured bird.

"Look, this is all a misunderstanding," Finias said, whispering into her hair. "Things are not what they seem, and they are certainly not what you think. Let's go back to my suite and talk about this. Okay?"

Francine simply nodded her head in the affirmative as Finias took her hand and the two of them set off.

When they reached his suite, Finias went to the bar and poured Francine a glass of wine, and the two of them took up space on his couch.

"Here take this," Finias said, "It will help to calm you."

"I didn't mean to tease you about the woman," Finias said. "She was here to see me on business which I'll explain to you later after you have had a chance to settle down okay?"

Francine simply nodded between sobs.

"Okay, good. Hand me your glass," Finias said, Francine having nearly drained her drink in one pull.

He took her glass and placed it on the table next to them. "Now come here," Finias said. He gently drew her to him and realized it was the only time, other than the forced hug at their last meeting, that they had any physical contact. It was exhilarating.

Finias couldn't help but wonder if Francine had a similar thought or feeling. He suddenly became very aware of her body pressed against him, her scent, and the feel of her breath on his neck. Along with this awareness came a feeling of warmth that spread throughout his being—thoughts of deep caring for this strong woman who now seemed so fragile.

As Finias pondered these newfound feelings, he noticed that Francine's shuddering sobs had begun to ebb. He pulled away just enough to look deep into her emerald eyes and kissed her softly on the forehead.

Seeing the tears on her face made his heart ache and he placed his hand on her cheek and, with his thumb, removed a single tear that had made its way to her chin. He then moved slowly to her and softly kissed away the remaining tears from either side of her lovely face. Francine looked up into his eyes, and he held her gaze for a moment before leaning forward and touching his forehead to hers, their mouths inches apart, and said in his softest voice, "You should consider anger management."

Francine began to laugh/cry and their heads bumped together as she convulsed.

"No, I mean seriously," Finias said. "Seek help for the sake of mankind."

Francine socked him in the arm.

"See, there it is right there," Finias said.

"Pitiful," she spluttered, and he kissed her. Softly at first, then more passionately. She smelled of peaches and vanilla, and her lips were as soft as rose petals. They embraced and Finias lowered her to the couch.

Side by side, only inches apart, Finias moved a strand of hair back over her smallish ear. They said nothing for a while, finding that it was enough just to be near.

Francine, her heart pounding, wasn't sure what comes next her not ever having been with a man. Her anxiety over her feelings for Finias, which seemed to have developed without thought now turned into a warmth she felt throughout and a sudden desire burned within.

Her want blossomed into a yearning which she was familiar with and which surpassed her trepidation and she whispered, "Finias, I'm frightened."

"Of what could you possibly be frightened?" Finias said.

"Of what I'm about to say..." Francine hesitated as she reached out and traced a finger along Finias's cheek. "I've never had a man...make love to me."

"Hmmm...Yes, a frightening thought indeed," Finias said, holding her gaze. "But fret not dear, as neither have I."

And with this, they fell into each other's arms and kissed, though laughing.

"You're an idiot," she said, pulling away.

"Sometimes, I suppose," Finias said. "Let's just say you bring out the best in me."

"So, being an idiot is your best?" Francine said, smiling.

"Being around you is difficult for me," Finias said. "The more I try to impress, the more I fail."

Francine moved so that she was on her back, and she pulled Finias to her.

"Maybe this time will be different," she said.

Chapter 18

Having made love, the two lay as one, reveling in the moment and enjoying the feel of each other's touch.

"If I were to share something with you which is wildly personal to me, would you promise to both not laugh, nor repeat it to anyone?" Finias said.

"Of course. That's a silly question," Francine said.

"I've never…done that before either," Finias admitted.

"What?" Francine said, somewhat shocked.

"You promised not to laugh."

"I'm not laughing at all. (To Finias, it sounded like she had said atoll). I must say, for your first time up to the plate, you really knocked it out of the park," Francine said, stretching out the "really."

"Yeah."

"Yeah."

"Well, you did a rather splendid, um, job yourself if I may use that term loosely, and I mean in an all-around sense. Not just the…," Finias paused.

"Yes, yes, I know. Please don't say it," Francine said.

"Okay, but just so you know, you were spectacular," Finias said.

"Yeah."

"Yeah."

"Well, good for us then," Francine said.

"What say we get dressed and go grab a bit of lunch?" offered Finias.

"I'd rather just lay here forever," Francine said, moving a finger along his chest.

"I as well, but I'm afraid your energetic performance has caused me to work up a bit of an appetite," Finias said.

"Yes, I suppose there will be no need for calisthenics for either of us today. And, I too have a bit of an appetite," Francine said.

"For round two?" Finias said, ever hopeful.

"No, you hound dog," Francine said. "For food."

"Pity," Finias said.

At that moment, Elzibeth popped up on the giant screen and shouted, "Hey, Finias, you in there?"

"Good lord, where are my clothes? Come on, out of the way," Francine said, as she hurried from the couch, shoving Finias away and unceremoniously dumping him to the floor.

"Quiet, she can hear you," whispered Finias.

"Francine, is that you?" Elzibeth said. "What are you doing in there and what is all this about your clothes?"

"Nothing dear, hold on just a minute," Francine said.

A mad scramble ensued, and after a few minutes, Finias had his shoes on, Francine had straightened in front of the mirror, and the cushions of the couch were fluffed up.

Finias went to the door and let Elzibeth in.

"What's going on? What's this about clothes? And why do you have lipstick everywhere?" Elzibeth said.

"What? How did? What?" Stammered Finias as he wiped his shirt sleeve across his mouth.

"You really need to work on that. I mean, for real," Elzibeth said.

"Yes, well, lipstick you say. You see, I had dropped something on the floor, and Francine and I both reached for it at the same time, and when we were coming back up, our faces bumped. Must have gotten a little on me."

"Uh huh," Elzibeth said.

"So, tell me what brings you here?"

"Wanted to see if you'd had lunch yet," Elzibeth said. "But it looks like you two skipped lunch and went straight for dessert."

"Elzibeth!" Francine said.

"Really!" Finias said.

"Uh huh," Elzibeth said, wearing a mischievous smile.

Neither Finias nor Francine knew what to say, so they both stood still for a moment, staring at the carpet. Elzibeth continued to smile, making them feel all the more uncomfortable when she offered.

"I'm guessing here, but I suspect you two have worked up an appetite. What say we go grab a bite?"

"You are beyond your years, child. But, yes, of course, let us go grab a bite," Finias said, not sure what else to say.

"Certainly, and as for you, young lady, I'll have you know that my appetite has nothing to do with my being with Finias; it's simply just well past lunch, and I had a rather light breakfast," Francine said, doing her best to cover her tracks.

"Uh huh," Elzibeth said, still smiling. "So, let's go."

And off the three of them went. There were others waiting in the Grand Entrance for the building to shift to gain access to the Great Dining Hall.

Finias, for his part, was wearing a broad grin, while Francine had the distinct feeling that everyone was staring at her with knowing looks. It was but a few moments until the doors opened with the now familiar whoosh, but to Francine, it seemed an eternity.

It was a bit late for lunch, and most of the usual crowd had thinned. They found seats readily available toward the front and settled into quiet conversation about anything under the sun that didn't involve lipstick or missing clothing.

On cue, a waiter floated near and offered his greetings.

"Francine, Elzibeth, so good to see you. And Finias, is it not?"

"It is," Finias said. "And what delectable items do you have in store for us today?"

"If you will allow, I would like to recommend something spicy."

Finias and Francine exchanged looks.

"Something to, shall we say, kick-start a fire in one's loins," he continued.

"Oh God," Francine said, under her breath.

Finias and Francine both found the napkins in their laps to be in need of attention.

"Ah, yes. A fire in our loins. Splendid," Finias said.

Francine shot him a look that said, "shut up about your spicy fired-up loins."

"Very well then, I recommend that you begin with the Spicy Avocado and Cucumber Soup with Lemon to be followed by Snapper Zarandeado with a grilled jalapeño pepper and vegetable salad."

"Sound hot enough for you?" said the waiter with a bit of emphasis on the word "hot."

"Yes, sounds hot, very, very hot," Finias said, as he took a sip of water and Francine rolled her eyes as she sighed. "Two of those if that is fine by you, Francine."

"Yes, fine, that's fine," Francine said, somewhat flustered.

"And for you, Miss Elzibeth?"

"I don't think I want anything that's going to be snapping at me," Elzibeth said. "I think I'll just have French toast with extra powdered sugar."

"Elzibeth, it's lunchtime, not breakfast," Francine said.

"So?" Elzibeth said.

"Not this again," Finias said.

"Okay, fine," Francine said. "But just this once."

Elzibeth flashed her most brilliant smile and said, "French Toast, please."

"Very well then, off I go."

And off he went.

Finias and Francine began an awkward conversation about Baltic weather patterns or some other nonsense, neither of them knowing exactly what they were talking about, but it seemed to them that the more they discussed something of disinterest to Elzibeth, the less likely it would be that she would interrupt with questions about what took place in Finias's suite.

The food arrived in due course, and the three of them settled into their meals to the delight of all.

Finias and Francine each, to their own, felt a sense of relief that to Elzibeth, it seemed, the memory of the day's prior goings-on was now lost in a puddle of maple syrup and buttery French toast.

"Is Finias going to be my brother-in-law?" Elzibeth said, without preamble.

Finias choked on a jalapeño, and Francine spilled her drink.

"What?" Both Francine and Finias said in unison.

"You know, if you guys get married," Elzibeth said.

"NO!" They both said as if synchronized.

"Why not?" Elzibeth said.

"What would make you ask such a question?" Francine said.

"Well, Shoop here is a pretty good egg as far as guys go, though his fireball wasn't much good. And I think from what I learned today he's pretty much done drooling on his shoes. Also, you are the strongest, smartest woman I know, and you'd make the greatest mum in the world. So, it seems like your strengths would make up for him being him, and you two would do OK," Elzibeth said.

"Thank you for that resounding vote of confidence. I shall have to put that on my resume," Finias said. "Listen, Elzibeth, I will admit Francine is very dear to me, but we hardly know each other."

"Seems to me that you would have to know a whole lot more than you knew a couple of hours ago," Elzibeth said, placing emphasis on the word "have."

"Alright, enough. We are not getting married, understood?" Francine said.

"Yeah, I guess," Elzibeth said. "Is it alright if I remain skeptical?"

"If that suits you and you drop this topic, then yes, that's fine. By the way, do you really think I would be a great mum?" Francine said.

"Of course," Elzibeth said.

"Ahhh...that is the sweetest thing I think I've ever heard. You never fail to surprise me, Elzibeth," Francine said.

"I hope not. Life would be boring without surprises," Elzibeth said.

Chapter 19

During dessert, in which Francine and Finias each had fresh berries and cream to cleanse their palates of spice, and Elzibeth dug into a small hot fudge sundae, Francine mentioned that she and Finias had never gotten around to discussing who it was that had come to visit him in his suite earlier that morning.

"What kept you all from discussing it?" Elzibeth asked between bites.

"Never you mind," Francine said.

"You must have been kissing and stuff because he had lipstick everywhere," Elzibeth said.

"You want to help me with this?" Francine said, giving Finias the evil eye.

"No, not at all," Finias said. "You're doing just fine."

Francine kicked him under the table.

"Ouch," he said. "I mean, of course. Look, Elzibeth, Francine and I have come to care for each other, and when two adults care for each other, their relationship takes on certain physical aspects…ouch…um, you know, like holding hands and things."

"What things? Like kissing and stuff, right?" Elzibeth said.

"Yes, but not like passionate…ouch. Will you stop that?"

"Elzibeth, Finias and I, in a moment of weakness and after I had a glass of wine, might have kissed. But just once, and it was just the corner of his mouth and mostly his cheek," Francine said. "That is why you should never, ever, drink alcohol when alone with a boy."

"So how did he get lipstick on his collar?" Elzibeth said.

"It's a messy business, lipstick," Finias said. "Have you ever broken an ink pen, then you get a tiny drop of ink on you and all of a sudden it's everywhere? Kind of like that."

"Uh huh," Elzibeth said. "So, it was the kiss on the part mouth cheek thing that kept you both from talking?" she asked.

"That's right," Francine said.

"For like an hour?" Elzibeth said.

"How do you know it to have been an hour?" Francine said.

"I was checking the monitor of the entry to see if there was a line for lunch," Elzibeth said. "I saw you yelling at Finias, then you weren't. Then you were walking with him toward a door in the wall that opened to the hallway to his room, and you were holding hands. When I went to get him for lunch about an hour later, you were still there."

"Well, that about covers it," Finias said.

"You're not being helpful," Francine said. "Look, let's just forget about this for now, sweetheart, okay?" Francine said, rubbing her temples.

"Okay, but you two are not making a whole lot of sense," Elzibeth said.

Afterward, the three of them made their way toward Francine's suite. Finias, being cautious, suggested that they go there as he did not want them to go back to his suite until he could make a clean sweep for incriminating evidence.

Stopping, Francine took Elzibeth aside and told her that she and Finias had important business to attend to, and that she should run off and find her friends for a bit. Fortunately, Elzibeth did so without a fuss and another round of questions.

Finias, sensing a potential opening, suggested that he and Francine backtrack to his suite so that they could settle in and maybe take the bed for a test drive this time rather than the couch.

"So, what? Now that we have been intimate this one time you think I'm going to sleep with you whenever you want?" Francine said, a look of incredulity on her face.

"Well...yes," Finias said.

"Not a chance, mister," Francine said. "First, you have some explaining to do about that woman in your room, and second, I'm not a toy. You don't just get to play with me whenever you like. Besides, as you were so eager to point out, we barely know each other."

"Let's be honest, I know every lovely inch of you," Finias said.

"I meant emotionally. And again. No," Francine said.

"Are you sure?" Finias said. "You heard Elzibeth, an hour. That means I'm not only quite the ladies' man, but I'm also a stud."

"Uh huh, you keep thinking that, big boy," Francine said.

"Big boy? I like the sound of that. I might have to get a tattoo."

"Good grief, though I have to admit I had no complaints," said Francine, giving him a sexy smile.

"You don't know it, but in my mind, I'm patting myself on the back."

"I was going to say something snarky, but after your performance, I think I'll join you. You deserve a pat on the back," Francine said, taking his hand in hers as they walked.

"Did I say back? I meant backside," Finias said.

"Men are pigs," Francine said.

Chapter 20

Upon their arrival at Francine's suite, Finias moved to sit in a black leather rocker/recliner, while Francine curled her legs up under her on the couch.

"So, what is it that you would like to know?" Finias said.

"Who was the pretty lady in your room, how long was she there, what was her purpose in being there, and did you do anything that you should be ashamed of while she was there?" Francine asked.

"Pretty, you say? I hadn't noticed," Finias said.

"Liar. Now, are you going to answer my questions, or do I need to bring Elzibeth back here to grill you?" Francine said.

"Oh God, please no. That was brutal," he said, and the two of them laughed.

"Hmmm…" Finias began. "I really don't know where to start. Now that I think about it, the whole thing seems a little preposterous, so hang in there with me, and I'll do my best to explain."

"I was shooting some hoops, you know, to keep my sexy body in shape for my lady."

Francine rolled her eyes but didn't interrupt.

"When Mary gave me a shout over the backboards," Finias said.

"Good thing you weren't in your skivvies," Francine said.

"That's what I said. I got the feeling that if I were, she might have barged in and tried to remove them," Finias said.

"Really?" Francine said. "At her age."

"Yes."

"Well, good for her," Francine said.

"Anyway, Mary informs me that there is a member of the order there to see me, and I say fine, send them in, and she tells me it's not what I think. The visitor is one of the Headminsters."

"Impossible," Francine said, startled at this revelation. "The Headminsters' anonymity is paramount to their safety. I doubt any of them would make such a public appearance."

"Briarwood is not exactly Disneyland, Francine," Finias said.

"That is true… but I believe not even mum nor dad have met any of the members of the council. Calderón is the only person I know who could identify any one of them."

Francine thought this over for a moment.

"So, okay, maybe it's not out of the question," Francine said. "I suppose she would appear to be just another member of the order on a visit to their child or for some other purpose. And she was dressed quite nicely in a modern sort of way. Not in a stuffy, dusty sweater wearing her hair in a bun sort of way."

"That's what I thought too," Finias said. "Why is it, do you think, we believe the members of the High Council to be decrepit old fuddy-duddies? I mean, couldn't they just be normal people like us with everyday problems, cares, and concerns?"

"I don't know?" Francine said. "I suppose they could. Being known as the Council of Old, I've created a mental image in my mind that is not apparently consistent with their reality."

"Me too. I had prejudiced myself in that regard," Finias said. "Then when she walked in, I was like, holy cow, she's hot."

"Did you now," Francine said.

"No, no. Not hot," Finias said, backtracking. "She walked with a limp and was somewhat stooped over, and she smelled of cheese and feet," Finias said.

"You're ridiculous," Francine said.

"But studly."

"I've no argument to counter that," Francine said, getting up from the couch and moving to sit on Finias's lap.

"So, Mr. Studly, do you think you could go another round?" she asked, her warm breath on his ear. "Or is your gun more like a musket, one shot then it takes forever to reload?"

"As you know, I'm new to this, so as I see it, there is only one way to find out."

And he stood with Francine in his arms as she began to unbutton his shirt on the way to her bed.

Chapter 21

"We really need to get a grip on ourselves," Francine said. "Or we'll never get anything done."

"I don't know, work is not nearly as much fun as the grip you had on me a moment ago," Finias said. "Nice touch in the playful department, and yes, pun intended."

"Stop that kind of talk," Francine said.

"Sorry." Finias said. "I guess I was getting a little full of myself thinking I'm a stud."

"No, you weren't," Francine said, kissing him lightly on the cheek. "Come, let's get dressed before Elzibeth stumbles along again."

And so, they did. The day was slipping into afternoon, and Finias had yet to tell Francine that he was having dinner with Lindsey later. He wasn't exactly jumping at the chance to dive into that pool but knew nonetheless that it was necessary that he do so.

"It's beautiful out, why don't we go for a walk, and I'll do my best to fill you in on the details of my meeting with Lindsey," Finias said. "Besides, we don't seem to do our best work when we are in the company of a sofa or mattress."

"I don't know, I would have to say that the work you performed was exemplary," Francine said.

"I think my musket just reloaded," Finias said.

"Jeez, we're like a couple of horny teenagers," Francine said. "Though proper girls are never to be referred to in such a way."

"There is nothing proper about you young lady from what I've learned," Finias said, moving to give her a hug.

"Perhaps, but that is only for you to know understood?" Francine said, while giving Finias a look that said she meant business.

"Snow cones in the arctic understood," Finias said.

Though a bit windy, the sun was shining brightly between high, thin clouds. The ocean air was crisp and clean and as they walked the perimeter of the plateau, an occasional wisp of mist reached them from the waves below, ever fierce in their determination as they crashed into the sheer rock face of the island. Gulls floated lazily in the currents of air pushing upward from the cliffs as another of the beautiful hawks which seemed countless on the island could be heard some ways off in the distance.

"So, what was interesting about her visit," continued Finias, as the two strolled along at a leisurely pace. "Was her air of casualness. She walked in as if she had known me forever, said I was handsome of all things, and touched my arm as we sat on the sofa and said something about anticipation and length. It was as if she was flirting with me but in a not so an obvious way."

"She said you were handsome?" Questioned Francine. "And what's this about length?"

"She confused me with that, so I don't know. You do find me handsome though, do you not?" Finias said.

"Of course, but that type of talk is a bit strange for a first meeting don't you think? Particularly coming from a member of the high council," Francine said. "So, how did you respond?"

"I told her she had nice lady parts?" Finias said.

"You what!" shouted Francine in surprise.

"Well, I didn't want to be rude," Finias said.

You are something else you know that" Francine said. "I'm not particularly sure I want to hear the rest, but I suppose it's necessary that I do so."

"So, she asked if I was hitting on her and I told her no, that if I were it would be recognizable by the clumsiness of my approach," Finias said.

"That is true," Francine said.

"Thanks," Finias said. "So anyway, she invited me to dinner tonight around 7:00."

Stopping, Francine turned, a look of surprise on her face. "For what purpose?" she said.

"She didn't say exactly, only that it was something she didn't feel comfortable discussing with Theodore or Teri," Finias said.

They had reached a point in their walk in which it was decided best to turn around and head back being aware of the time and the distance they had traveled.

"Something about this just doesn't feel right," Francine said.

"How so?"

"I just can't wrap my mind around the fact that a member of the high council came to your chambers, which is highly inappropriate to begin with by the way, flirted with you, then talked you into a dinner date."

"It's not a date," Finias said.

"Trust me, it's a date," Francine said. "I understand these things better than you, my being a woman. Especially if she is anticipating your length."

"That's not what she said, though I do suppose that its fate that you have worn me out today in case she does begin to get frisky with me," Finias said.

"Oh please. And if I hadn't, what would you have done," Francine said.

"I'd probably have made in my pants and run home crying," Finias said.

The two of them laughed a little at this before he continued.

"Besides, I would have no interest in her as my heart had already been devoted to you my dear Francine, the loveliest of all," Finias said.

"Why thank you," Francine said. "That is so sweet. So, I have your heart, do I?" Francine said.

"You've had it from the moment we met. Aside from your obvious anger issues, there is this delightful, hard to describe, brave and bright-eyed girlish quality to you," Finias said.

"Ahhh..." Francine said. Stopping, she moved to him, and putting her arms around his neck, gave him an extended warm kiss.

"You know you had better allow me to concentrate on things other than you at the moment, or I may be tempted to take you right here," Finias said.

"Is that right? You think you could just take me?" Francine said, starring into his eyes.

"Yes."

Francine flushed and moved away gathering herself.

"Anyway, as I was saying," Francine began, "so she asked you to meet her for dinner in a place isolated from the protections of Briarwood, a place where if she had any serious business to attend to could have been wrapped up here on the grounds. And proper protocol would dictate that she meet with the Headmaster first with you to be called in for introductions. It just smells fishy that's all."

"We live by the ocean, it always smells fishy around here," Finias said.

"God you are impossible. Did you not hear a word I said?"

"I have to admit it is difficult for me to concentrate when you are wearing those terribly short shorts. Do you even have panties on?" Finias said.

"These are my running shorts and are meant to be of this length and never you mind what I'm wearing," Francine said. "And don't you have an off switch for that libido of yours."

"Yes, but it malfunctions when I'm around you. And, by the way If they were any shorter, half the men on the island might inadvertently walk off the edge, having been thoroughly distracted," Finias said.

"Well, never mind my shorts," Francine said. "Just try and pay attention."

"I was," Finias said.

"Not to my bum. To my words...Idiot." She said.

"Oh...Gotcha. You know, idiot is not known to be a term of endearment," Finias said.

"I know, it just slips out as with you it seems so natural to do so," Francine said.

"Well, as long as we understand each other," Finias said. "So, where were you going with your theory. Do you suspect her of being an impostor?"

"I'm not sure," Francine said. "If indeed she is not the true Headminster, that would be a rather bold move, marching straight away into Briarwood and introducing herself as a member of the High Council. And she must be from the gifted community because the road is not visible today, and I noticed she had arrived by car as she had a driver waiting when you walked her out. If she was not of the Order, how would she know the road to be there?"

"I wonder how he navigated that?" Finias said.

"Once through the arch, he probably picked a point in the distance and hoped for the best. The road is rather wide," Francine said.

"I see," Finias said.

"Anyway, her driver would not have been able to get through the protections without her unless he is of the gifted community himself," Francine said.

"I'm almost positive he was carrying a gun," Finias said. "If he were of the Order, what would be the need of that?"

"Suppose he was involved with non-gifted people and had to carry on the pretense of being one of them," Francine said.

"Possible," Finias said. "As for Lindsey, do you understand there to be any pictures of her on the grounds that I could take a look at to try and identify her?"

"Doubtful. I've been here since childhood and I've never seen a picture of any High Council members, present or past. Again, their privacy is held in the strictest of confidence lending more credence to my theory that something about this just doesn't smell right. She is now identifiable by at least three people, and who knows how many Mary might have alerted to her little visit prior to you parading her out the front door," Francine said.

"I did not parade her," Finias said.

"You kind of did, and you were not inconspicuous about it, having left a trail of drool on the floor," Francine said.

"Good grief," Finias said. "Am I never going to live that down?"

"Nope," Was all Francine said, pulling Finias close by his arm and resting her head on his shoulder as they walked.

Chapter 22

Upon their return to Briarwood, Finias and Francine met up with Elzibeth and her friends. Elzibeth looked a little worse for wear, having spent time with her friends in the school art studio molding clay and playing with paints. To Francine, she and her friends looked as if they had been in a food fight, only with art supplies. She had clay and paint in her hair and on her face, and it was splattered across her front. Her friends were covered in varying colors of paint and clay, looking a bit cartoonish.

"Hey sis," Elzibeth said.

"What in heaven's name happened to you?" Francine asked.

"Oh, this? Nothing really. We were just goofing around over at the art school," Elzibeth replied.

One of her young friends, a pretty brown-haired girl named Missy, spoke up and said, "You should have seen it, it was so cool."

"What was so cool?" Francine asked.

"Elzibeth was using the potter's wheel and she was making this big bowl, and we thought the clay was boring just being all grey, so we dumped a bunch of paint in it. Elzibeth, using magic or something, got it spinning so fast it just blew apart. It was awesome," Missy explained in one rushed sentence.

"I see," Francine said. "So, after this awesome explosion, did you clean up the awesome mess you made?"

"Elzibeth did," said Missy. "I don't know how, but suddenly everything was back as it was, and we got the heck out of there."

"Elzibeth, if you are now so capable in the use of your gifts, would it not have been prudent to also clean up yourself and your friends as well?" Francine asked.

"Sure, I suppose. But what fun is that? It's a great story to tell, and if we'd cleaned up, it would be less believable. So, we have been walking around to the other dorms kind of showing off," Elzibeth said.

"Sounds like you have had quite the day," Francine said. "What say we go get you cleaned up?"

"Yeah, the clay in my hair is all dried up, and it's starting to bounce off my head when I walk," Elzibeth said.

Finias let out a chuckle.

"Since you find this so amusing, would you care to do the honors?" Francine asked.

"She's a bit old for me to bathe, don't you think?" Finias said.

"Not if you take them out back and hose them down," Francine suggested.

"I'd love to, but I need to get ready for my date," Finias said.

"I thought you said it wasn't a date," Francine remarked.

"I didn't think so at first, but you've convinced me of the errors of my ways," Finias said.

"I'll give you errors of my ways upside your head if you don't behave yourself tonight," Francine warned.

"And how will you know?" Finias asked.

"Because now that you have just let on that there is a possibility that you are not to be trusted, I think I'll be coming with you," Francine declared.

"You most certainly will not," Finias countered.

"What's all this about a date, Shoop?" Elzibeth interjected.

"It's a complicated matter, one that I think we should give some attention to before I leave," Finias said.

"Before we leave," Francine corrected.

"To be discussed," Finias said. "Why don't we all go get cleaned up and meet back in my quarters in half an hour?"

"Half an hour? Are you mad?" Francine exclaimed. "It will take at least that long to get the clay out of Elzibeth's hair."

"Okay, yes. You are certainly correct on that," Finias conceded. "How long do you suppose then?"

"It's just a bit past 2:00 now. Let's say we meet at your suite at 6:30?" Francine proposed.

"6:30?" Finias exclaimed. "Rome was built in less time."

"There he goes with the drama again," Elzibeth said.

"Most unbecoming, isn't it?" Francine agreed.

"Most," Elzibeth concurred.

"I'm not being dramatic; I'm simply making the point that you girls fuss around too much. Get in, get out and be done with it is what I say," Finias argued.

"Yes, I've recently become familiar with that approach," Francine said, giving Finias a playful look.

Finias flushed.

"Yes, well, first time for everything, am I right?" Finias returned.

Now it was Francine's turn to blush.

"Look, it takes a girl time to prepare for such a thing as being an uninvited guest of two people out on a date," Francine explained. "Besides, I want to make sure that Elzibeth has something to eat before we go."

"Fine," Finias agreed. "But it's not really a date if you are going to tag along."

"Tag along? Is that what I am to you? Your little pet on a leash? I'll have you know that there are dangerous things going on that involve me just as much as you, and if you want to go carrying on this little affair of yours with miss touched my arm, it may well be that you are walking into something that is beyond your measure and I'll not stand idly by while you get in over your head for something as silly as your bravado or stupidity," Francine said, with an emphasis on stupidity.

"I'll do some research for you tomorrow on the anger management thing," Finias said. "Maybe there are some free classes at the local college."

"Awph," Francine said, and she stormed off. "Come, Elzibeth, leave that grizzled pig of a man to himself."

Chapter 23

Six thirty rolled around, and the girls were nowhere to be found. Finias simply stood in his room and watched the minute hand spin until somewhere around 6:38 when Francine and Elzibeth finally appeared on the television and said, "We're here."

"About time," Finias said, though somewhat under his breath, aware of being heard. "Come in."

Francine was dressed to the nines in a stunning, tight-fitting red dress with thin straps and color-matched heels. She wore an elegant necklace of diamonds and sapphires which accentuated her ample breasts, with her hair pulled back and clipped in a way that made Finias's knees go weak.

"My God, you are stunning. And that dress," Finias said. "You didn't perchance wear something so dramatic, and somewhat short I notice, to simply show off your great legs and other...um, assets, to give Lindsey a bit of what for, now did you?"

"Oh, this old thing," Francine said. "And, yes, of course."

"That's my girl," Finias said, and as he moved to take her into his arms, Elzibeth suddenly came through the door, to his surprise.

"Hey, Shoop," Elzibeth said.

"Elzibeth...so good to see you," Finias said, trying hard and failing to hide his surprise. "You clean up rather nicely," Finias said.

"Oh, this old thing," Elzibeth said, obviously having just overheard Francine. She was wearing bib overalls with a T-shirt under and her now-familiar tennies.

"So, being that you arrived right on time as scheduled," Finias said, giving Francine a look. "I think it best we get down to business straight away."

And that they did. Finias began by seating everyone comfortably, offered beverages which were declined, and began in this way.

"So, I take it by your dress that you still intend to be a part of this...meeting I am to have with the Headminster?" Finias said.

"No, I dressed this way so that I could play chess with Elzibeth," Francine said, shooting him a look.

"Chess?" Finias said. Huh, I didn't even know you played. And Elzibeth, when was it that you learned?

"Do you actually hear the words that come out of your mouth? Or do you just not have a filter for that tiny little brain of yours?" Francine said.

"Look, if you two are going to fight, I think I'll go watch a movie or something," Elzibeth said.

"No, Francine is right. I apologize to each of you. I'm a bit nervous about this whole affair, and when I get nervous, my brain sometimes kicks into neutral. Please, let us carry on with the business at hand," Finias said.

"As I see it, this can go one of two ways. Either Lindsey is working for whatever forces are behind the continued aggression toward the underground or drug cartels, or she is looking for a way to stop it," Finias said.

"Or she may be in fear for her life," Francine said. "It was either Mum or Dad, I don't recall at this moment, who suggested that Thaime was putting pressure on the council to grant him a seat. If he is involved with this violence, that in and of itself is providing pressure, but what if he has ramped it up and made it personal, possibly targeting Lindsey?"

"Okay, so how do we play this?" Finias said.

"Well, you are going to think this is a ridiculous idea, but it is why I've brought Elzibeth along with me tonight. You see, during training the other day, I noticed that while Elzibeth was teleporting about, she was able to pause at will during any portion of her transfer. A gift yet unheard of," Francine said.

"Bravo to you then, Elzibeth, but what does that have to do with our meeting tonight?" Finias said.

"It occurred to me that if this is some kind of setup by Lindsey or whoever that woman was, that she may not be truthful with her intentions. Maybe she will be just trying to ply information from you regarding what we know of the details of the attacks and our position as to who we feel is responsible, and how we intend to act," Francine said.

"And that brings Elzibeth into play how?" Finias said.

"She can tail her. It would be interesting to see if she simply goes home, as well as to know where it is she lives so that we can use her address in a background check to see if she is who she says she is. And heaven forbid if she doesn't go home and ends up going to Marcon's or to Thaime's place, then we know she is either in cahoots or indeed an impostor, in which case we have big trouble on our hands," Francine said.

"Cahoots?" Finias said, laughing.

"Yes, cahoots. It's a word," Francine said, somewhat crossly.

Finias smiled, then said, "I see you've given this a lot of thought."

"I knew one of us would have to, and I find that between the two of us, I'm better suited to the task," Francine said, returning the smile.

"You are some piece of work, you know that?"

"So I've been told by other handsome gentlemen."

"That's not what I meant, but sadly, point well made."

"So, Elzibeth, how do you feel about all this?" Finias said.

"I really don't know what you are talking about, and really don't care about all that, but I've followed people around before without them knowing, and it's kinda fun," Elzibeth said.

Finias and Francine exchanged a look that suggested this was unwelcome news.

"So, do you think you could come with us to the restaurant, get a look at the woman we are to meet, follow her home or to wherever she ends up, and report back to us the location?" Finias said.

"Sure," Elzibeth said.

"Look, Finias, I know that sounds like a bit much to ask from a six-year-old girl," began Francine.

"Six and a half," corrected Elzibeth.

"A six-and-a-half-year-old girl," continued Francine. "But you have to take into consideration that she is no ordinary six-and-a-half-year-old. She has extraordinary gifts, though undeveloped, that neither you, nor I, nor anyone of our world, has ever known. I not only have faith that this will work out fine, but I'm also assured by what I know of her that it will."

"I have to admit to being less than comfortable with the idea, but the potential of the information to be gleaned by her success is too great to ignore. Besides, if this goes badly, and God forbid harm comes to her, we are on an island. It would be a simple matter to simply throw myself off a cliff," Finias said.

"That's not funny," Francine said. "Believe me, this is a last resort option in my mind as well, but I know that she can do this and do it well. I'm confident of that."

Dinner being at 7:00 required that a decision be made quickly. It was agreed that the three of them would arrive by taxi a half a block from the restaurant where they would disembark, and Elzibeth would find the space in the zone between dimensions that allows for her to traverse along at whatever pace is necessary, and Francine and Finias would walk the rest of the way.

The three of them left the protections of Briarwood, and not having time to walk the mile or so across the land bridge, opted to teleport to the bench outside of Bob's Baked Goods and Crab Shack, where Elzibeth had been taken, to await a taxi.

Chapter 24

It wasn't long before a taxi happened by, and Finias stood to hail its services. The three of them climbed into the back, which was an easier task for Finias and Elzibeth than it was for Francine, who found her tight-fitting dress a bit restrictive for such a maneuver.

The ride was uneventful and Finias asked the taxi to drop them off a short way from Akita. He paid the fare with a generous tip and then asked the cabbie for a phone number he might use for a return trip home.

Francine, after wiggling her way out of the taxi, asked why they wouldn't simply teleport home. Finias suggested that if Lindsey both arrived and left with a driver, it would be prudent to follow her as a backup to Elzibeth.

"So, there is a brain in that pretty little head of yours," Francine said.

"I know I fumble about a bit, but I am actually quite intelligent," Finias said. "I don't know why you go on about me being somehow simple-minded."

"Mostly because it's fun and partly to annoy you so that you'll pay attention to me," Francine said.

"Trust me, you are hard not to pay attention to. Particularly in that dress," Finias said.

"Ahhh, aren't you sweet. It is a bit on the tight side. Do you think you would have difficulty getting me out of it?" Francine said, giving him a suggestive smile.

"I would use my teeth or whatever means necessary," Finias said.

"Comforting to know. It's so snug that I was a little afraid it may never come off, and I'd have to wear it like body paint until it became so threadbare that it would eventually shed," Francine said.

"Not to worry, Finias to the rescue," he said.

"Again, good to know," Francine said as they walked, she holding him close by his arm.

Their playful banter brought them to the entrance of Akita, and Finias asked Francine if she would wait outside for a bit as he went around to the rear of the restaurant to check the parking lot for Lindsey's limousine. It was there, with the same driver behind the wheel, and Finias, being careful not to be seen, returned to the restaurant.

Upon entering, they were met by a Japanese man in a tuxedo, which, Finias thought, was odd attire for a sushi restaurant. And, he thought some more, he wasn't sure he had ever seen a Japanese man in a tuxedo before. Maybe Jackie Chan in some movie of his. Wait, he thought again, Jackie Chan was from Hong Kong right? Or, Japan. He turned to ask Francine but thought better of it as she would most assuredly make some remark about him being brainless for thinking such things at such a time.

The tuxedoed man asked for their names and then checked his seating chart against the reservations list.

"It says here that the reservation is for two, but I've already seated one other person."

"Yes, we had a last-minute addition," Finias explained.

"Very well. We don't offer tables for two as couples usually sit at the sushi bar, so there will be room for all as the table assigned has seating for four."

This he explained while reaching for two menus, then asked politely if they would please follow him to their table. Along the way, Finias asked the man if he knew if it was common for Japanese men to wear tuxedos while eating sushi.

"I don't eat the stuff myself," the man said. "The tux is supposed to be a play on a James Bond movie. One of the characters wore a tux and threw his hat as a weapon. Goldfinger, I think it was."

"So, no hat for you?"

"No, they wanted me to wear one, but I thought it a bit much."

"Is Jackie Chan Japanese? I think I saw a movie where he wore a tuxedo."

"No, he's originally from Hong Kong, and he starred in a movie called 'The Tuxedo.'"

"Ah, yes. Superpowers or something, right?" Finias said.

"What on earth are you two going on about?" Francine interrupted, as she made her way along behind the pair of men, half stopping occasionally to tug at the hem of her dress.

"What? Oh, nothing." Finias said, just idle chit-chat.

Lindsey had been seated and was sipping from a glass of wine as they approached. She stood, and upon seeing Francine, seemed a bit taken aback.

Greetings were exchanged all around, and Finias introduced Francine as an interested party and an associate of his at Briarwood. Lindsey then asked Finias, quite pointedly, what this was all about, him having brought an uninvited guest.

Finias knew this to be a delicate matter and before answering, took the opportunity to inject a little flattery by stating that Lindsey looked stunning. Francine shot him a look at this remark, which Finias chose to ignore, as it was true that she did indeed look fabulous.

Lindsey was wearing a dress not dissimilar to Francine's but low cut in the front with wide straps crossing her open back, and was black rather than red. This was accompanied by dangling diamond earrings, a diamond bracelet on her left wrist, and a diamond pendant that lay smoothly in the middle of her plentiful breasts. Her hair remained as he remembered, though her makeup appeared expertly applied as one might do for a special occasion or maybe in preparation to be photographed. Though she was tall, she was again wearing four-inch heels which made her look considerably taller than Francine's five-foot, six-inch frame.

"You don't look so bad yourself, handsome, but your flattery in and of itself did not answer my question now, did it?"

Finias, for his part, did look quite the part as he was dressed in all black. Black suit, black shoes, black shirt, and tie in various shades, which when put together looked rather striking. Especially when paired side by side with Francine's bright red dress and brilliant blonde hair.

"In answer, my only defense in having Francine here," Finias began, "is to protect me from making a fool of myself if after a glass of wine or two, I should become untoward and begin to ply you with unwanted advances."

"Cut the crap, Finias. Her being here puts me at risk, and I'll not have it. This meeting is over," said Lindsey, who looked as if to leave.

"No, it's not," Finias said to everyone's surprise. "I'm afraid I will not allow you to leave under such false pretense. I sense it may be that you've asked me here because you are under threat or in trouble. If there is truth in this, there is no one more capable of helping you than Francine. Now, if you would be so kind as to take your seat, there are some questions we would like to ask and some things we need to discuss."

Francine, for her part, was very impressed by this and made a mental note to lay off calling Finias a stupid dolt or other such names in the future. Maybe halfwit or something less hurtful, she thought.

Lindsey, after taking a deep breath, decided the damage had already been done, her now having been identified by Francine, so she took her seat and asked what specifically Finias wanted to discuss.

"We would like to discuss why it was that when you came to Briarwood, you did not go to the headmaster's office to seek my introduction rather than coming straight away to my suite, among other things," Finias said.

Francine had noticed and was appreciative of Finias's use of the word "we" and made another mental note to perhaps reward him in a newfound and special way later.

"Believe me, I gave much thought to bringing this matter to Calderón first, but I knew there would be nothing more to be gained from that than stock political answers or information that he has already shared with the Council. Calderón is adept enough at such things to avoid showing his cards too early, if at all," said Lindsey.

"Yet, you thought it would be a simple matter to extract such information from me," Finias said.

Lindsey leaned toward Finias, allowing him a view of her plentiful cleavage while placing her hand on his and said, "Not simple, but you being a very good-looking young man, and I with what did you call it? A pretty nice lady setup or something to that effect, was confident in tonight ending with all the information I would need."

Finias pulled his glance away from Lindsey's cleavage, which he found not to be a simple matter, toward Francine, who was practically levitating from this little exchange.

"I'm flattered to have been considered a pawn in whatever game you believe you are playing," Finias said, removing his hand from under hers. "But this is no game to me. There is some connection between the recent gangland-style hits and the two attempted abductions of a little girl who means the world to me, and I intend to put a stop to both."

Francine blew off a little steam at this and settled back into her chair.

"You," said Lindsey, with a laugh. "And how do you propose to do that?"

"At the moment, I have no idea," Finias said. "To tell you the truth, I'm not sure that it's possible. But what I can do is provide protection to an asset of great gifts and power who will grow to be strong enough to someday do what I cannot."

"The girl?" said Lindsey.

Finias did not answer.

"Tell me what you know about Marcon," Finias said.

"I know everything about Marcon," said Lindsey. "I'm his mistress."

Finias choked on his water and Francine said, "What?" so loudly that it got the attention of the full house.

The host in the tuxedo was escorting a group to a nearby table and, startled by Francine's outburst, jumped backward as he dropped a handful of menus and knocked a small Asian woman to the floor.

There was a small fuss over this, and Francine, embarrassed, offered her apologies as Finias continued.

"So then, you are a fraud," Finias said.

"Not at all," said Lindsey. "What? Do you think that members of the council are not allowed to live a normal life outside of chambers?"

"You call being the mistress of the head of one of the largest crime syndicates in the country normal?" Francine said.

"Actually, as of a few days ago, I'm no longer his mistress," said Lindsey. "I didn't know the man I was involved with to be Marcon. The man I knew as Marco Perino was an east coast guy and I out west, though he does have a lovely home here. We would see each other on occasion. It wasn't until recently when the news of his son's death went public and Marcon himself was shown on the news and in the paper that I discovered the truth. I was very upset, as I'm sure you can understand, Francine. I could not bring myself to speak to him, so I drafted a letter to his wife explaining my situation and disappointment, and obviously broke things off, though I doubt the wife would care much. Turns out, if you can believe the press, that Marcon had women in every city in which he does business. So, I, in the throes of betrayal, sent a few less-than-lovely photos of us in various stages of...how should I say...undress, with...only my face blacked out. It was a simple matter to change my phone numbers, both home and cell," continued Lindsey, "but he had been to my home on occasion when we did not stay in a hotel or visit his mansion. So, he knows where I live, and I fear that my adolescent need to poke a stick in the fire by attaching those photos may not have been the smartest thing to do. The messages I received from Marcon before changing my phone numbers were rather nasty to the point of being very disturbing."

A waiter happened by and, seeming to sense that the pot at this particular table was done boiling over, asked if they were ready to order.

"Not now," snapped Francine, and the waiter, somewhat startled, slunk off.

"How was it that you got involved with Marcon?" Francine said.

"I don't see that as being relevant to this conversation," said Lindsey.

"It's not," Francine said. "I'm just curious as to how such things get started."

"Oh, to be young and naive about such things again," said Lindsey. "We met at a formal affair featuring collections of rare antiquities from ancient Persia. What we know now to be Iran, Iraq, and Syria, I believe. Marcon purchased a piece for a dreadful amount of money, and I, being the sort attracted to handsome men, especially those with money, took it upon myself to introduce Marcon to my considerable charms. Does that answer your question?"

"Who else was in attendance?" Francine asked.

"Just the two of us, darling. I haven't introduced my considerable charms to more than one man at a time since college," Lindsey said, much to the surprise of her two table mates, and possibly the people occupying the table next to them.

"No, I...um, well, okay. I meant at the function, not in the bedroom," Francine said, a bit surprised by Lindsey's candor.

"Why does that matter?" said Lindsey.

"Again, I'm curious," Francine said. "How well connected do you think Marcon might be to politics, for instance?"

"I see. Yes, there were a number of high-ranking government officials, members of the cabinet, and heads of state as well as representatives from leading law enforcement agencies in attendance," said Lindsey.

"Do you know if any of them had their hands in Marcon's pockets?" Francine said.

"Again, I didn't know him as Marcon," said Lindsey. "The man I knew, or rather, thought I knew, pretended, I suppose, to be a shipping magnate of some sort and bragged that he controlled one of the largest ports on the west coast outside of the influence of the coastal guard."

"What if that's the truth?" Finias said. "What if he wasn't pretending?"

"Then he would be able to receive shipments of God knows what from all over the world without oversight," Francine said.

"My God, you are right," said Lindsey. "Something I should have considered, but again it was just a few days ago that I didn't know the man that I was involved with to be Marcon."

"Not to muddy the waters any more than they already are, but what information were you hoping to glean from us?" Finias said.

"I wanted to know if members of the order with whom you are connected at Briarwood are concerned with these events," said Lindsey. "And if there is a widely held belief that somehow Thaime is involved with the killings that have taken place recently. You see, Thaime has been blackmailing me, suggesting that if I do not relinquish my seat held with the Council of Old, he will come forth with my involvement with Marcon."

"So let him," Francine said. "Screw that piece of poo. You had an adult liaison with a man you did not know to be Marcon. So what?"

"I wish it were that simple. Members of the High Council are held to an impossibly high standard," Lindsey said. "If this information were to come out, I would most assuredly be asked to step down, possibly opening a seat for Thaime, who has been applying similar pressure to others on the council to grant him their vote. Additionally, I would be stripped of my gifted powers and all influence I would have both within and outside of the order. Without those things, I am powerless to do anything about what I know to be terrible wrongs, and I fear that the Order itself will be forced to go to war as we are the only leverage against what seems to be a rising tide of violence within the leadership of warring factions.

My fear is that at the conclusion of such violence, an opening will appear for one man to take control of all, giving rise to a syndicate so powerful the government will be powerless against it, and it will begin to become a government unto itself. Anarchy will reign, and the mostly peaceful world as we know it today will cease to exist."

Chapter 25

The three of them sat in silence for a while, digesting what had been said. Finias, for his part, was mulling over what to do next, while Francine was lost in thoughts of Elzibeth floating about in the netherworld. She was worried, as the dangers to her now, with the threat of involvement by Thaime and Marcon in relation to Lindsey, had not been predicted prior to her decision to have Elzibeth participate in what now seemed to be a very dangerous undertaking.

"Might I ask why it is you need a driver?" Finias said, breaking the silence.

Francine rolled her eyes involuntarily and was about to remind Finias that it was not necessary to speak every stupid thought that might be rolling around in that empty head of his when Lindsey said, "Council members are forbidden to teleport. Actually, in the technical sense of the Order, we are not to use our gifts at all. It is feared, you see, that if I were to, say, pop up in a grocery store and be seen by someone with connections to one of the various associations or political factions that we support and interact with, it would raise questions we would not want to have to answer."

"I see," Finias said. "That also answers the question of why your driver carries a firearm. It presents the look of normalcy to non-gifted folk. To them, it would be considered appropriate for a driver to provide security, and carrying a gun supports the guise of your having influence or being in a position of power, which are both true, of course, but in a form acceptable to them."

"Precisely."

It was at this point that the waiter, having grown impatient, came to the table and asked if they would indeed be dining this evening.

"I don't know about you two lovely ladies, but I have no appetite at the moment. Do either of you care to order?" Finias said. Both Francine and Lindsey declined, and Finias offered his apologies to the waiter.

Francine, her anxiety over Elzibeth mounting, suggested that they be going but that the three of them should meet again in one week's time, with Lindsey again coming to Briarwood so that they might share additional findings and begin to formulate a plan.

Finias paid for their drinks, and the three of them exchanged goodbyes at the entrance. Francine was not so preoccupied with Elzibeth to notice the prolonged hug between Lindsey and Finias, nor the less-than-formal kiss on the cheek she had given him.

"Would the two of you like a lift home?" Lindsey offered. "Perhaps we could drop Miss Francine off at Briarwood, and Finias and I could go out for a nightcap."

"That's very kind of you," Finias said. "But I think we will just teleport home. Some other time, perhaps."

"Let's not say perhaps and instead I shall say I look forward to an evening out with you...alone," Lindsey said, while looking at Francine.

Francine, for her part, looked about to come out of her shoes, so Finias thought it best to hurry things along.

"Very well then, goodnight," Finias said.

"Are you not going to walk me to my car?" Lindsey said.

Finias heard something which sounded like a low growl coming from Francine.

"Yes, yes, of course," Finias said. "Francine, why don't you wait here?" The better, he thought, to keep the two separated so as to avoid Francine knocking Lindsey's block off.

"I shall not," Francine said.

"No, of course, you won't."

So, the three of them moved off. After another hug and a quick kiss on the mouth from Lindsey, and after an extraction of a promise for that drink, she climbed into the backseat of her car and blew Finias a kiss as they drove off.

"So, that was nice," Finias said.

"Shut up," snapped Francine.

"Why are you mad at me?" Finias said.

"'Some other time perhaps'? 'Very well then'? Did the word NO ever pop into that pea-sized brain of yours when this woman asked you out for a nightcap? You know what a nightcap means? It means take you to a hotel room and screw your brains out, that's what it means. God, you are dim," Francine said.

"Look, I was just being polite," Finias said.

"The hell with polite," Francine raged. "I want you to practice saying this as I know you can't spell it. NO, got it? N freaking O. And wipe that stupid lipstick off your face."

"You're upset," Finias said. "What say we go back to my suite for a nightcap, and I'll do my best to see if I can relieve some of that tension."

This seemed to take all the steam out of Francine. She stood facing Finias, considering what to say. She thought perhaps an apology was in order, but instead of offering one, she simply moved in to hug him and said, "That sounds wonderful, but what about Elzibeth? At this point, with no way to contact her, I'm not sure what to do. Should we try and catch up to Lindsey and try to intercept her somehow?"

"It's too late for that now. I thought about telling Lindsey that we were having her followed, but that would reveal too much about Elzibeth's capabilities and I still don't know if what she told us is the truth. It seems a bit far-fetched not to be, but still, there is a chance that if Marcon were to pressure Lindsey, she might not be able to withhold that knowledge. I think we should trust our instinct that Elzibeth is capable of returning home safely."

"I suppose, though I feel as if things have turned sour and I wish I hadn't sent her at all. Still, there is not much to be done at this point, so it's probably best that we are waiting for her when she arrives."

"Agreed."

Chapter 26

Back at Briarwood, Finias found that by having skipped dinner, he was now famished. He gave Francine a call and suggested ordering some food, which she thought was a wonderful idea. He said he would have dinner sent to his room and for her to join him when she was done changing. With that, he ordered Fava Bean Pasta e Fagioli topped with bacon and Parmigiano-Reggiano for two, along with a side of Romaine salad with cracked olives and salted lemon yogurt to be delivered to his suite.

Francine, wanting to be out of her dress as quickly as possible to enjoy the pleasure of breathing again, teleported directly to her suite to change. Finding that she couldn't manage the zipper, she grabbed a handful of clothes and a pair of slippers and made her way to the Grand Entrance to gain access to Finias's suite. Not wanting anyone to see her moving off from her room with a handful of overnight clothing, Francine wished she could teleport, but knowing she could not. The headmaster forbade inner-structure teleportation, as he felt such behavior to be lackadaisical. Instead, she stealthily made her way to the control panel and soon found herself alone outside of Finias's room.

Francine came to life on the television over the bar and said, "Finias, quickly, let me in."

Finias was pleased to see that Francine was still in her dress, as he might have an opportunity to help her out of it. He moved to the door to let her in.

"What's the password?"

"Just open the door," Francine hissed under her breath.

Finias was quick to oblige, and Francine rushed in.

The food had arrived prior, and its aroma filled the room. Francine was suddenly famished and instructed Finias to hurry her out of her blasted dress so that they could sit down to eat. Finias was, of course, most eager to cooperate, and he moved to unzip her.

"Why, Francine, you are not wearing a brassiere, or panties for that matter," Finias was pleased to see as she shed the dress to the floor.

"Of course not," Francine said. "One doesn't wear a bra with spaghetti straps. And that dress was so tight my panty lines would have shown through."

"How silly of me not to know," Finias said.

Francine smiled at him and asked, "So, do you like what has been delivered?"

"More than life itself," Finias said.

"Not me, you dullard, the food. You'll have to wait for this until we are finished eating," she said, using her hands to indicate her body. "I'm starved."

"Me too, but I'm not the least bit hungry," Finias said.

"Keep it in your shorts, big boy. Momma's gotta eat," Francine said with a grin.

"Momma's gotta eat?" Finias said.

"Just mixing it up a little. Wouldn't want you to tire of the same old Francine so soon into our little romance," Francine said.

"Fat chance," Finias said as he set the table and retrieved a bottle of champagne from the bar.

Francine, not bothering to dress, simply grabbed a towel from the kitchen and placed it on the seat of a chair, sat down, and began digging into her meal with gusto.

Finias was too stunned by the fact that she hadn't slipped into at least a little something before she sat down to eat, that he was unable to eat himself. So, he simply sat opposite her and stared.

"That is the sexiest thing I have ever seen," Finias said.

"What, Romaine salad with cracked olives?" Francine said.

"Yes, that too, but I was referring to the stunning nude woman at the table," Finias said. "I'm not sure I can wait to bed you."

"I'm not nude, I'm wearing a necklace," Francine said with a smile. "And what makes you think you can just bed me?"

"I'm thinking a locked door and chloroform would do the trick," Finias said.

"Too close to necrophilia for me," Francine said. "I may have to just suck it up and let you do me."

"Don't say suck it up," Finias said. "I might pop a cork."

And with that, he opened the champagne.

"Clever," Francine said.

"Ah, a small victory for my intelligence."

"Oh, I'm sure you'll disappoint me sometime later."

"I certainly hope not," Finias said, and she smiled.

"I certainly hope not as well."

"How do you suppose Elzibeth is getting along?" Finias said.

"Oh, I'm sure she is fine," Francine said, so as not to upset the mood, though she was quite concerned indeed.

And with that, Elzibeth appeared on the television screen.

"Hey Shoop, you in there?" Elzibeth shouted in her typical way. "Open up. It's kind of important."

"Good lord," Francine said. "Isn't there a way to shut that thing off?"

A similar fire drill ensued as to last time, and it was Francine again doing most of the scramble. Finias, for his part, picked up whatever clothes Francine had left behind as she hurried to the bathroom to change and then moved to the door to welcome Elzibeth.

"Well, kiddo, how did it go?" Finias said, as Elzibeth hurried inside.

"Not so good, not so good at all," Elzibeth said. "I went by Francine's, but she wasn't there, so I dropped off a guest and came straight here."

"What do you mean by a guest?" Finias asked.

By this time, Francine had pulled herself together somewhat and had come into the room.

"Why are you wearing your nighty?" Elzibeth asked, as Francine pulled her robe closed around her.

"I, um, couldn't rest having had a stressful meeting with that awful woman, so I came to see if Finias would like to have a bite to eat," Francine said.

"But didn't you just have dinner?"

"Well, yes. We went to dinner, but things got to be a little too strange for us to have much of an appetite."

"Strange how?"

"Look, just strange, okay? Now, what is this about a guest?" Francine said, frustrated with Elzibeth's constant questioning.

"Oh, just the lady you had dinner with. She's waiting for you guys in your room," Elzibeth said.

"What? Lindsey? Why on earth would that terrible woman be in my room?" Francine said.

"I brought her with me," Elzibeth said.

"Brought her with you?" Finias said, surprised.

"Yeah, after the fire," Elzibeth said.

"Fire? What fire?" Francine said.

"The one that burnt her house down," Elzibeth said.

"WHAT?" Both Finias and Francine shouted in unison.

"Yeah, well, first there was the explosion, then the fire," Elzibeth said. "Do you think we could go to your room and see that lady before I go too far with this? She doesn't know what's going on and is kinda freaking out. Plus, I don't want to have to tell you this stuff all over again."

"Yes, of course, but," Francine hesitated.

"But what?" Elzibeth said.

"Give us a minute, will you?" Francine said to Elzibeth while taking Finias aside.

"I don't want her to see us together."

"Elzibeth? She's standing right there."

Francine took a deep breath and remembered her mental note to go easy on her brainless remarks toward Finias.

"Not Elzibeth, Lindsey."

"Oh yes, of course. But, why not?"

"I don't know. I'm still a little shy about all this between us, and being dressed this way, she'll suspect I'm sleeping around."

"There are others?" Finias said, grinning.

Francine punched him in the arm.

"No, there are no others. You know that," Francine said. "I misspoke."

"I'm not so sure. You do seem rather well-versed in certain things," Finias said.

Francine reached out and twisted his nipples.

"Ouch."

"You take that back."

"Okay, let's just say you have done exceptionally well in the pursuit of your first romantic interlude," Finias said.

"That's better," Francine said.

"Look, I understand where you are coming from. Fair or not, perception is different for girls than it is for guys. You take Elzibeth and give me a ring later to join you," Finias said.

"Are you guys coming or not?" Elzibeth said.

"I will be coming with you, and we will need to have a little talk along the way about some lies I'm about to tell, okay?" Francine said.

"Sure," Elzibeth said.

Chapter 27

Francine pressed the intercom button to her suite from the hallway outside her door with Elzibeth by her side. They waited a moment, and sensing that maybe Lindsey didn't hear the buzzer, she pressed it again, this time asking if Lindsey was there. A moment later, the door was opened, and Lindsey appeared. Francine noticed that she was disheveled, her hair blown about, and her mascara having run in black rivulets down her cheeks. She had been crying.

In not one of her proudest moments, Francine couldn't help but rejoice in the fact that Finias would be joining them soon and would get a gander at Lindsey in her current state. Francine and Elzibeth stepped inside. The tension between Francine and Lindsey was palpable, and, feeling the need to somehow break the current of ice between the two, Elzibeth suggested they have a seat so that she could give them an account of what had happened.

"Elzibeth, be a dear and give Finias a call first, will you? I suspect he will be in need of hearing this at some point and it might as well be now," Francine said.

"Sure," Elzibeth said.

While they awaited Finias's arrival, Lindsey said, "Do you always stroll about in a robe and nighty?"

"Only when I am on the prowl for younger men," Francine said with an obvious jab.

"Younger than you?" said Lindsey. "What are you, twelve?"

"Why you overbearing b—"

"Francine, are you in there?" Finias said, as his picture filled the television screen in her room, saving the day for the moment.

"Yes, just a sec," Francine said, and she moved to the door to let him in.

"Hello," Finias said. "What's with the getup? Out trolling for young men?"

"Oh, just shut up and get in here," Francine said.

"What? I was trying to provide you with a little cover, being that you are running around in a nighty," Finias whispered.

"And robe, but we are past that now, so just come in," Francine said. "Besides, I'm in my home, not out trolling around, so that doesn't even make sense, moron."

Finias gave her a look but chose to ignore it.

"Lindsey, what on earth brings you here?" Finias said, pretending not to know about the fire. "And you have been crying. Here, let me get you a towel and we'll see if we can't get you cleaned up a bit."

Finias moved to the bathroom and came out with one of Francine's nice bright white custom-embroidered hand towels, which he had dampened, and taking a seat next to Lindsey, began moving her hair back in place with his fingers and, using the towel, began gently removing the mascara from her face. When finished, Francine noticed that if it were not for her puffy red eyes, Lindsey was mostly back to her normal attractive self, and she wanted to jump out of her chair and go smack Finias upside his big dumb head for being so helpful.

"Get a hold of yourself, Francine," she thought. "It's just Finias being Finias."

Elzibeth, for her part, sat quietly and watched this go on and thought to herself, "Oh, this isn't going to be good."

Again, wishing to carve a channel through the glacier that had now formed between Francine and Lindsey, Elzibeth said, "Anybody want some ice cream?"

Everyone looked at her as if they had forgotten she was there.

"No? Okay, I'm going to have some," Elzibeth said as she moved to the kitchen.

Finias, having finished fussing over Lindsey, stood to place the towel in the laundry, but Francine instructed him to just throw it in the trash as it was now ruined. From the kitchen, they could hear Elzibeth complain that the only ice cream she could find was soy-based and that she wasn't eating any of that.

"Who eats soy ice cream?" she said loud enough for all to hear.

"Lindsey, again might I ask what you are doing here? And why were you crying?" Finias said upon his return. He chose to ignore Elizabeth's empty chair and instead moved to sit next to Lindsey on the sofa.

Francine knew Finias was being a jerk on purpose just to get her goat, and she thought she knew exactly how to turn the tables on that later on.

"It's terrible, Finias," Lindsey said. "Someone blew up my house and almost killed me. Us...both of us."

Lindsey leaned over and put her head onto Finias's shoulder and began crying again. Finias, not knowing what to do, brought her to him, and they embraced as he allowed her to cry. Francine could see Lindsey's bosom bob up and down in her low-cut dress as she pressed into Finias with each heaving sob, and she wanted to scratch her eyes out.

"This is too much. Let me know when this little love fest is over," Francine said, who then joined Elzibeth in the kitchen.

Finias held Lindsey this way for some time, and when her sobs began to subside, Francine could hear him saying little things like, "There, there," and "Everything is going to be alright," and "Hush

"You OK sis? You look like you are going to be sick," Elzibeth said.

"You don't know the half of it," Francine said.

From the main room, Finias asked Francine to bring him another damp towel.

"Dig it out of the trash," she yelled.

"I'm not digging anything out of the trash. Here, let me get you a fresh towel," Finias said as he moved away from Lindsey to the kitchen.

Francine had already dug the towel out of the trash and had rinsed it.

"Here," Francine said as Finias entered. "This will do fine."

"What has gotten into you? She is a guest in your home having just gone through a very traumatic experience. Have some decency," Finias said.

"Oh, blow it out your backside," Francine said. "Hush now, ssshhh, there, there. You're making me sick with all this boo-freaking-hoo business. So her house blew up, so her life is in the crapper. Tell her to shake it off and wake the hell up to reality. She's created this mess herself."

"You frighten me sometimes, you know that," Finias said. "Come, Elzibeth. Time for you to tell us a tale."

Elzibeth came out of the kitchen and took a seat. Francine reluctantly followed and found that Finias again had taken up a seat next to Lindsey, though she had stopped crying. Lindsey, for her part, had shifted and was leaning into Finias with her head on his shoulder and an arm draped across his waist.

"That's enough with you two," Francine said. "Finias, why don't you take this chair and I'll sit on the couch."

"Are you two lovers?" Lindsey said, out of the blue.

"NO, no, no," Francine said. "As a matter of fact, since we've had the misfortune of meeting you, I can't even say that we are friends."

"Lovers? No, of course not," Finias said, shooting Francine a look. "Just colleagues. Nothing more, thank goodness. In case you haven't noticed, she can be difficult to get along with. Might I ask what would make you think that?"

"Well, first, that's good to know," said Lindsey, snuggling up closer to Finias. "Really good to know. And second, little miss bitchy pants there seems not to like me being here next to you."

"She's probably just tired, it being late and all," Finias said. "Isn't that right, Francine?"

"No, I'm not tired at all. I am disgusted that this old lady is hanging all over you on my couch, though."

"Why, you little…just how old do you think I am?" Lindsey said.

"Old enough to be his mother," Francine said.

"Yes, well, you've got me in a box there," Lindsey said. "But I'm not too old to know how to please a younger man."

"Ladies, ladies, please," Finias said, obviously enjoying having two women fight over him. "Elzibeth has important information to share, and I think it's best that we hear it."

"Finias, are you sure you wouldn't be more comfortable over here in this chair?" Francine said, her voice as cold as death.

"No, Lindsey is in obvious need of comfort at the moment."

Oh, you are so dead, thought Francine.

"Elzibeth, why don't you go ahead and tell us what happened," Finias said.

"Okay, so I was floating around outside of the restaurant," Elzibeth began. "Oh, did you guys know the Chicken Shack next door has a real chicken coop on the roof?"

"Really," Finias said. "Cool."

"Maybe it would be best if you just told us what happened at the house, sweetheart," Francine said.

"Yeah, so I was floating around thinking maybe I should drop in for a look inside where you guys were so that I could get to see what this lady looked like, but I got distracted by the chickens. Anyway, you guys came out and I saw that lady there give Finias a really long hug, and then she kissed him pretty good. Then you guys walked around back, and that lady there hugged him some more and then kissed him some more."

"Yes dear, maybe we should skip forward to the house," Francine said, rubbing her temples.

"Right, so there I was watching this lady blow Finias a kiss from this big black car (Ughhh groaned Francine), then they took off, so I followed them for what seemed a long time. Then, they pulled up to a gate and went through, and these guys behind them snuck through the gate before it could close. So, the lady there and her car pulled up to this really nice house, and that lady went inside. Then the guys that snuck through the gate pulled in behind the lady's car and got out with these big guns strapped over their shoulders. When the driver guy got out of the lady's car, he had a gun too, and he shot one of the guys with the big guns in the side. So, one guy grabs the shot guy and throws him back in their car while the other guys shot the driver a whole bunch of times."

"Sweet Jesus," Finias said, as Lindsey buried her face in her hands and again began to cry.

"I'm sorry to have put you through that, Elzibeth. That must have been terrible for you to see," Francine said.

"It wasn't so bad; it wasn't like on television. Except for the driver, the other guys' guns hardly made any noise, and the driver guy, he just dropped on the ground and stopped moving," Elzibeth said.

"The gun guys then ran around the house. One guy was carrying a big green canvas bag, and he went to the porch first then around to the back. Then all of a sudden, they all came running back real fast and jumped into their car and drove away in a hurry. So, I was thinking something bad was going on, so I just went into the house and grabbed that lady there and brought her back here, figuring maybe she could spend the night or something until this all gets figured out."

"You teleported with another person?" Francine said.

"I didn't know if I could, but I just had a feeling she was in trouble, so I had to try. Then when I went to pick her up, she wasn't any heavier than a bag of popcorn. I don't know how it works, but it did," Elzibeth said.

"I've never heard of such a thing. You are indeed a gifted child, do you understand that, Elzibeth?" Francine said.

"I suppose," Elzibeth said. "I don't think any of my friends could have picked up a lady from a house that was blowing up."

"What do you mean the house was blowing up? Do you mean to tell me the house was blowing up while you were inside?" Francine said, shock registering in her voice.

"Yeah, it was a close one too. I had just grabbed that lady there into kind of a hug, then there was this big explosion that would have blown us through the roof, but the roof had just disappeared. Then there was this big rush of air, and we shot forward really fast which was awesome. I didn't stick around to watch the house burn because my backside was really hot, but I looked back, and it was a mess of flames."

"Jesus," Francine said, as she plucked Elzibeth from her seat and gave her a hug, kissing the top of her head. "My poor, sweet, wonderful girl. I'm so sorry to have put you through that. Please forgive me."

"Sure, sis," Elzibeth said, as Francine sat holding Elzibeth on her lap. "It's really no big deal though, so don't get all upset, okay? Plus, my friends are going to freak out. I can't wait to tell them I almost got blown up."

"Yes, about that, Elzibeth, I'm going to ask something of you that I have no right to ask, so it is up to you to choose whether you think it's the right thing to do. When you relate this story to the headmaster, which you will most certainly be asked to do, I would ask you not to let on about the house blowing up while you were inside and your narrow escape. Simply say that you were able to rescue Lindsey from the bad men that you had seen and brought her back here with you. Will you do that for me?" Francine said.

"Because you don't want to get in trouble, right?" Elzibeth said.

"Yes, because I don't want to get into any more trouble than I already am," Francine said.

"Sure, sis, anything for you," Elzibeth said, and Francine gave her the longest hug of her life. "Can I still tell my friends what really happened? I mean, I'm just a kid, so even if it gets around, nobody's going to believe it."

"Sure," Francine said, and kissed her cheek. "Thank you for being you. I love you so much," Francine said, as she too started to cry.

"Finias, will you dig that towel out of the trash for me?" Francine said.

"Of course," Finias said. "Anything for you."

Chapter 28

Finias set off to retrieve the towel, and when he returned, the crying had subsided. As he moved to take his seat on the couch, he tossed the towel to Francine.

"You're a real gentleman, you know that," Francine said.

"I brought you a towel," Finias said.

"Just, never mind," Francine said. "And Elzibeth, I suppose it's time for you to be off to bed."

"What are you going to do about the lady there?" Elzibeth asked.

"Please, Elzibeth, call me Lindsey. I mean, you did just save my life, and I want to thank you for that. Calling me 'that lady' seems a little distant considering what we have been through."

"I don't know," Elzibeth said, pausing. "Sis doesn't seem to like you much. So, if I have to choose... you know where I'm going with this, right?"

"It's okay, Elzibeth," Francine said. "It looks like she may be hanging around here for a little while until some things get sorted out, so you might as well begin to address her by her proper name. She is, or was—I don't know, considering she is supposed to be dead—a current or former member of the High Council."

"Why doesn't she just go to a hotel or stay with a friend or something?" Elzibeth said.

"It's complicated, dear, but the bad men that blew up my house obviously intended to kill me. And if they were involved with a really, really bad man who now thinks I'm dead, if I were to show myself to a friend, or if I were to use my credit card at a hotel, they would be sure to find this out and those bad men would hunt me down," said Lindsey.

"How would they track your credit card?" Finias said. "That's a police matter, isn't it?"

Lindsey gave him a look as if to say, do you not think these people wouldn't have access to such things through contacts inside the department.

"If Marcon or whoever couldn't track it themselves, I'm sure they have informants within the police department," Francine said. "If her name were to pop up on a computer somewhere showing that she was, let's say, staying at the Ritz, whoever did this would probably get to her first. If she perchance were able to escape, it would then be known that she was indeed alive, and her picture would be in every newspaper in the country, and the search for her would be 24/7 cable news. Her life would be effectively over outside of the protections of Briarwood."

"Oh God," said Lindsey. "What have I done? Finias, would you be a dear and have the kitchen send in some rhubarb leaves?"

"Rhubarb?" Finias said, perplexed.

"Yes, I understand the leaves to be quite poisonous," said Lindsey.

Lindsey and Finias remained seated together on the couch, and at this, Finias put his arm around her shoulder and pulled her in tight.

"I'll not have that kind of talk, you hear me," Finias said. "We need to work on a plan to take these people out of the picture, and once that's done, you'll have your life back and things will return to normal."

"Do you really think so?" Lindsey said.

"No, not really. But life will go on, and you being a strong, capable woman will find your place again," Finias said.

With that, Lindsey took Finias's face in her hands and, before he could object, kissed him squarely on the mouth.

"Thank you, Finias. Your support means the world to me, especially now when I'm so vulnerable and feel so alone," said Lindsey. "Would you be a dear and allow me to stay with you tonight? I've really no place to go, and it's clear Francine does not favor the pleasure of my company."

"NO, ABSOLUTELY NOT," Francine said, rather sharply. "There will be no staying with Finias tonight or any night. No nightcaps, none of that. As long as I remain on staff here at Briarwood, I shall see to it that no such behavior exists between members of staff or those who deal with important matters with the High Council. Relationships of this kind cannot be tolerated as their demise often leads to bad feelings which become disruptive to our process and frankly to others involved with the same work. Is that clear?"

Finias and Lindsey turned to Francine, both stunned at this little outburst.

"I suppose, but there is no reason to be upset. If not with Finias, then where shall I sleep?" said Lindsey.

"You can have my couch," offered Francine.

"I shall not sleep on a couch," said Lindsey.

"Fine, then take the floor," Francine said.

"I will not."

"Look, you two, it's just the one night. Francine, why don't you take the couch? I'm sure tomorrow Lindsey will take a suite of her own, one preferably close to mine so that I may provide her protection if it should come to that," Finias said, his arm now around Lindsey's shoulder.

"Well, aren't you sweet," Lindsey said.

"He's an idiot," Francine said. "An idiot on his deathbed, he just doesn't know it. And no, I will not be sleeping on the couch, thank you."

"Fine, Lindsey, why don't you come stay in my suite tonight, and I'll take the couch," Finias offered.

"YOU HAVE GOT TO BE KIDDING ME," Francine said, in a voice loud enough to be heard in the hall. "Did you not hear a word I said? She is never to set foot in your room, EVER. Do you understand me? If I even hear a rumor of her passing by your door, I will personally serve you your balls on a platter for breakfast. You got that?"

"Yes, I think I do," Finias said.

"Are you sure that there isn't something going on between you two?" Lindsey said.

"Yes, I can tell you without hesitation that there is nothing going on now or EVER. You understand me, Finias. EVER," Francine said.

"As she said, nothing," Finias said, rather meekly. "Francine, if you'll not allow Lindsey into my suite, why doesn't she stay here in your room tonight. You can come stay with me and have my bed, and I'll take the couch?"

"Too bad there is no bed of nails handy for you to sleep on, Lindsey, but yes, I suppose that will do," Francine said.

"Charming, but yes, thank you," said Lindsey. "That will be fine. We are about the same size. Francine, would it be alright if I borrowed some clothes and took a shower? I'm still a little smokey from our narrow escape."

"Yeah, I guess," Francine said. "Just look around for whatever you need. You'll find personal care products for tonight as well as makeup for tomorrow in the bath.

"Thank you, Francine. That is very generous of you. I really don't know how we got off to such a bad start, but maybe someday we can be friends," said Lindsey.

"Doubtful, but bully for wishful thinking," Francine said.

"Francine, really, can't you try to be nice?" Finias said. "And Elzibeth, didn't Francine ask you to go to bed? This is no kind of talk for a child to hear."

"Not a chance, I wouldn't miss this for all the ice cream in the world," Elzibeth said.

"Come, Elzibeth, that's enough," Francine said. "If you are up early, wake us for breakfast. I'm sure Finias will be more than happy to be up off the couch."

"Alright," Elzibeth said. "But if there's any more good fighting between you guys, you'll tell me about it, right, sis?"

"In all of its gory detail," Francine said.

"Cool," Elzibeth said. "Well, goodnight."

Everyone said their goodbyes, and she left.

"Tomorrow will have its difficulties, no doubt," Finias said. "We will have much to explain, and unfortunately our explanations are not very good. I suggest we meet for breakfast around 7:00 a.m. to prepare a game plan."

"7:00 a.m.?" Lindsey said. "I've not been up that early since I had to wake before my parents to shoo my prom date out of my room."

"My turn to say charming," Francine said.

"Okay, whenever you get up and about, just have me paged. I'll be with Francine and Elzibeth anyway, then we can meet up," Finias said.

That is if he lives that long, thought Francine.

"Sounds perfect. See you in the morning," said Lindsey.

Francine was the first to move. She got up quickly from her chair and marched straight out of the door. Finias, having been caught off guard, said a quick goodbye to Lindsey, who would not allow him to leave without a hug and a kiss goodnight.

Finias thought at this point that maybe he had opened the Lindsey door up a wee bit too much just to annoy Francine. He wasn't sure why he was enjoying Francine's discomfort so much. Probably something to do with all of her nitwit comments to him.

Finias gave Lindsey her kiss and set off after Francine. Being late, the building was quiet, so its shifting of rooms took no time at all. Francine had cleared the Grand Entrance and stood waiting by the time he arrived at his door, and with this being so, her not having waited for him, he knew did not bode well.

Francine, who did not have access to his suite, stood standing with her back to him. Finias moved up behind her and said, "trapped again, I see. This storming off thing of yours just doesn't seem to be working well for you."

Francine turned and slapped him hard across the face.

"How dare you belittle me so," she shouted. "And in front of Elzibeth. You should be ashamed of yourself."

Finias was stunned at this outburst but knew the truth behind it.

"I'm sorry," Finias began.

"Oh, please, you heard what Calderón said about the word 'sorry.' It's an empty token and will not be accepted," Francine said.

"Then I am at a loss for words," Finias said.

"How about admitting that you are the world's most giantest jackass?" Francine stammered.

"Giantest?" Finias said.

"I'm upset. Leave me alone," Francine said.

"OK, I admit to being the giantest jackass in the world. What was it that you told me when I had asked you why you took such pleasure in torturing me with your little digs at my intelligence? You said that you did it because it was fun to annoy me, and that you were looking for attention. I guess I went too far tonight, but I felt a little of that myself," Finias said.

"So, you admit to being the giantest?" Francine said, now with a hint of a smile.

"World's giantest, and yes, I do," Finias said.

"And you promise not to embarrass me so in the future?" Francine said.

"I will do my best, but being that I'm also the world's most giantest idiot, I'll probably stumble now and again," Finias said.

"Undoubtedly," Francine said. "How about you open the door so we can go to bed?"

Finias, having heard the word "bed," moved with the quickness of a ninja, and had the door open before she could blink. He swept Francine off of her feet and carried her off to the bed.

Francine stood after having been placed at its foot and loosed the belt on her robe. She left it to drop to the floor, then turning from him, slowly lowered her nighty, legs straight, to her feet.

Turning to face him she asked, "Like what you see?"

"I already used 'more than life itself,' but let me say that still holds true," Finias said. "And do you ever wear panties?"

"Sometimes, but not always," Francine said. "It will be up to you to find out."

At this, she moved to him, and their bodies pressed together as one as she kissed him hard, passionately. As her hands roamed his most intimate areas, she could feel his excitement grow to full measure as she toyed with him before saying, "So, goodnight."

Breaking away and leaving Finias in a state of stunned silence, Francine moved to the middle of the bed, turning off the bedside lamp as she went, and pulled the covers up tight around her.

"I suppose this means I get the couch," Finias said.

"Yep," was all she said.

Chapter 29

"Hey, Finias, it's me. Open up," Elzibeth said into the intercom.

Finias, not yet fully awake, was startled to see Elzibeth at his door through the television screen. "Blimey, what time is it?" Finias asked.

"It's time for you to open the door, that's what time it is," Elzibeth replied.

Finias rolled off the couch with a crick in his back and a creak in more than one part of his body. He hobbled to the door and let Elzibeth in.

"Enjoy your little slumber party, Shoop?" she asked.

"Good morning to you too, and no, not so much," Finias said.

Sensing an opportunity to get back at Francine for last night's little charade, Finias said, "Hey, I have an idea. Francine missed you so much last night, I'm sure she would be delighted to see you. Why don't you go surprise her by jumping on the bed and quickly pulling off her covers? And don't be quiet about it."

"Okay, cool," Elzibeth said.

So that's what she did. Finias thought she looked practiced at this as she moved carefully to the door and opened it very slowly. Then, with a bloodcurdling yell, she jumped on the bed and stripped the covers off of Francine.

"AAAAAHHHHHHH, what the hell!" Francine shouted, bolting upright and providing Finias with a nice mental image as he watched the proceedings from just outside the door.

"Morning, sis. Hey, you lost all of your clothes. Did they get stuck in the covers or something?" Elzibeth said.

"Oh my God, you scared me to death. Here, hand me my covers before Finias comes in," Francine said, ever playing the part.

"He put you up to this, didn't he?" Francine said.

"Yeah, pretty good, right?" Elzibeth said.

"I did no such thing," Finias lied from just outside the door.

"Did too, I swear," Elzibeth said.

"I know, dear. You see, what you need to understand about Finias is that he's an idiot," Francine said.

"Oh, I knew that already. I've heard you say that plenty of times," Elzibeth said.

"You two are hurting my feelings," Finias said.

"Why don't you go see if Lindsey can soothe them for you," Francine said.

"Cheap shot, but not a bad idea after last night," Finias said.

"Elzibeth, would you be so kind as to hand me my robe? I need to kill Finias now," Francine said.

"Sure, sis, but maybe not kill him. How about if you just wound him a little?" Elzibeth said with a grin.

"My God, it's like the Manson family," Finias said. "Come, Elzibeth. Francine, you get dressed and we'll go see if we can scare the crap out of Lindsey."

"Alright," both Elzibeth and Francine shouted with delight.

And so, they did.

Chapter 30

"What is wrong with you people being up before 9:00 am?" Lindsey said from the kitchen where she was making coffee. "And what's with scaring me to death like that? That was so mean."

Upon arriving at Francine's suite, Finias had pounded on the door and, in a loud gravelly voice, said through the intercom, "Lindsey, open up. It's Marcon; we need to talk. Come on, get up and open the fricking door."

Finias wasn't sure if Marcon had a gravelly voice, but it seemed to fit the part.

"I see you on the television, Finias," Lindsey said. "Not funny."

Lindsey, to Francine's delight, had opened the door with bed head the likes of which she had never seen. The longish part on top was a tangled mess that stood almost straight up, and she was never more pleased. Francine noticed too that Lindsey was without makeup and was wearing sweatpants and an old ratty T-shirt Francine used when cleaning the bath and the like. Her only plus was being without a bra, which she was sure to be the only thing that Finias would notice.

Having opened the door, Lindsey moved quickly to give Finias a good morning hug, pressing her bra-less breasts to him while twisting side to side.

Way to take the attention away from that rat's nest of hair, Francine thought.

"Good morning, good morning, good morning," Lindsey said while hugging Finias. "Come in, come in."

And with that, they entered. After their little prank, Francine, still in her bedclothes, went to change out of her nighty, and Lindsey fixed her hair and dressed while Finias and Elzibeth settled in on the couch.

When they returned, Lindsey asked if anyone would care for coffee.

"Sure," said both Finias and Francine.

Francine took a seat beside Finias on the sofa after having changed into blue nylon running shorts and a matching color sports bra, leaving her feet bare for a sexier appeal.

Two can play this game, she had thought while she changed clothes.

Lindsey made coffee, and the four moved to the kitchen and took a seat at the dinette. Elzibeth found a packet of hot chocolate, which she mixed in an oversized glass before placing it into the microwave to heat.

"So, what's with all that Marcon nonsense?" Lindsey said.

"Finias wanted to scare the crap out of you," Elzibeth said.

"Elzibeth, you are too young to use such language," Francine said.

"What? Crap? Is that a bad word? I don't even know what it means," Elzibeth said.

"It is an impolite word, and I'll explain later what it means, okay?" Francine said.

"Why would you want to scare me?" Lindsey said. "Haven't I been through enough?"

"Lindsey, what you need to understand about Finias is that he's an idiot," Francine said.

"I'm beginning to see your point," Lindsey said.

"Hmmm... Maybe we could be friends after all," Francine said.

"You know, I do need to go shopping for, well, everything," Lindsey said. "I won't have access to funds until this mess is cleared up, but if you think you could front me, I will certainly pay you back."

"Of course, but you know, Briarwood pays for all of our personal needs. I'll set up a Briarwood account for you so you can maintain your anonymity and shop till you drop," Francine said.

"You would do that for me? After all the... well, water under the bridge. Thank you very much. That's very kind of you," Lindsey said.

"Thank Briarwood. You will be one of us for the foreseeable future, so you might as well take advantage of all the benefits," Francine said. "But thank you all the same. And yes, water under the bridge."

What on earth is going on here? thought Finias.

"Delightful, maybe we could go shopping today," Lindsey said. "I would have to teleport some distance away so as not to be identified, which I can do now that I'm dead."

"It would be nice to do something fun after such a horrid day yesterday," Francine said. "So, I think that's a wonderful idea. How about you, Elzibeth? Would you like to join us?"

"Sure, why not," Elzibeth said.

"Excellent, it's settled then."

"Great, three against one," Finias said.

But they didn't hear him as they were already busy making lists of stores to visit and things to buy, and Finias felt as though his bit of fun with Lindsey had come to an abrupt end.

"I hate to break up your little shopping party, but we should talk about how we are going to explain to Calderón just how Lindsey and I met, why we would schedule a private meeting outside of the protections of Briarwood, and how Elzibeth had to rescue Lindsey from a burning building," Finias said.

"If you guys lie, they'll know," Elzibeth said.

Everyone turned to look at her.

"I'm just sayin', I've tried a bunch of times, and it never works out," Elzibeth said.

"We'll talk about that later, young lady," Francine said. "But I believe she is right. The truth will set us free, or so they say, and if not, then we're in trouble anyway even with a good lie."

"You are right, of course," Lindsey said. "For me, being truthful will be turning over a new leaf as it appears my life lately, though unwittingly, has been wrapped up in lies. So, I may as well begin being truthful now. I would like to tell you, Francine, that I was upset that Finias had brought you to our meeting. I had meant to seduce him that night, and when you showed up looking like you do, I suddenly felt bad about myself. Like I'm beyond my prime and too old to measure up. So, I went out of my way to annoy you, and I'm sorry."

"Missed it by one day," Finias said.

"Missed what by one day?" Francine said.

"What? Oh, nothing. Just talking to myself," Finias said.

"Yeah, I know what you think you missed by one day," Francine said.

"Finias, I'm flattered. Would a night with me have been something you would have looked forward to?" Lindsey said. "If that's okay of me to ask, Francine?"

"Sure, I see where you are coming from," Francine said. "But if he answers, he's a dead man, and will never, ever, have anything of that nature to look forward to ever again. So, what say you, Finias?"

"I've suddenly become deaf and dumb," Finias said.

"Really? You believe the dumb part to be all of the sudden?" Francine said.

"Come on, knock that off, and let's just get on with this," Finias said.

"Okay, so if we are being truthful, and Elzibeth, you might as well hear this now as well. Deaf and dumb here and I are kind of an item," Francine said.

"I knew it," Elzibeth said. "You don't get all that lipstick everywhere without something going on."

"Correction, we were kind of an item. After last night, I'm beginning to consider other options," Finias said.

"You be quiet. Women are talking," Francine said. "Why don't you go make a pencil holder out of a toilet paper roll or something."

"I feel rather foolish," Lindsey began. "It did feel odd to me that you were being so overly guarded of him, but you had me convinced that there was no relationship. I just thought you had a crush on him, and that's why you were acting so jealously. Do forgive my behavior."

"Of course. I forgive you if you forgive me. It's just that with you being so outgoing and the attraction I felt between the two of you, it made me feel inadequate. You are so pretty and charming and sophisticated, and look at me, I'm a raving lunatic pretending I have all the answers when I don't even understand the questions just so I can feel good about myself," Francine said.

"I think I'm going to cry," said Lindsey.

"Me too," Francine said.

And the two stood and hugged and cried and spoke of each other's incredible qualities. This went on for some time. For his part, Finias leaned into Elzibeth and said, "Oh brother," to which Elzibeth answered, "You said it," as they waited for the two women to shed whatever self-imposed demons they allowed to reside within the depths of their self-esteem.

Chapter 31

At the conclusion of their meeting, the girls decided to meet later at the Grand Entrance so that the three of them could go shopping. Having a little time left, Lindsey changed and freshened up, as did Francine, and the two left to meet with the Head of Housing at Briarwood to arrange to have one of the several guest suites shifted to be located next to Francine's.

Finias set off to visit Mary for only the second time to request a formal meeting with the headmaster later that evening and asked that she place a request to both Theodore and Teri to attend. Mary said that she would make the arrangements and suggested to Finias that it was not necessary to visit her in person with such a request, hinting that it was much more fun to chat over the television in his room or the backboards in his gym so that he might be more comfortable in his choice of clothing or lack thereof.

"Why, Mary, are you flirting with me?" Finias said, with a wry smile.

"I'm too old to waste time diddling around with flirting. I'm suggesting that the next time you are playing basketball, let's say shirtless and wearing little else, you give ole Mary a ring and give me a thrill."

"Why, Mary, you are brazen," Finias said.

"You should have known me when I was younger," Mary said. "You would have been as worn out as a threadbare tire after spending a weekend with me."

"What a shame to have missed out on that," Finias said.

"Yes, for both of us," Mary said.

"I'm afraid to say I must be off," Finias said, who then went around the desk and kissed Mary on the cheek. "You'll be a dear and make the arrangements for tonight?"

"Yes, of course. Will you be having dinner prior to, or should I arrange for this to be a dinner meeting?" Mary asked.

"Hmmm...good question. No, let's set the meeting for 9:00 pm this evening so that dinner will be out of the way. I'm afraid that what we have to discuss would not go well with dinner," Finias said.

"Bad?" Mary said.

"The outcome of what we are to share, though with some unfortunate conclusions, came out somewhat better than one would expect, all things considered. But overall, yes, it's bad," Finias said.

"Well then, good luck to you. I will see that it's done," Mary said.

"Oh, and if you would be so kind, I am in need of the home address of one Thaime Pregmierar," Finias said.

"I can give you the address he left on file from the current members' registry, but Thaime has been shunned with no requirement to report a change of address," Mary said.

"It's a start, I suppose," Finias said.

"Might I ask why it is you wish to speak with such a despicable man?" Mary said.

"It has to do with the business of tonight. Everything is a bit up in the air right now with more questions than answers, but when things get cleared up a little more, I'll play some basketball in but a pair of sneakers and give you a call with all the juicy details," Finias said.

"Don't tease an old lady," Mary said. "Though that's an image I'll be falling asleep with tonight."

"You are quite something, Miss Mary," Finias said. "I think you and I are going to be good friends."

"Here is the address I have on file. Good luck to you," Mary said. "And Finias, do be careful. You'll find Thaime to be not only an unpleasant man but also unpredictable. I'm not sure which is worse."

Chapter 32

Finias set off to the Arlington address of Thaime. Having teleported to just inside the massive steel gate at the entry.

Finias made a clean visual sweep of his surroundings, prepared to teleport back to...anywhere, he supposed, if an angry Thaime or a gang of his goons became aware of his presence and looked to do a Thomas Huerta and knock his block off.

Sensing no immediate danger, Finias took a deep, "thank you, Lord" breath and turned his attention up the drive to a rather large colonial-style home. Moving ever cautiously, still acutely aware of potential danger, Finias trekked up the long and curving cobblestone drive to the turnaround at the top.

The house itself, though large, would not, at least to Finias' mind, be considered a mansion. It was well-kept and attractive with its grey slate roof and white entry colonnade. But the overwhelming size of his single yet extravagant room was of similar size, and Finias doubted that Thaime's home would contain a full-sized basketball court.

Hah... One up on you already, Finias thought. Not a bad home, though, he considered to himself. Too bad I'm going to blow it up.

Along the way, Finias could smell the faint scent of jasmine, which he now noticed growing behind planters of blue hydrangea along the side of an outbuilding to the left of the drive, with tall Italian cypress trees lining the downhill side of the drive opposite the house, better to block the view from below, Finias supposed.

Upon arrival at the entry, Finias was not sure what to do next. He had come with a singular purpose, which he was anxious to get on with, but to do so with the potential for others to be inside, or heaven forbid, Thaime had pets, so he put his fears aside, stepped to the door, and rang the bell. He waited a moment, preparing himself to jet out of there at the slightest hint of sound or movement from the side windows, and rang the bell again.

Nothing. Finias could feel his heart rate slow from the pounding it had given his chest. Having had no reply to the door, noticing no movement, and hearing no noise, he made his way around to the back of the house to gain a further glimpse inside.

The rear of the property backed up to sparse woods, with more Italian cypress creating a border between the woods and a large pool deck. It was a typical rear area with a kidney-shaped pool, outdoor BBQ, lounge chairs, and the like. Nothing fancy. It could have been the rear yard of any middle-class home in America and seemed oddly unsuited to the size and style of the house.

"To each his own, I guess," Finias found himself saying out loud. "A little disappointed there are no sharks swimming in the pool, or a torture rack, or maybe a pit of vipers somewhere," he continued.

Finias moved to a set of glass French Style doors at the rear of the home and looked inside. On the wall to the left of the dinette set just inside the door was a large framed picture of Thaime in a suit with another gentleman Finias did not recognize. They were shaking hands and holding court in front of an audience while being the recipients of some kind of plaque.

For Finias, this was a good sign as it told him that Thaime had indeed not changed his address. Finias banged cautiously on the glass door a couple of times, thinking then he had no alibi for being there, but when it was clear that the residence was vacant of either occupants or pets, he went back the way he had come and strolled casually down the winding drive, enjoying again the scent of jasmine and the cool breeze of the morning.

Stopping not yet at the gate but at a point in which the house was still in view, Finias, with the utmost concentration, conjured a massive ball of pure energy more powerful than a lightning bolt and with it, struck the house. A massive explosion followed with another, which Finias suspected to be a propane tank. Finias strolled the rest of the way down the drive, turned to take in his good work, then left to return to the confines of Briarwood.

Chapter 33

It was early evening when Francine found Finias in the Hall of Records and Library. Finias was looking into ownership of shipping slips along the massive Grand Port Harbor when Francine walked in wearing white nylon running shorts and a black tank top that Finias had not seen before, with color-coordinated running shoes.

"Enjoy your shopping?" Finias asked.

"Yes, very much so," Francine said. "She really is a hoot to be around, Lindsey is. She's so bold and curious and finds everything to be fun and interesting. I really enjoyed our time together. I think even Elzibeth had a good time, Lindsey being so playful."

"Well, good for you three then," Finias said.

"So, what have you been up to?" Francine asked.

"I've been trying to find out if there are records of ownership in Marcon's name or his other name, Perino, of a slip in the Grand Port Harbor. Also, I took a stroll and blew up Thaime's house in Arlington," Finias said.

"You what?" Francine shrieked.

"Quiet, we are in a library," Finias said.

"I thought it was the Hall of Records," Francine said. "Besides, the only other person in here is the guard way up front."

"Hall of Records and Library. But, I suppose, it's just that blowing up the home of one of the Order, though shunned, is not something I want to be associated with outside of those in our tight little group," Finias said.

"What would possess you to do that?" Francine asked.

"Revenge for Thaime having blackmailed Lindsey, and to a lesser extent, to send a message. For if Thaime wasn't involved with blowing up Lindsey's home, it was only because she is a member of the Order and his involvement carried too much risk to Marcon," Finias said.

"How so?" Francine asked.

"Having Thaime involved in such action against a member of the Order, a high-ranking member at that, brings us into play. Marcon would have to understand that we would not sit idly by and allow such behavior to go unpunished," Finias said.

"My word, Finias, I'm stunned you would do such a thing," Francine said. "I'm feeling a little turned on."

"My blowing up a house turns you on?" Finias asked.

"Well...yes. I don't know. It's just so...dangerous," Francine said.

"Every instinct in my body tells me you are trouble and that I should stay away from you," Finias said.

"And yet you are unable," Francine said.

"Entirely," Finias said.

Chapter 34

"Tell me, what else has my brave little soldier been up to while I've been out protecting a valued, though reportedly dead, member of the High Council under the pretense of shopping?" Francine said, moving close and kissing his cheek.

"I've been sitting here thinking of getting a dog," Finias said.

"A dog? What on earth for?" Francine said, surprised.

"To keep me company now that I know I will be forever lonely with you having a newfound friend," Finias said.

"Oh, you poor baby. Here, let momma give you a kiss to make it all better," Francine said, teasing him as she brought her chair in tight and leaned in to kiss him again.

"That was nice, thank you, but I think you'll have to do a little better than that later on," Finias said. "I'm feeling most neglected."

"Later on? I think not," Francine said.

"No? Is there a reason why?" Finias said, suddenly disappointed.

"Because I can do better than that right here," whispered Francine, moving her hand to his lap.

"What are you doing? Stop that. We are in the library, for crying out loud," Finias said.

"Hall of Records and Library, and so what? There is not a soul around. Relax and enjoy this as you'll never know when I might have time for you now that Lindsey and I have become besties," Francine teased.

"But..."

"But what?" Francine cooed in his ear. "It doesn't appear by how things are shaping up that you are experiencing performance anxiety."

"No, it's not that," Finias whispered. "It's just that, you know, if you keep up with this, I'll end up... well, making a mess."

"You just sit back and let momma worry about that," Francine said.

"What's with all this momma business?" Finias asked.

"Shush, you'll spoil my fun," Francine said.

And with that, she picked up Finias's pencil and dropped it to the floor.

"Oops, look at that. I seem to have dropped my pencil," Francine said, as she moved her chair back and crawled under the table.

"Oh my God, what are you doing?" Finias said in a harsh whisper. "Stop that and get back up here."

"Quiet. You just relax and enjoy this. The only person here has his back to us, so nobody is going to know," Francine said. "Now just be still and pretend to be playing with your little computer there as if you are preparing studiously for a different type of job."

"You're crazy. And, a little scary. And, oh my, incredibly good at that," Finias said.

"Shush, just relax," Francine said.

"Oh God," Finias groaned.

"That's a good boy."

A number of minutes later Francine stood and said, "Oh look, I've found my pencil."

"You are indescribable," Finias said.

"I'll take that as a compliment to my developing talents and not to my having frightened you. Now, what say we get out of this stuffy place and go somewhere more comfortable?" Francine said.

"And what did you have in mind?" Finias said.

"Well, as ours is a reciprocal relationship, I was hoping to take advantage of that," Francine said, having regained her seat while bumping her shoulder into his.

"You're insatiable, thank goodness for me," Finias said. "Are you ready to go?"

"After that, I've never been more ready," Francine said.

As they moved to leave, the security guard asked where Francine had disappeared to.

"What the devil do you mean?" Francine said, alarmed.

"It's my job to keep track of people in here," he said, pointing to a bank of security monitors to his left. "You disappeared for a while, and I know you didn't use the ladies' room."

The guard directed her attention to the restroom locations at the front.

"Oh, yes. Well, you see, I had dropped my pencil," Francine said. "It rolled under the table."

"You must have had difficulty finding it then," the guard said with a small grin.

"Oh, no. I found it just fine," Francine said, rather shyly, while looking around at anything but the guard.

"I'm sure you did," he said, again with a grin. "Good day to you."

"Yes, good day," they both said, then left.

"Oh my God, I'm so embarrassed," Francine said as they made their way back to Finias's suite.

"As well you should be," Finias said. "As you remember, I'd begged you to stop."

Francine slugged his shoulder.

"You did no such thing. This is partly your fault anyway, you know," Francine said.

"My fault? How is it my fault?" Finias said.

"Well, if you had taken care of business last night, I wouldn't have had to spend the day feeling... rather pent up," Francine said.

"What? You teased me and put me out on the couch," Finias said.

"Well, yes, but what man doesn't wait a while then sneak into bed with his naked lover?" Francine said. "Especially when I purposely left my clothes on the floor as a hint. I waited nearly an hour before falling asleep."

"Really? Well, that would have been good information to know."

"That's alright. Lesson learned. I expect you to make up for it when we reach your suite."

"I believe I see your meaning and trust me, I will be most delighted," Finias said.

And so they went. Finias could actually feel Francine's excitement as she pulled him along in anticipation.

A short time later, they arrived at Finias's suite and upon opening the door, they found Elzibeth in the middle of coming off the couch.

"Hey there, kiddo. What are you doing here? And how did you get into my room?" Finias said.

"I asked Mary for a key so I could hide here and scare the cra… um… stuffing out of you," Elzibeth said. "But I fell asleep after all that shopping."

"And she just gave you a key?" Finias said.

"She didn't want to at first," Elzibeth said. "But when I told her I was going to try and scare you to death she said, 'bully for you,' or something like that and she gave it to me."

"Huh, I shall have to have a talk with Mary about that," Finias said.

"You'll do no such thing," Francine said. "I'll need this for later it appears now, so hand over the key, Elzibeth."

"Really? I'd planned a surprise attack later when he was sleeping," Elzibeth said.

"There will be no more surprise attacks," Francine said. "You nearly ended my life this morning."

"Alright," Elzibeth said as she handed Francine the card key.

"So, why do you need a key?" Elzibeth said. "If you're not planning a surprise attack."

"What? No, not a surprise attack. Um, Finias owes me a favor, which I was hoping to collect on before we stumbled into you. But it now looks like I will need to come back... later, for that... favor," Francine said, somewhat lamely.

"What kind of favor?" asked Elzibeth.

"What? Oh, favor? Yes, well you see, Finias is known to be quite the cook and he was going to prepare dinner for me," Francine said.

"Why did he owe you a favor?" asked Elzibeth.

"Favor yes, why is it that you owed me a favor again?" she asked Finias, while staring him down with a withering gaze.

"What favor?" Finias said, appearing perplexed though relishing in her discomfort.

"Oh my God, you know what favor. The favor that you owed me. Oh, never mind," Francine said, angry now, and not sure what to do next.

"Oh, of course, the favor," Finias said, hurrying to make up for his blunder knowing if he didn't he would surely receive a good sock later. "You see, I owed Francine a favor as she helped me with a little job I was afraid of finishing without her help."

"What kind of job?" Elzibeth said.

"I may pass out so be a dear and catch me, please," Francine said.

"Research, yes, she was very busy exploring a certain region for me. At the library," Finias said. "So enough about that. Why don't you run off and find your friends so that Francine and I can get busy cooking?"

"I thought you were doing the cooking," Elzibeth said.

"What? Yes, that's what I meant, while I get busy with Francine. Busy cooking, I mean," Finias said, flustered.

"You guys came here to kiss and stuff, didn't you?" Elzibeth said.

"No, most certainly not. Now why don't you head on out and find your friends for dinner. It's about that time anyway," Francine said, hoping beyond hope that she takes her up on this.

"I'd rather have dinner with you guys if that's okay," Elzibeth said. "I'm wearing these funny clothes and I don't want my friends to see me if I can help it."

"What? Why, you look adorable," Finias said. "And rather grown up. I would think that your friends would be most envious."

Elzibeth was wearing an embroidered flutter sleeve tee, white, with pink and blue flowers, black yoga pants to above her ankle, and grey Ked flat-bottom tennies.

"Really?" Elzibeth said.

"Absolutely," Francine said, "So, run along now."

"Okay, so listen, I have an idea," Elzibeth said, apparently ignoring Francine. "When we go to dinner, let's walk the full length of the center aisle to see if my friends notice my clothes."

"I think I'm going to cry," Francine said.

"Why, sis?" Elzibeth said.

"Hmm, oh, I'm just terribly frustrated at the moment," Francine said. "In more ways than one."

"Maybe we should go to dinner so that you can have some wine and relax," Finias suggested.

"I suppose... There really is no way around this, is there?" pleaded Francine.

"Not that I can see," Finias said.

"Alright, let's go then," Francine said, snatching up her purse in frustration.

And the three of them set off to the Great Dining Hall.

Chapter 35

As promised, Elzibeth made quite the show of things, taking her time walking up the center aisle while stopping to visit with friends along the way. She was greeted with "oohs," "ahhs," and "wow, that outfit looks great, Elzibeth."

Being very pleased with herself, she made one more round before the three of them settled in to eat.

"That was fun," Elzibeth said. "Thanks for buying me stuff today."

"You are welcome. And don't forget to thank Lindsey. She both found your stretchy pants and talked you into wearing them," Francine said.

"Okay," Elzibeth said.

As was the norm, a waiter arrived in short order and recommended oysters on the half shell with a mignonette sauce of shallots, lemon juice, peppercorns, and vinegar to start; these to be accompanied by a bottle of champagne for the lovely couple.

"Oh, we are not a couple," Francine said.

"But I thought you said," Elzibeth began.

"No, dear, we certainly are not," Francine said, winking at Elzibeth.

"Oh, got it," Elzibeth said.

"My apologies," said the waiter. "Perhaps, if I might suggest you give them a try. As you know, oysters are said to have certain qualities that may be sufficient to allow you to enjoy each other's company all the more, perhaps with an after-dinner stroll in this lovely near-moonless night. Near-moonless, of course, being all the better for a little privacy, don't you think?"

Francine and Finias just looked at each other and did not reply.

"Very well then, to follow, I would suggest that you allow yourselves to fully explore the unadorned nature of each other's being by sharing in a most lovely dish of baked salmon with capers and lemon, to be accompanied by sautéed haricots verts, morel mushrooms with scallions, and a delicious pea consommé with mint and white chocolate. This to be followed by a light grapefruit-pomegranate salad."

"Yes, okay, that will be fine," Francine said.

"Fine by me as well," Finias added.

"Most excellent," said the waiter. "To finish, dessert tonight will be chocolate volcano cake simply gushing from deep within served with vanilla ice cream."

"You've got to be kidding me. It's molten chocolate cake, simple as that. No volcano gushing anything. This can't be by accident," Francine whispered in a most annoyed voice to Finias.

"I think you are just being overly sensitive," Finias whispered back.

Francine leaned into Finias and said, "I know you don't see it even with that magnificent brain of yours, but something is going on with these suggestive remarks."

Finias, knowing better than to argue, simply shrugged his shoulders.

"I'll go ahead and have that chocolate thing," Elzibeth said.

"No, you will not," Francine said. "First dinner, then dessert."

"Saving dessert for later, what shall I bring you for dinner, Miss Elzibeth?" asked the waiter.

"Mac and cheese with extra cheese, please," Elzibeth said.

Francine was going to comment but really just wanted to get on with things before the waiter had a chance to suggest any additional sexual innuendo.

It wasn't long before the waiter arrived with the oysters for Finias and Francine, along with a rather extravagant dimpled solid silver cup full of French fries with sides of roasted garlic aioli and, of course, ketchup for Elzibeth to snack on while the oysters were served.

As the remaining dishes arrived, the conversation was sparse as the three enjoyed their food and the mood in the room, which seemed light, all things considered.

Finias took a moment to point out to Elzibeth and Francine a constellation of stars through the glass ceiling of the Great Dining Hall with a tragic yet, some say, starry-eyed history.

Gathering their limited attention, Finias began by telling a tale of two stars said to be the romantic partners Perseus and Andromeda. "During his return from a successful trip to kill Medusa," Finias said, "Perseus spotted a beautiful young woman chained to a seaside rock. He rescued her and learned she'd been tied there by her parents, King Cepheus and Queen Cassiopeia.

"You see, Poseidon had sent the sea monster Cetus to destroy Cepheus's kingdom as punishment for Cassiopeia boasting about how beautiful Andromeda was," he continued. "Cepheus and Cassiopeia sought the counsel of an oracle who advised them to sacrifice their daughter in order to save their kingdom. Perseus found another way out. He killed the monster Cetus. Then asked to marry Andromeda.

"However, Andromeda had already been promised to her uncle Phineas. So, Perseus had to kill him too. Perseus and Andromeda are said to still be together today, going around the northern pole together forever."

"Good story, but too bad you had to go," Elzibeth said.

"Different Phineas," Finias said. "But thank you for the sentiment."

Chapter 36

After dinner, it was suggested that they go to their respective suites to change for the meeting with Calderón, which was scheduled to begin shortly. Elzibeth argued that she was just going to wear what she had on and asked Francine if she could simply stay with her for a while.

"No, I would like you to go back to your room and brush your teeth after dinner and chocolate cake," Francine said. "Freshen up a bit, then come back to meet me in my room."

"Okay, I guess," Elzibeth said. "I'm going to go visit Missy for a bit when I'm done, OK?"

"Sure, but don't be long," Francine said.

Francine waited until the doors of the Grand Entrance had closed behind Elzibeth, then grasping Finias's hand, she said, "Come on, let's do this. We don't have much time."

And off they hurried to Finias's suite.

"Francine, we really don't have time for this now," Finias said, unlocking his door. "I promise to make it up to you later."

Francine shoved Finias through the door and said, "Let's go, big boy, this is happening. Besides, trust me, it will not take long."

This did indeed turn out to be true. As Finias gave his full attention to her, Francine moved with him in obvious delight until she could stand no more, and her body erupted into multiple prolonged seizures of gratification.

"Oh, my good God, that was amazing," Francine said as she lay back, melting into the bed, panting heavily. "Where has that been all my life?"

"So, I did okay?" Finias said.

"Finias, I swear I almost passed out that was so good," Francine said. "You don't suppose you'll ever forget how you did that, do you? Maybe you should write it down. As a matter of fact, write it down twice in case you miss a step, then send a copy to the Library of Congress or something as a national treasure."

Finias laughed.

"Forget how to do that? Not a chance. I Googled it," Finias said. "But, I'm glad you were pleased. Now, we need to get a move on."

"Pleased?" Francine said. "Finias, you have no idea."

Moving quickly, though on somewhat shaky legs, Francine gave Finias a thank-you hug and a quick kiss, said a hasty goodbye, and headed off to her room to change for the evening.

It wasn't long before Elzibeth arrived to see after Francine.

"Hey, sis, it's me," Elzibeth said into the intercom.

Francine answered the door yet undressed.

"What's taking you so long?" Elzibeth said. "We're going to be late, you know."

"Yes, I couldn't decide what to wear," Francine said, by way of excuse for the time spent with Finias.

"Well, get a move on," Elzibeth said.

"Do me a favor, give Finias a call and let him know we are running late and that we will be along shortly and for him to go ahead along without us," Francine said.

"Okay," Elzibeth said, and so she did.

As for the meeting, Finias arrived soon after Theodore and Teri and exchanged greetings. Lindsey came through the door not long after, wearing a stunning all-white shirt dress with long sleeves and tabs, a black belt, and matching high heels, giving her a casual-chic look. Her jet-black hair highlighted the stark contrast of her white dress, and her cover-page face left everyone present seated and simply staring at the true essence of Lindsey Sterling fully on display.

Calderón, upon seeing her, was first up out of his seat and seemed to be in a hurry to greet her.

"Lindsey, I understood you to be here tonight, but a part of me did not believe this to be true," Calderón said. "Might I say that you look absolutely fabulous and much different than I expected, considering I've only seen your beauty on those dreadful monitors in that circular chamber you call a conference room."

"Delighted to see you in person as well," said Lindsey. "Yes, I must say I am most delighted. You are much taller than I expected, and I have to say, considerably more handsome than the monitors would suggest."

Lindsey extended her hand in greeting and instead of taking it in his, Calderón bowed slightly, raised her hand to his lips, and kissed it lightly.

"Oh my, how charming," said Lindsey, feigning slightly as she touched a hand to her plentiful cleavage.

Elzibeth came through the door at this moment, breaking the air of stunned silence surrounding Finias, Theodore, and Teri, having witnessed this little interchange between the two.

"Sorry we're late," Elzibeth said. "Sis couldn't figure out what to wear."

Elzibeth had not changed from her morning's outfit, yet, and as adorable as she was, it was Francine who caught the attention of all. Francine seemed to float into the room, looking marvelous as always, wearing a simple white tank top with a pleated black skirt ending just below her knee, surrounded by a striped purple wrap tied at the waist with color-matched sandals.

"My, I wasn't expecting a fashion show, but you three lovely ladies look terrific," Theodore said.

"And Elzibeth, look at you. You look so grown up," Teri said. "Come here and let me see what you are wearing."

The conversation drifted around this topic for a while as it was explained how they had gone shopping earlier in the day and thought there might be no better time to show off their wares than now.

Calderón, being ever clever, understood this to be a bit of a diversion from the trouble he suspected they might be in but was glad of it. There had been enough tension among the group as of late and he saw no harm in them providing a bit of levity to an otherwise tense situation.

Introductions having been made; the group settled in. Calderón had taken it upon himself to have a small conference table brought in to seat the group, and it being ultra-modern, clashed terribly with the room's old-world décor.

"I suppose it best that we begin without delay," Calderón said. "Being the hour that it is, I propose we get straight to the heart of the matter. I would like to know how and why it is, Lindsey, that you have come to join us here in your stay at Briarwood."

"I came here seeking information of the type and level that I was afraid I would not be able to obtain from you. You see, I myself was in a spot of trouble, having been in the process of being blackmailed by Thaime for my ill-advised affair with a man who I did not know to be Francis Marcon," said Lindsey directly.

"You are or were Marcon's mistress then, I take it," Calderón said.

"Yes, but not with a man I knew to be Marcon. I was deceived," said Lindsey.

"I see," Calderón said. "Please continue."

"I convinced Finias here, without much effort I must say, to meet me for dinner so that I might seduce him in an attempt to extract information. Fortunately, it turns out, Francine became aware of our little outing and decided to join us, thus spoiling my plans," said Lindsey.

"I... you didn't... there was some effort... oh, never mind," Finias said.

Francine shot Finias a glance and rolled her eyes as if to say, yeah, like you would have put up a fight.

"I wasn't sure if she was who she said she was or an impostor," Francine said, ignoring Finias's dramatic silence. "I had Elzibeth tail her to find out her address, or to see where she might go after departing the restaurant."

"You what?" Teri said, startled. "You involved my little girl in this adventure?"

"Yes, mother, a terrible mistake on my part," Francine said.

"Thank goodness you are okay, Elzibeth. You are okay, aren't you?" Teri said.

"Sure, it was no big deal after the explosion," Elzibeth said.

"What?" Those not in the know yelled in unison.

"Yeah, these guys came along after Lindsey got home and shot up her driver, then blew her house up," Elzibeth said rather factually.

"Oh my God, is this true?" Teri said.

"I'm afraid that it is," said Lindsey.

"What on earth did you mean by 'tail her'?" Theodore said.

"You see, Dad, while I was instructing Elzibeth and Finias in teleportation, I learned that Elzibeth was able to pause as she wished anywhere along her path of travel. She just seemed to float until it was decided where she wanted to go. My thinking was that it seemed a simple matter for her to follow Lindsey home," Francine said.

"Remarkable," Theodore said. "I've never heard of such a thing."

"Nor I," Calderón said. "How could this be?"

"She is an incredible little girl," Francine said. "In more ways than any of us could imagine. She, having seen the gunmen leave, suspected Lindsey of being in some trouble and made the decision to try and remove her from the home to bring her back here for the night in order to sort things out."

"So, out of nowhere, I'm suddenly being carried away by this little girl as my house was blowing up around us," said Lindsey.

"My God," Teri said.

"Yeah, it was a close one too. My bottom is still a little red," Elzibeth said. "Hey, would you guys mind if I left now? I told Missy I'd watch Toy Story III with her. We've seen it a million times, but she still cries."

"No, please, you go right ahead," Calderón said. "I believe you've told us more than I myself can digest in one night."

"Come here and give us a hug first," Francine said as Finias, Teri, and Theodore joined in.

Goodnight wishes were shared by all, and Elzibeth made off to find Missy.

"My, that is some tale indeed, and a very gifted little girl who told it," Calderón said. "Do any of you have any other misadventures to add to this little misadventure?"

"I blew up Thaime's house today," Finias said.

Chapter 37

Thaime was furious, though it was hard to tell at what. He seemed to be furious most of the time. He had been across the border after spending the majority of the day meeting with various cartel factions when later that evening he had been called on a tip about a breach in the port authorities' database at Grand Port Harbor.

The information he received he knew not to be good news, as it appeared that someone had hacked into the system and was looking to retrieve information regarding the current ownership of each of the docks along the harbor.

"What did they get?" he'd asked the data analyst at the port.

"Nothing that we could see. It seems like whoever was snooping around wasn't sure where to look, so they were simply opening random folders in the hope of stumbling across something. Then, the exchange was just dropped. He or she must have been interrupted. Ten more minutes, and they might have been onto something."

"Were you able to trace the location of the connection?" Thaime said.

"No," said the analyst. "It didn't seem to come from anywhere."

"What do you mean, it had to come from somewhere," Thaime said, kicking a chair across the room.

"Not that we have been able to determine," the analyst said, cowering at the outburst.

This raised alarm bells with Thaime. Bells he was not eager to share with Marcon.

"Keep an eye out and let me know the minute you find something. Understood?" Thaime said.

"Yes, of course. I will keep you posted," the analyst said, nervously.

"You do that," Thaime said. "Both of our lives may depend on it."

Chapter 38

Thaime wasn't sure what to make of the information he had received about the hacking of the port's records. His plan was proceeding as he had expected, and he didn't appreciate any setbacks or deviations, especially from an unknown source.

Of course, Thaime thought to himself, Marcon's eventual demise was an unfortunate reality he would have to come to terms with. Marcon had brought him in when he was left with nothing but the clothes on his back after being shunned by the Order. He owed him, he supposed. Marcon had made him a very rich man, and he had moved up the ranks in Marcon's operation rapidly, becoming his right-hand man with oversight of all business entities and transactions.

So, why didn't he feel any overwhelming sense of loyalty, he thought to himself. And why did he feel no remorse for the life of a friend that he knew he would eventually have to take?

Thaime decided to simply go back to his home, have a drink, and think things through. Yet upon his arrival, he became instantly aware that this was not to be.

Chapter 39

Thaime arrived at Marcon's western mansion soon after discovering the pile of ash and rubble that had been his home. He had discovered the destruction soon after leaving the port, having gone there to settle in for the night. Outraged at his findings, Thaime chose to teleport straight into Marcon's mansion, which he was not allowed to do under any circumstances, but at the moment he didn't care. He was in no mood to be polite.

"What the hell do you think you are doing?" Marcon said as Thaime appeared just inside the front door. Marcon was seated across the entry in an expansive space known as a great room or combination room.

Marcon had his feet up, glass of scotch in hand, and was watching a baseball game on a television too large for viewing without splitting the screen in two or moving one's head side to side.

Thaime, without hesitation, moved to block Marcon's view.

"What have I said about you dropping in like this?" Marcon said.

"Forget about that for now, I have an emergency," Thaime said.

"Then I suggest you handle it," Marcon said. "That's what I pay you for. Do not involve me with petty details."

"Someone blew up my fricking house," Thaime said.

"Pity, it was a rather nice house if I remember correctly," Marcon said.

"That's it? That's all you have to say?"

"And, what pray tell would you have me say?"

"Well, you can begin by telling what you are going to do about it?" Thaime said. "Or, did you have something to do with it?"

"Don't be silly," Marcon said. "Why would I have an interest in blowing up your home?"

"Seems like you have had an interest in me and my guys blowing up a lot of things lately," Thaime said.

"Only in the interest of progress, my good man," Marcon said. "Not in the interest of my own personal gratification."

"If not you, then who? I want answers, Marcon. And I want you to build me a new damn house. Greater than the equal of this squalid sandbox," Thaime said.

"You dare come to my home and threaten me?" Marcon said. "And insult my beautiful home?"

"I do not simply threaten," Thaime said. "This you should know by now."

"Look, what do you want from me?" Marcon said. "You want me to build you another house with my hard-earned fortune? If I were to do that for everyone looking for a handout, where would I be? Answer me that."

"You've earned your fortune off the backs of others like me, Marcon," Thaime said.

"Yes, this is true. But you have done very well for yourself, have you not?" Marcon said.

"Not so well that I wish to spend millions rebuilding my home," Thaime said. "You owe me, Marcon."

"See, there it is. This ungrateful attitude of yours, which had you chase me down begging for an opportunity to earn more than the substantial salary the Order had been paying you before being ousted," Marcon said. "I do suppose that I understand, though. There is never enough for men like us, is there, Thaime?"

"I will get what I seek one way or the other, Marcon," Thaime said.

"Do you really wish to play this kind of dangerous game with me?" Marcon said.

"I'm not playing," said Thaime. "I want fifteen million in cash for my new home and the trouble it will be to rebuild it. As I see it, this is your fault whether you were directly responsible or not."

"My fault?" shouted Marcon. "You are insane. Go, get out of here before I lose my patience with you."

"Me insane? Perhaps. But you know that I am a target of this aggression simply by my association with you. Nobody outside of your influence would dare mess with me if they weren't trying to get to me in order to have a better shot at getting to you. You need me, Marcon. I'm your best protection," Thaime said. "Or did you forget how my men and I saved your behind from that lovely gang of mercenaries with their color-coded hats that stormed your little castle here? And don't forget the successful mission that I alone planned and executed with your son and his family."

"He was not my son. And his wife, as was my wife, were whores. The only loss I regret is the loss of the dog, not that man and his bastard son and what he thought of as a wife."

"How do you know this? Any of this, Marcon."

"How do you think? The child was mine, Thaime. That's how I know. And that little whore tried to blackmail me into making Anthony, a bastard himself, head of my operations. Well, she and the lot of them got what they had coming."

"As for your good works, and yes, I will say you did an admirable job both in the execution and cover-up. Yet, aside from that, it seems it is you who has forgotten, Thaime. Remember, I hired you just for that purpose: to protect me. And, truth be told, you were very good at it.

"And now, I feel nothing but pity for you. Coming here to my home unannounced, threatening me, though with hat in hand like a beggar. Such a shame you have become so full of yourself, Thaime. It is a pity to have to kill you," Marcon said, suddenly raising a nine-millimeter pistol from between the cushions of the couch.

Thaime seemed ready for this. Suddenly, Marcon was lifted off the couch, arm outstretched, yet seemingly frozen in time; the gun in his hand now useless. Thaime twisted Marcon's head from his body and set it next to the glass of scotch Marcon had left on the coffee table.

"And just who did you say was so full of himself?" Thaime said to the headless body as he walked to the front door and stepped outside to admire the view from his new front porch.

Chapter 40

"You what?" Everyone but Francine shouted in unison.

"I blew up his house," Finias said, a little less boastful this time.

"To what end, my dear boy?" Theodore said.

"Retribution for his blackmail of Lindsey," Finias said. "And to send a message that not even someone as powerful as Thaime is safe."

"I admire your stones, my good man, but these types of decisions should not be made in a vacuum. The consequences of such actions need to be carefully measured prior to such activities. You do see my point I hope," Theodore said.

"Of course. I know I should have consulted with this group prior to acting, but truth be told, I was afraid of being overruled, which would have forced me to act on my own outside of the wishes of this council," Finias said.

"Hubris such as this can be terribly dangerous," Teri said. "And in the future, will not be tolerated. Is that understood?"

"Yes and no," Finias said. "I certainly understand the concept, but I've been told that it is my heart that has brought me here to Briarwood, and it is my heart I will follow outside of the politics of group decision. Please understand, I could not simply, in all good conscience, stand idly by and allow the near-death of two people who have become quite dear to me and the loss of a home to go unpunished. In the future, I will attempt to bring other similar matters to your attention if timing allows, but I do not promise to remain silent in the way of my actions if I feel in my heart that it is indeed the right thing to do and it becomes necessary that I do so."

Francine was stunned by the boldness of his statement, him having challenged Teri directly, as well as the strength of his convictions and the character he had shown in this revelation. She no longer measured her impression of Finias as simply her young boyfriend but found him now to be a proud man of principle and inner strength. Her heart swelled with pride in knowing that it is indeed within the heart that such ferocity of predisposition resides. Francine stood suddenly, gathering the attention of the group as she did so, and addressed Finias directly.

"I've been wrong about you, Finias, and for this, I am sorry. So much so that I do not have the capacity to explain," Francine said to the surprise of all. "You are so much more and a much greater man than I've given you credit for, and I'm ashamed of myself for not having seen it sooner."

And with this, she moved to him, and he stood as she kissed him unashamed in front of all. Finias and Francine hugged each other for a while as the others in the room roundly applauded their newfound fondness for each other.

"I must say it is about time with the two of you."

Both Finias and Francine turned to see that it was Calderón who spoke. "The unfortunate waitstaff of the Great Dining Hall were tiring of me asking them to conjure up additional sophomoric suggestions to kindle the fire of romance under you," he said, unable to hold back a grin.

"It was you?" Francine said. "I kept telling Finias that something was going on with all the sexual innuendo, but he didn't believe me."

"I believed that you believed," Finias said, spinning his finger at his temple to suggest she was a little whacky.

"Stop that," Francine said, slapping at his hand. "And you be quiet. Just stand there and look pretty for me for a moment, will you?"

There was laughter and some applause at this, and a hoot or two from the women.

"Well, that was short-lived," Finias said, and everyone renewed their energetic laughter.

"Get used to it, my man," Theodore said, as he pointed his thumb at Teri. "Gets it from her mother."

Teri smacked Theodore on the back of his head.

"See what I mean," Theodore said, as everyone continued to laugh.

Calderón, for his part, moved to embrace them both and, after wishing them luck, offered his apologies if either of them had been the least bit offended.

Francine broke from Finias and, to Calderón's great surprise, she turned and hugged him tight and whispered in his ear, "You were a little too late. The fire had already been lit and had become incredibly hot at least once before the first suggestions by the waitstaff to, what did they say, light a fire in our loins."

"Is that so?" he whispered. "Well, bully for you," Calderón said, while hugging her back, then gave her a bit of a quick squeeze around her shoulder as old friends might do after sharing a personal insight.

Francine kissed him on the cheek. "Thank you," Francine said. "For caring enough to have tried."

Calderón looked at her with a smile and a twinkle in his eye before moving away as he turned to address the group.

"Oh, to be young and in love again."

"Here, here," the group said in unison.

"Why, I don't believe you have to be young to begin to fall in love," said Lindsey, looking Calderón in the eye. "It is actually somewhat simpler when one has experience in such matters, don't you think?"

"Yes, I have found this to be true," Calderón said. "Though it has been some time for me."

"For me as well," said Lindsey. "Pity, because discovering love can be so rewarding. And, so much fun."

"Indeed," Calderón said, not breaking eye contact.

"Ah hmmm, I believe we have additional pressing matters to attend to if I may be so bold as to interrupt," Theodore said.

"Yes, quite. Does anyone care to remember where we left off?" Calderón said.

"I believe we were discussing the matter of Finias's risky but somewhat warranted behavior, in blowing up Thaimes home" Teri said, apparently acquiescing somewhat in her position on the matter.

"Ah yes, and where did we end with that? I seem to have lost my place with such things having been most distracted," Calderón said again, making eye contact with Lindsey.

"I have an idea if you all will allow," said Lindsey, interrupting. "It is rather late, and I too have lost my train of thought and fear that even if it could be recovered, it would do me little good as I don't believe I could make sense of it now. What say we meet again in the morning with a fresh start, say around 9:00, which is dreadfully early I know, but that way everyone can have breakfast and will be ready to go."

"I think that to be a most splendid idea," Calderón said, rather quickly in order not to allow Theodore or Teri to object.

Calderón knew that for both Theodore and Teri, staying another night meant pushing off the next day's business at hand, and that they would not be happy about having to now re-juggle the juggling they did to their schedules simply to be here tonight. He also knew that they had been working nearly around the clock gathering as much information as they could on the infrastructure of Marcon's operations.

"Please do not look so glum, Theodore. You as well, Teri. We all live to fight another day, do we not?" Calderón said. "The two of you have been going at it quite hard these past months, and I fear that the lack of rest and the stress you are under must be taking a toll. I insist you stay. The ugliness of the world will not go away overnight, I'm afraid."

Theodore and Teri both looked resigned to this at first, then they appeared to be relieved at the prospect of ignoring their immense responsibilities to the outside world if for just one day.

"Actually, to be able to sleep in past 5:00am for once sounds rather marvelous," Teri said.

"FIVE AM?" blurted Lindsey. "I don't know if I have ever noticed there to be a five on my clock at all, morning or evening."

Everyone laughed at this, then began to understand a bit of the flavor and charm of Lindsey Sterling.

"So, without objection, it's settled then," Calderón said. "Plus, I am sure that our newfound couple must be most eager to retire for the evening."

"Headmaster!" Francine said, with a look of shock.

"Oh, it's quite alright, Francine," Teri said. "Frankly, since you have never had a boyfriend, particularly at your age, your father and I had begun to think that maybe we should not continue to treat you so much as a girl."

"WHAT?" Francine fairly shouted.

"Trust me, she is very much a girl," Finias said.

"You be quiet with that kind of talk," Francine said.

"Look, honey, you are a grown woman, and we are very pleased to see the beginnings of a romance for you," Theodore said. "Now that we are sure that you prefer the company of men, if you should tire of him or perhaps were to simply wear him out, I've met a fine young chap who I hope to instill as a spy of sorts into the grounds crew over at the port."

"Dad!"

"Don't worry, darling, he means no harm with such stupid remarks," Teri said. "You don't know this because I've been rather careful about saying it in front of you, but something you need to understand about your father is that he's an idiot."

Francine and Lindsey exchanged knowing looks at this, and they both turned to Finias.

"Join the club, old chap," Finias said, and again laughter took hold of them.

Everyone began to say their goodbyes amid hugs and promises to see each other in the morning. Theodore and Teri made their way out first with Francine and Finias lagging behind a bit to finalize plans with Lindsey to meet for breakfast.

On their way out the door, both Finias and Francine could hear Calderón ask Lindsey if she would do him the honor of joining him for a nightcap.

"I would have been terribly disappointed if you hadn't asked," they heard her say as they then hurried outside so as not to interrupt the moment.

"How about that? Calderón and Lindsey? Didn't see that one coming," Finias said.

"You're kidding, right?" Francine said. "Didn't you see how they were practically devouring each other with their eyes?"

"No, can't say that I did," Finias said.

"Nitwit," Francine said.

"Good to see that some things never change," Finias said.

Francine pulled him in close and hugged his arm as they walked.

"Yes, but you are my nitwit, and I love you," Francine said.

Finias stopped at this and turned to Francine.

"You love me?" Finias said.

"I've not ever been in love, but yes, I believe I do," Francine said.

"Hmm, well, thanks," Finias said.

"THANKS?" Francine said, her voice rising. "That's it?"

Finias laughed and pulled her in close.

"I've loved you since the first time you called me an idiot," Finias said. "I mean, what guy wouldn't fall in love with a woman with your obvious warmth and charm."

Francine socked him in the arm.

"See what I mean?" Finias said.

"And when exactly was that?" Francine said, ignoring him.

"The first time you called me an idiot?" Finias asked.

"Yes," Francine said.

"It was the first time we made love," Finias said.

"Well, that would make sense," Francine said, then shoulder-bumped him to let him know she was kidding.

"I think you should begin to take note of which arm you sock so that you can rotate. This one is beginning to be a little sore," Finias said.

"Then you shouldn't give me reason to sock you," Francine said.

"But I never know what it is I might say that deserves a sock," Finias said.

"See, variety and the unknown are what keep a relationship fresh," Francine said as they moved to continue on with their walk, her having snuggled up to his arm again.

"I'm rather glad that you love me," Francine said, after a bit.

"Is that so?" Finias said.

"Yes, it seems less hurtful to sock the one you love," Francine said. "Socking a complete stranger would make me feel dreadful."

"You are a very confused young woman," Finias said.

"I know."

"So, what do you propose we do now?" Finias asked, more than hopeful.

"As I see it, since it seems that we have the blessing of my mum and dad as well as the others, I think it best that we take advantage of the opportunity at hand for me to stay with you tonight lest they change their minds come morning," Francine said.

"Shall we stop by your room first so that you might grab a nighty or something?" Finias said.

"What on earth for," Francine said, who then stopped again and pulled Finias to her, kissing him deeply.

"Yes, what on earth for," he said.

Chapter 41

The morning began to unfold unlike any other as Finias awoke to find, to his great pleasure, Francine asleep by his side. Moving quietly, he went to the kitchen and started a pot of coffee, preparing to serve Francine breakfast in bed.

It was early, just a little after 7:00, but he knew that Elzibeth would most likely be along shortly. He put a note on the door for her to knock lightly to let him know she was there rather than use the intercom so as not to wake Francine. He then, as an extra precaution, unplugged the television.

Returning to the kitchen, he removed an assortment of fresh berries and a kiwi from the refrigerator, sliced strawberries into a bowl with a touch of sugar, and left them to macerate. Finias then set about hand-whipping, so as not to disturb Francine with the sound of the mixer, heavy cream with a spot of vanilla extract, a pinch of nutmeg, and powdered sugar to stiff peaks. He set it aside while he prepared a light crêpe batter, heated a pan with a touch of clarified butter, and began making batches of individual crepes.

Straining the strawberries, he added plump blueberries, blackberries, and red raspberries, mixed them with a portion of the cream, and rolled them into the crêpes. Finias quickly moved to the bath, gathered a fluffy white robe, and put it in the dryer on high. Returning to the kitchen, he plated the crêpes, added a topping of cream and a few of the berries with kiwi slices as garnish, drizzled a bit of honey over the top, then grabbed the robe out of the dryer and took the tray to a sleeping Francine, complete with coffee and orange juice.

Setting the tray on the side table next to the bed, he leaned over and kissed Francine gently on the cheek. She awoke quietly and, looking a bit as if she was seeing Finias for the first time, came to somewhat and said, "Good morning," in a sleepy voice.

"Good morning, sweet you," Finias said.

"Honey, I know it's the first time we have spent the night together, but do you think you could wait a while to have at me again? I would like to shower first if it's all the same to you," Francine said, as she rested her head on her pillow and closed her eyes.

Finias pulled the covers down just far enough to expose her to just below her breasts and, touching her soft skin, said, "I've brought you a lovely breakfast, but I suppose I shall have to wait to enjoy the fruits of you."

"Don't, it's cold," Francine said, pulling the covers back to cover herself.

"Here, I've brought you this knowing you didn't bring anything comfortable to slip into first thing," Finias said, handing her the robe.

"Oh my gosh, it's so warm, and soft and smells wonderful" Francine said. "I can't wait to put it on."

Francine got out of bed, as Finias helped her into her robe. Francine lifted her hair from its collar, and as it draped down her back, Finias thought her to be lovelier than any sunset. They hugged for an extended period, but when Finias moved to kiss her, she pushed him away. "Not till I've brushed my teeth and have cleaned up a bit."

"Here then, you might want to sample this first before brushing your teeth," Finias said.

"Oh my, what have we here," Francine said. "Breakfast in bed for me? And, a warmed, fluffy robe? I think I might cry; you are so sweet."

At this, she kissed Finias on the cheek, said thank you, and asked that if he wouldn't mind, she would prefer that he join her at the table so they might share. Finias moved to the door and removed the note he had placed for Elzibeth, plugged the television back in, then moved to the table to sit across from Francine.

"What was that all about?" Francine said.

"Oh, I had just left a little note for Elzibeth to politely knock rather than use the intercom so as not to wake you. Then I had pulled the plug on the tele just in case."

"Ahhh, it's no wonder I love you," Francine said.

"You look incredible in the morning. Are you sure you don't want to return to bed," Finias said, "however briefly?"

"Past experience would indicate that it would not be brief. And, I do love you, but not as much as these delicious-looking crêpes at the moment, I'm afraid," Francine said, with her most beautiful smile.

"What it is I see in you is still not clear to me," Finias said, shaking his head.

"I suspect these might have something to do with it," Francine said as she opened her robe.

"You are quite the tease, aren't you," Finias said.

Francine flashed her award-winning smile again but said nothing as she went back to her breakfast.

"And, just so you know, if you were closer, I would have socked you for that," Francine said.

"Good to know, but for which comment?" Finias said.

"The first one, I rather delight in the second one," Francine said, still smiling.

The morning was shaping up rather nicely, Finias noted, looking out the window behind Francine. There was just a little breeze ruffling the leaves of the trees beyond, and the ever-present gulls were busy as always doing what it is they do. As the direction he was looking faced to the west this morning, and out over the plateau, there was no sunrise to be seen. Just high cumulus clouds floating lazily about.

"I rather expected Elzibeth to be by before now," Finias said. "Should I give her a call?"

"I love that you worry about her, and yes, I suppose it is time we move on from this silly charade we have been playing and sit her down for a little talk," Francine said.

Finias picked up the phone and dialed, and Elzibeth answered on the first ring.

"Hello."

"Elzibeth, Finias."

"Yeah, I know, about time you called," Elzibeth said.

"Again, good morning to you too. It's considered a polite greeting at this time of day in case you have forgotten," Finias said.

"Okay, good morning. So, is Francine up too?" Elzibeth said.

"Why yes, but how did you know she was here?" Finias said.

"I couldn't sleep last night," Elzibeth said. "I kept thinking about almost getting blown up, so I went to her room to see if I could stay with her. Checked again this morning, and she wasn't there, so I figured she was with you doing grown-up stuff. I didn't want to come by too early and bother you."

"Yes, she is awake. Why don't you come?"

"Okay," she said, and hung up.

"She sounded a little sad," Finias said. "Also, she came by to see you last night as she was having bad thoughts about what happened at Lindsey's."

"Oh no, we should have given that more attention than we did," Francine said. "She is so beyond her years that sometimes I forget that she is only six."

"Six and a half."

"Yes."

It wasn't long before Elzibeth came to the door wearing another of her new outfits, this time a tie-sleeve tee in pink and white stripes, grey yoga pants, and, of course, her grey Keds.

"Look at you," Finias said. "Only six and already as pretty as her sister."

"Six and a half," she corrected.

"Right."

"Good morning," Francine said as Elzibeth joined her at the kitchenette. "Here, sit down and help me with this."

"Good morning, and no thanks, I ate already," Elzibeth said.

"You did?" Francine sounded surprised. "By yourself?"

"No, I woke Missy up and made her come with me," Elzibeth said.

"Why didn't you come wake us?" Francine said.

"I figured you and Finias didn't want me around while you spent the night," Elzibeth said.

"Elzibeth, Finias and I need to speak to you candidly about something. We have discovered that we have become very fond of each other over these last months, to the point of being in love," Francine said. "I know that may be something you don't fully understand, and if you are uncomfortable with that, I need you to tell me so that we can talk about it, okay?"

"No, it's not that," Elzibeth said. "I knew something was up with you two. I just felt lonely last night when I couldn't find you and again this morning is all."

"Oh, sweetheart, come here," Francine said, placing Elzibeth on her lap. "As long as I'm on this planet, I want you to never feel alone. Finias and I haven't changed as people. You may see us hold hands and kiss on occasion, but the relationship the three of us share is special and unchanging. You should never feel that you have to wait for us to get up from bed or be afraid of interrupting. I would drop anything for you at a moment's notice, including Finias off of the couch one time when we weren't expecting you."

"That was when he had lipstick on his collar, right?" Elzibeth said.

"Yes, it was, and I must say your powers of deduction are very well developed for your age," Francine said.

"I don't know. Seemed pretty obvious," Elzibeth said.

"Not to most six-year-old girls it wouldn't," Francine said.

"Six and a half."

"Yes, six and a half."

Chapter 42

"Oh no, Finias, I forgot we were to meet with Lindsey at 8:00 am for breakfast," Francine said. "I better give her a call."

"It's almost 8:15, and though early for her, I'm surprised she hasn't tried to reach us," Finias said.

There was no answer to Francine's call, so they both assumed she had gone on without them. Francine returned to her room to shower and change while Elzibeth helped Finias in the kitchen. When they were done, Elzibeth settled herself on the couch and turned on the television as Finias showered and dressed.

To save time, the three of them met up in the Grand Entrance with Francine looking as if she had just stepped off the cover of a leading fashion magazine. She was wearing an embellished mini dress in white with grey accents in a paisley print trim both front and back, with color-coordinated sandals.

"I don't know if it is the clothes, but each time I see you, it's as if for the first time. You never cease to amaze me," Finias said, as he moved to her and, taking both of her hands in his, kissed her lightly on the cheek so as not to disturb her makeup.

"Oh, just a little something I threw together last minute," Francine said.

"Last minute? It's not been my experience that you've done anything with regard to getting ready in under an hour," Finias said. "I bet you take an hour to change just to take out the trash."

"That's a lie. I've never taken out the trash. Housekeeping does it for me so that I don't have to take the hour to change," Francine said, smiling.

Finias laughed. "I would kiss you, but I might get lipstick on my collar," Finias said. "Then I would never hear the end of it from this one."

"Well, if you wouldn't mess up trying to talk your way out of things, I wouldn't have to try so hard to figure things out," Elzibeth said.

"True. I'll try and do better," Finias said.

"At trying to not mess up telling lies, or telling the truth for once," Elzibeth said.

"What is it with you and questions? Don't you know questions make people uncomfortable?" Finias said.

"Not for people who tell the truth," Elzibeth said.

"She's kind of got you there," Francine said. "You'll not outsmart her, that's for sure, so you might as well give up."

As they continued to walk, having chosen to take the hall rather than shift rooms, Finias said, "I miss being alone in my home back at ½ Humbleton Place. No women to call me names, no little girls to outsmart me."

"Oh please," Francine said.

"No Thaime, no Marcon, no little girls questioning me," Finias continued as they approached the door to Calderón's chambers. "No blown-up houses or houses on fire…"

They had arrived just as Finias finally ran out of things to complain about.

"You need to come up with an off button for this guy, sis," Elzibeth said. "Before he drives both of us mad."

"I usually just sock him a good one, but today he just seemed too pathetic to punch," Francine said.

"Just ring the bell, would you?" Finias said, as the two of them sniggered.

Having left a little early, they were the first to arrive and were welcomed at the door by Lindsey. She looked terrific as always, though wearing the same outfit as the night before. Hugs were exchanged, and Finias could smell alcohol on her breath, the reason for which became clear as they moved inside to greet

Calderón, who was clearing away the remains of breakfast, complete with Champagne.

"Ah, a bright and cheery good morning to you all," Calderón said. "Please forgive me for not offering a more formal greeting. I'm in the process of sprucing up a bit after a late breakfast."

Finias moved to give Calderón a hand, as did Elzibeth, while Francine pulled Lindsey aside.

"Sooo," Francine whispered.

"I'll have to wait to tell you later, but he is fantastic," said Lindsey. "And, not just in bed."

The two of them squealed a little in the way only women can and grasped each other's hands in delight.

"I had an amazing experience with Finias last night before the meeting that I have to tell you about," Francine said.

"Before the meeting?" said Lindsey.

"Right before. My knees are still weak from it," Francine said.

"Good for Finias," said Lindsey.

"I was thinking more 'good for me,'" Francine said, as they squealed some more.

"You ladies want to shut down the gossip mill and lend a hand?" asked Finias.

"Of course not," said Lindsey.

"You know better than to ask such a silly question," Francine said.

"Just checking," Finias said.

"Now, ladies, you go on and enjoy yourselves. There is no such thing as gossip among friends," Calderón said. "It is the duty of men to care for their lady friends, and I, for one, will not allow such wonderful hands as yours, my dear Lindsey, to be soiled by the remains of our meal."

"See, I told you he's fantastic," said Lindsey, as they squealed and bounced still holding hands.

"I'm so happy for you," Francine said.

"And I you," said Lindsey, as they hugged.

Elzibeth turned to Finias and said, "Good grief," Finias answered with an "Oh brother," and Calderón couldn't seem to stop smiling.

"By the way," Lindsey began, "I'm sorry I didn't let you know about not meeting for breakfast this morning. Calderón and I were having seconds, and I'm not talking about the food that was delivered."

"Really, how marvelous for you," Francine said. "Finias tried to mount me again this morning, but he'd made me breakfast in bed, and I was more interested in the food. I didn't think I would be able to function today if I'd allowed him to have another go at me."

"Oh, by the way, speaking of breakfast in bed, that's the reason I didn't call you. Of course, it was after eight anyway before I remembered," Francine said.

"Well, it sounds as if each of us were fulfilled in our own way," said Lindsey.

"Do you think we should go lend a hand?" Francine said.

"Heavens no, that would be a terrible precedent to set," said Lindsey.

"Good point," Francine said. "Like puppies, we need to begin training them early."

With this, the chime at the door sounded the arrival of Theodore and Teri. They both looked well-rested, and Teri looked comfortable in a pleated navy skirt and white sleeveless top. Finias couldn't help but notice Teri's resemblance to Francine, which was all the more evident with her having had a good night's rest. She seemed more youthful this morning, the stress of the prior week having faded.

Proper greetings were passed out all around this time as the table-clearing crew had just finished up.

"Please, let's all take a seat," Calderón began. "I would like to thank everyone for being here this morning, as I'm sure the expectation of all was that we would have finished with this business last night.

"Before I begin, and please forgive me Teri, Theodore, as I would never question your judgment, but I find I must ask. Do you believe it to be okay that Elzibeth hear what it is that we are about to discuss? No offense, dear Elzibeth, but as Theodore and Teri know, the content of what is about to be shared is rather graphic," Calderón said.

"We discussed this at length last night," Teri began, "and came to the conclusion that as Elzibeth is gifted with powers beyond us, it may be that we may be forced to involve her in the solution to problems we are unable to solve alone. So, as unfortunate as it is for you to say and for you to hear, Elzibeth, we find it necessary that you do so."

"Very well then," Calderón said. "As it turns out, it was fortuitous on my part to have been able to hold the two of you over until this morning; and as we have discussed, and the others have yet to know, it has come to my attention that one Francis Marcon is now deceased."

It was clear to Francine that Lindsey knew of this ahead of time, as she did not react. But it was stunning news to both herself and to Finias. It just didn't make sense, and they both felt a feeling of discomfort. As if a boat changing direction abruptly on the water, the direction they were heading had just shifted dramatically and without warning, throwing them both entirely off balance.

Chapter 43

"When did this happen?" Finias asked.

"That has yet to be determined precisely," answered Calderón. "But it is believed to have been within the last twenty-four to thirty-six hours."

"Has the cause of death been determined?" Francine asked.

"Preliminary reports indicate that Marcon's head was twisted off of his body," Theodore said. "His headless body was left on the steps of police headquarters with a note from the perpetrator suggesting the police not thank him. It said he had only done the right thing in the service of his civic duty."

"Twisted?" Finias said, incredulously.

"Yes," Calderón confirmed.

"Twisted off? My God," Francine said. "How did they know?"

"Apparently what was left of his neck looked quite like the end of a licorice stick," Theodore said.

"That was unnecessary for you to share," Teri said.

"Yes, I apologize for that, Elzibeth," Theodore said.

"For what?" Elzibeth asked.

"Well, for that description. As your mother pointed out, it was unnecessarily graphic," Theodore said.

"I thought it was pretty cool," Elzibeth said. "I mean, how else would you describe someone's head being twisted off? I thought pretzel at first, but you nailed it with licorice."

Theodore and Teri exchanged a nervous glance, and, without a proper answer, Theodore cleared his throat and simply said, "Yes, I suppose pretzel doesn't quite fit, does it?"

"Idiot," Teri mumbled under her breath.

"Let us continue, shall we?" Theodore said, giving Teri a sideways look.

"What happened to his head?" Finias asked.

"Nobody knows at this point," Theodore said. "The body's identity was determined by fingerprints. Though I'm sure if they have a DNA sample in their database, they will do a comparison test."

"My, this is absolutely stunning news," Francine said.

"I suppose we should rejoice as it sounds as if the head of the snake has been severed," Lindsey said. "And when I say snake, I mean in more ways than one with that lying bastard."

"Please, dear, do not allow this news to upset you," Calderón said. "Shall I prepare you a Bellini perhaps?"

"That would be lovely," said Lindsey.

"Would anyone else care for a little something to settle the nerves?"

There were no other takers, and Calderón finished shortly with Lindsey's drink and returned with one for himself as well. He then took up his seat on the sofa next to Lindsey. They clinked glasses, and Calderón placed his arm around Lindsey's shoulder and pulled her in close for a quick peck on the lips.

Teri gave Francine a look of surprise at this, and Francine nodded her head quickly to confirm that yes, they were a couple. Teri brightened at the news, then turned to whisper what she now knew to Theodore, suspecting he would not have noticed, which of course he had not. Theodore took the news with a small shrug of his shoulders as if to say, "So what?" Teri looked down and shook her head slightly as she rolled her eyes, which indicated to Francine that she had silently called him an idiot.

Finias broke the silence. "It seems to me that with both Marcon and his son now dead, someone will move to fill the void," he said. "And quickly. Such a power vacuum will attract other syndicates to take over Marcon's territory."

"I believe the void has already been filled," Theodore said. "Teri and I have been trying to untangle the ball of thread that makes up Marcon's extensive reach into legitimate business and his spread into the underworld in order for us to attempt to infiltrate his syndicate. A large part of that effort was to establish his ownership in various enterprises, their properties, other real estate holdings, and ownership or at least control of properties without stringent government oversight, such as various rail spurs to onshore holding areas and his slip at the Grand Port Harbor.

"In the short time since Marcon's demise, several of the enterprises believed to be held by Marcon, though listed as being owned by layers of false corporations, have suddenly become the property of one Thaime Pregmierar."

"He certainly doesn't seem to be hiding his intent," Calderón said.

"Not at all," Teri said. "I believe that rather than hiding the takeover of Marcon's assets, he is indeed flaunting them as a signal to others who might maintain thoughts of stepping into Marcon's territory. He is openly showing the other syndicates that he is indeed the new sheriff in town."

"If it's true that indeed Marcon's head was twisted from his body, it's clear that aside from the use of some machinery, this was not done by an ordinary man," Francine said. "Could it be that we have been looking at this thing all wrong? Our thinking was centered on Marcon being responsible for the attacks on Huerta as revenge for his son and the attack on Marcon's son as a power play by Huerta. Now follow me on this. What if Thaime had taken it upon himself to take out Marcon's son, leaving Marcon to believe the hit was sanctioned by Huerta. Thaime goes in, takes out Huerta on Marcon's order, then bides his time with Marcon to learn of his various business ventures."

"Are you suggesting that Thaime knows in-depth the labyrinth of Marcon's dealings?" Teri said. "Honey, I just don't see how that is possible."

"But what if he knows enough," Francine said. "And let's say that he doesn't. There would be no way for, say, the Yakuza, or

Zanetti to the north, or Fuentes across the border to know that. They would have to assume that Marcon's power and influence were now under the control of Thaime."

"We're assuming, of course, that these other syndicates even know who Thaime is," Finias said. "Until he makes a name for himself, he would be known, if at all, as simply being a heavy for Marcon. Nothing more."

"Then, it makes sense for Thaime to have killed Marcon in such a bizarre and public fashion," Francine said. "He needed to make a splash and to spread the rumor of his involvement. Clearly, the other factions will be looking into Marcon's holdings to see what they could get a piece of and will discover Thaime's new ownership."

"If it is true that Thaime is targeting Marcon's assets," said Lindsey, "he would surely have taken ownership of his west coast mansion. Especially since our young Finias here thought it wise to employ a biblical approach to retribution."

"West coast mansion?" Teri said. "I've not uncovered ownership records for such a property by Marcon."

"I'm sure the property is in the name of some Saudi prince, or shell company if at all," said Lindsey. "But I've been there, and it does exist."

"An eye for an eye," Calderón said. "Your reference to a biblical approach, Lindsey. For someone as ill-tempered and unpredictable as Thaime, might I suggest that upon the discovery of his home's destruction, he placed unfair blame on Marcon, thus taking Marcon's home as recompense for his perceived slight? Or it's possible that he simply needed a new home, and knowing that his goal was to take down Marcon anyway, simply seized the opportunity to kill two birds with one stone."

"Lindsey, you wouldn't happen to have an address for this property?" Finias said.

"I'm not sure that it has an address," said Lindsey. "I'm sure Marcon would have had all records of its construction destroyed as well as the people who built it. He bragged about having a natural gas line direct from his refinery to the property, and all power was generated on the grounds. He owns hundreds if not thousands of acres around him, so I doubt that a map was ever filed. If it was, that too would have been destroyed. That Teri was unable to discover Marcon's ownership is no coincidence. There probably are no records."

"Do you remember where it is?" Finias said.

"Not exactly," said Lindsey, and everyone's hearts dropped. "I don't think I could find it on a map, but I've been there several times in Perino... excuse me, Marcon's limo, and though I wasn't always paying attention, I do believe I remember enough of the route to possibly find it by car."

"Does anyone here know how to drive?" Francine said.

All in the room unfortunately shook their heads a disappointing no.

"But," Calderón said, "I know someone who does."

Chapter 44

"Mary!" Finias was the first to say. Everyone turned to look at him at this suggestion.

"I've only met her twice. Well, three times if you include her appearance on my backboards, but I noticed a photo of her on her desk in what I believe to be a race car," Finias said.

"Yes, you are quite correct. It is Mary of whom I first thought," Calderón said. "This is not to be repeated, but when Mary was young, she was very popular with the young gents, both gifted and not. She has many wild tales of drag racing for pink slips and the like."

"Our Mary?" Francine said.

"Oh yes," Calderón said. "She was quite something, I understand. And these stories are not just from Mary. I've heard many a fond memory of her from the lips of several men. Apparently, she was fearless and could race with the best of them, having been taught by non-gifted boys seeking to engage her in her non-driving talents."

"My, that sounds so exciting," said Lindsey.

"It is my hope that I have not opened up a can of worms with you on this, my dear," Calderón said.

"Not to worry," said Lindsey. "You seem entirely capable of providing all the excitement I need."

The group, as if one, like a flock of birds suddenly changing direction in flight, looked down at the floor, then to the left, and away from Lindsey. Calderón, noticing this display of discomfort, chuckled and said, "Come now. All of you are surely aware that Lindsey and I have become friends. Please do not feel uncomfortable with that fact."

"No, of course not," the group said in unison, sounding as uncomfortable as they felt, and so disingenuous that they all broke out laughing… again, as one.

"Very well, then. I will assume this newfound friendship between Lindsey and me will not be a problem for our little group. Now, I wish to move on to the matter at hand," Calderón said.

"Teri, would you be a dear and ask Mary to join us?" Theodore interrupted.

"I suppose, though I don't see that any of your fingers are broken," Teri said. "Yet."

"I'm sorry, dear. You stay put," Theodore said as he got up and moved to the telephone to make the call.

"So, what's our next step?" Finias said.

"Good question. I believe we may need to determine if Thaime has indeed taken control of Marcon's mansion," Teri said. "Having Thaime's name on documents suggesting ownership of other properties previously held by Marcon does not provide enough proof that Thaime is taking control of Marcon's territory. Taking ownership of his mansion with Marcon dead certainly does and sends a loud and clear signal that Thaime intends to continue down Marcon's path of total domination."

"That being said, I believe it is time for us to conduct an old-fashioned stakeout," Theodore said.

"Before we go too far with a plan, might I suggest that I do a test run first with this Mary," said Lindsey. "It seems it would be best that I'm sure that I could find it first."

"You've met Mary," Finias said. "She's the receptionist."

"Oh," said Lindsey. "Well, that may be a bit of a problem. She didn't seem to care much for me."

"That's because she has a thing for me," Finias said. "She probably wasn't too keen on sending you to my suite."

"Mary has a thing for you?" Francine said.

"Nothing serious, we just banter about," Finias said. "I did promise her that she could watch me on the backboards playing basketball in nothing but my sneakers while I filled her in on all the juicy gossip from our meeting."

"You what?" Francine said.

"It was just a little joke and some harmless flirting between the two of us," Finias said. "I doubt that she would actually take me up on it."

"I believe you may have underestimated her," Calderón said.

"Good lord," Francine said. "First, you're hot for Lindsey, now you promise to be naked for Mary. It's clear that I need to keep a closer eye on you."

"Really, he was indeed hot for me?" Lindsey said.

"Are you kidding," Francine said. "He was practically falling all over himself trying to find a way to keep me from coming to that meeting with you. I'm surprised I wasn't found tied up in the basement."

"That is so sweet," said Lindsey.

At this, Mary knocked on the door, and Finias, partly to save himself from Francine, moved to answer.

Opening the door, Finias greeted Mary with a simple good morning, and they exchanged a quick kiss on the cheek. Mary was tall and trim, with brightly colored blonde hair cut short but stylish. She looked as if she would be more comfortable on a tennis court than behind the wheel of a race car. She wore tan Capri pants to above the ankle, a light-colored blouse, and sensible flat white tennis shoes. Finias thought her attractive, and she had a look of being comfortable just being Mary. As if by chance the leader of the free world had just walked in, she wouldn't have given him or her any additional consideration other than the usual pleasantries.

"Calderón, so good to see you. Theodore, Teri, Francine, and of course, dear Elzibeth."

Everyone answered their good mornings, but it was not lost on the group that Mary had either purposely skipped or simply glossed over saying good morning to Lindsey.

Lindsey stood and moved to introduce herself to Mary. "Good morning, Mary, I don't suppose you remember, but we met the other day. Lindsey Sterling," she said, offering her hand.

"I'm not so old that I can't remember two days ago," Mary said, ignoring her greeting.

"Yes, of course," said Lindsey. "That's not what I meant at all."

"Mary, please take a seat," offered Calderón. "We have some things to discuss, some information to share, and a favor to ask."

At this, Mary took a seat next to Elzibeth and far away from Lindsey.

"Ah, Mary, where to start," Calderón said once everyone had settled in.

"If I may, sir, you once told me that the beginning is always the best place to start," Finias said, as Francine elbowed him in the arm.

"Of course," Calderón said, shooting Finias a look. "Mary, there have been a number of disturbances within organized crime recently, with one man making a power play to take over all with the express purpose of developing a crime network so vast and powerful that the government itself would be powerless to stop them. Recently, the man who we believed to be behind this power play was killed in a most unusual manner. We believe the man who killed him to be Thaime Pregmierar, as he has used his gifts to change ownership of several properties previously held by Francis Marcon, the recently deceased, to his name. Thaime, by all appearances, seemed to have crafted a plan to pit warring factions against themselves to weaken their leadership and individual structures so that he could step in and join them as one. There is one singular property which, if taken by Thaime, would indicate to all other syndicates that he had taken control of Marcon's empire. His mansion. We would like your help in finding it."

"Me? What on earth do you expect me to do?" Mary said. "I suppose you wish me to pull up Google Earth and poke a pin in every square inch of this territory."

Mary gave Calderón a playful look.

"Much simpler than that," Calderón said. "We need a driver."

"A driver. I see. So rather than poking pins, you think it best that I simply drive every inch of the road looking for what I believe to be a mansion," Mary said.

Calderón smiled at Mary, as he knew her to be toying with him.

"Better yet, it seems our Lindsey here has been to this property, and though she doesn't remember exactly where it is, she is hopeful of spotting certain markers along the way with the expectation of taking us to its location," Calderón said.

"Interesting," Mary said. "I must tell you it has been a number of years since I've driven."

"Wouldn't it be like riding a bike?" Finias said. "You're never too old to remember."

Francine banged her elbow off his ribs this time.

"And you are not too old to be taken over my knee for such remarks," Mary said. "Just how old do you think I am?"

"I think it best that he not answer as you see, he's an idiot," Francine said. "He will most certainly just dig himself in deeper."

"But she's been here for like forty years or more," Finias said, as Francine gave him another shot to the ribs.

"That's not true," Mary said. "And I'm a young fifty-six for your information and perfectly capable of driving. I might just be a little rusty is all."

"Excellent," Calderón said. "I take it then that you are willing to join our little expedition?"

"I don't know," Mary said. "I rather live to sit at my cramped desk in my dusty office each day."

"Help us with this, and your office will be made to be the envy of Briarwood," Calderón said.

"Deal," Mary said. "And how do you propose we go about obtaining a car?"

The group was giving some thought to this when Lindsey spoke.

"I have a car," said Lindsey. "Or did. I'm not sure if it's still at what's left of my house. But if it hasn't been towed away, it has forward and rear-facing seats in the back, so it seats up to eight comfortably. And I hid a spare key in there somewhere. The glove box or center console, I think. Or maybe check over the visors."

"So, you hid the key but don't remember where?" said Mary.

"Well, yes. That's the problem with hiding stuff. Remembering where you hid it."

"Jesus," Mary sighed. "Ok, I'll find it if it's indeed there."

"Then may I suggest Mary teleport over and take a look. Mary, if the car is there, do you feel confident that you could bring it back here safely?" Calderón said.

"I know I can bring it back," Mary began. "Safely? I don't know. I may feel the need for speed."

Chapter 45

Lindsey gave Mary the location of what had been her home, and Mary, concentrating on the address, suddenly vanished from the room.

"Shouldn't be long now, I lived less than twenty minutes outside of Brighton Beach," said Lindsey. "If the car is there, she should be back within the hour."

"Hopefully, it will be more than a few minutes, or we'll have to find another form of transportation," Teri said, suggesting that if Mary were to return soon, the car obviously wasn't there.

Everyone thought about that for a moment, then Teri suggested they begin to work on a plan. Assuming Mary was successful in returning with Lindsey's car, it was decided that Francine and Finias would ride along with Lindsey and Mary as another set of eyes to pick out certain landmarks on the way and to memorize those that Lindsey could recall.

"What if the car is not there?" Finias said.

"Then I suppose we take Mary car shopping," said Lindsey. "It wouldn't do for us to hire a service to pick us up knowing where we are going."

A number of minutes had passed, and Mary had not returned. This, though early, was thought by all to be a good sign, and they returned to fine-tuning their plan.

"Teri, if you will agree, I would like to outfit Elzibeth with a camera," Theodore said.

"What in heaven's name for?" Teri said.

"I was getting to that, I had just lost the courage to say it for the moment," Theodore said. "I would like for you, Elzibeth, if of course you agree to this, to follow behind them with a video camera mounted to your head."

"Mounted how?" Elzibeth said, looking worried. "You mean with screws and stuff."

Everyone chuckled at this.

"No, dear, just a strap around your head and one under your chin," Theodore said. "They have become rather popular with sporting people wishing to memorialize their most memorable wipeouts."

"You want me to wear a camera so I can crash into stuff?" Elzibeth said.

"No sweetheart," Teri said. "Your father was giving you an example of what some people use them for, only in a most idiotic fashion."

"Yes, I apologize," Theodore said. "What I propose is that you use the camera to give us a bird's eye view of the route. A car, it would seem, would have an obstructed view, but it would be to our benefit to see associated landmarks at each turn from an aerial perspective. Also, I would like to suggest to Mary that if you are indeed successful in finding the property, that you turn around prior to its entrance and wait for Elzibeth to tour the grounds."

"No, absolutely not," Teri said. "I'll not have our daughter exposed to that danger. If she is seen, and if what we believe to be true about Thaime having taken up residence there, his minions will most assuredly take her or worse kill her."

"But mum, she won't be seen," Francine said.

"You yourself said that you could track her movements during her version of teleportation as you were training her," Teri said.

"Only if she pauses," Francine said. "As long as she is moving, no matter how slowly, she is as invisible as any of us during teleportation."

"Most excellent," Theodore said. "Elzibeth, once you see the car turn around at the gate, I want you to first circle the grounds to give us an overall view, then circle again at a lower altitude to look for guards or other personnel. As you identify their location, I want you then to circle back to each of them and look at them directly from a distance of, say, you to me, so that we might identify them. Do you think you could do that?"

"Sure," Elzibeth said.

"But you must remember to keep moving," Francine said. "You must keep moving at all times, okay? You'll remember to do that, right?"

"Of course," Elzibeth said. "If these guys are going to kill me if I stop, I kinda think I'll just keep moving."

"That's my girl," Theodore said.

"Why the need to risk her possibly stopping by accident trying to get a close-up of the guards?" Finias said. "Who they are or what they look like will have no bearing on what we are trying to find out."

"Unless one of them is Thaime," Theodore pointed out.

Calderón, who was quiet during these discussions, spoke.

"What if he is there?" Calderón said. "Let's assume first that he is proven to be in possession of the mansion. What then?"

"We whack him," Finias said, unable to resist slipping in a mob reference.

"Oh please, I'll give you a whack," Francine said. "We are not killers."

"But what if we are forced to be," Calderón said. "What if we discover that Thaime, with his well-established gifted power, is crazy enough to believe that he can generate a force of men large enough to follow his path to the destruction of civilized society? Would our participation in his death be much different than Oppenheimer and the others who developed the atomic bomb? Or, would it not have been better for the sake of mankind if some brave soul had taken it upon themselves to end the life of Hitler before it was too late for the six million people who died at his hand?"

To take the life or lives of the few to protect the lives of the many? I do not hold the answer, but history does, and I think there are lessons to be learned from that."

The group grew quiet as they considered what it was that Calderón had said.

"Let us not dwell on such an important issue as this at the moment," Calderón said. "It is too weighty to be considered lightly, though I would suggest you keep the thought in your mind and allow it to steep. I often find my best solutions come after a day or two of reflection."

"Theodore, Teri, I've asked that you look into Marcon's supply chain. Do you have any update on that?" Calderón asked.

"The answer is both simple and complicated," Teri began. "Simple in that being on the west coast, Marcon's smuggling operations receive goods from the port and from across the border. Complicated in that Marcon is a major player in shipping, having owned his own fleet of carrier trucks, an ocean container vessel named the Marcon, of course, and various rail spurs to warehouses throughout the country."

"Tracking shipments from across the border has become problematic. It's like trying to track a colony of individual ants," Theodore said. "But the port is a static entity. So, it seemed the most logical of the two to focus our efforts."

"Ah yes," Calderón said. "I believe it was the great general Patton who said that a fortress is a monument to man's stupidity, or something to that effect. I do agree that a stationary target such as the port is the best place to start. Now, how do we shut it down?"

"As Marcon's operations at the port seem to go unchecked, if we were to be successful in locating a container of drugs or other illegal shipment and were to bring it somehow to the attention of the authorities in a public way, there would be no way for them to cover it up, no matter how deep their hands might have been in

Marcon's pockets," Teri said. "That is why I have been trying to determine which portion of the port is or was owned by Marcon. If we were to determine that, we could possibly get the shipping manifest for incoming arrivals, search the containers, and hopefully stumble upon a shipment of drugs or something illegal."

"Why just drugs?" Finias said. "Why not stolen cars, or bearer bonds, or whatever else he might be into?"

"The profit margin on drugs is staggering," Teri said. "They are cheaply made, mostly in impoverished countries, and Marcon would sell the shipment to buyers who purchase in bulk. The transfer happens rapidly. Marcon, or whoever it is now, gets paid, and if all goes smoothly, his hands are clean."

"And putting an end to his ability to transport large quantities of drugs from overseas not only disrupts his supply chain, it discredits him with his buyers and sellers. Marcon or whoever it is now would take a huge financial hit as well as a hit to their reputation, which leads to diminished power and control of their operations," Theodore said.

"I was in the Hall of Records the other day trying to find information on port ownership," Finias said. "I hacked into their database, and I think I was getting close to finding the information I was looking for. I left a backdoor on their server, so it will be a simple thing for me to go back and look again."

"You hacked into the port authorities' database?" Teri said.

"Why, yes," Finias said.

"Their protections are legendary. Marcon spared no expense in providing for the highest level of data security. How do you know how to do this?" Teri said.

"Study and practice, I guess. It's really just a hobby of mine," Finias said.

"Huh, how about that dad," Francine said. Grasping Finias's arm lightly, she leaned in and said, "He's been telling me all this time that you are good for nothing, and now look at you, all good for something."

"Theodore, you didn't," Teri said.

"At first maybe. Just being protective of my little girl," Theodore said. "But I've changed my mind on that front just so you know, Finias."

"Thank you, sir," Finias said.

"This talent of yours might have been a good piece of information to have shared, though," Theodore said.

"I suppose you're right. Not being involved with the daily activities of yourself and Teri, I was unaware that such a thing could be useful," Finias said.

"Might I ask why you didn't finish the task while in the Hall of Records?" Theodore said.

"Oh, I finished alright," Finias said, as Francine pinched his arm hard. "Ouch, I meant for the night. Something came up. Ouch, stop that."

"Well, I suggest you give it another go," Theodore said.

"I would like nothing more," Finias said, putting his arm around Francine. "It would be my great pleasure. Again."

"Do you guys mind if I go? I'm bored," Elzibeth said.

"Yes, of course, dear, you are free to go," Teri said.

"Will we see you at lunch?" Francine said.

"I may stop by," Elzibeth said. "I've got a lot to tell my friends."

"Elzibeth, I think it best that we not share what we have learned here today. Alright?" Teri said.

"Teri, if I may, I believe that Elzibeth has earned the right to speak freely to her friends. After all, what fun are great adventures and knowing what us adults do in these little meetings of ours if the information cannot be shared? With your mother's permission, Elzibeth, I suggest that you not only share what it is that you know but embellish a bit as well," Calderón said.

"What's embellish?" Elzibeth said.

"It means to add a little to the story to make it seem more dangerous or exciting than it may actually have been," Calderón said.

"Cool, I'm good at that," Elzibeth said.

"Well, I suppose if it's okay with the Headmaster, it's okay with me," Teri said.

"Thanks, Mum, thanks, Mr. Calderón," Elzibeth said. "I can't wait to embellish some stuff."

Elzibeth was hugged and kissed and fussed over by all before departing.

Calderón, noting the time, suggested that since it was just past noon, they break for lunch with the hope that when they return, Mary might be back with good news.

Chapter 46

"Shall we go see what is available for lunch now that the waiters no longer have to try and light your fire?" Finias said, teasingly.

"My pilot has been lit since puberty, so they must have been directing their remarks to you," Francine said, as they strolled down the hall away from Calderón's quarters.

"Then why no boyfriends?" Finias said.

"I suppose I was just waiting for the right knucklehead to come along," Francine said.

"Lucky for me I'm a knucklehead then," Finias said.

"Very," Francine said.

"I have an idea," Finias said.

"I'm sorry, does it hurt your little heady poo?" Francine said in a pouty voice.

"You just never stop with that, do you?" Finias said, exasperated.

"Nope, though I know how I can make up for it," Francine said.

"Do you now?" Finias said.

"You know from the Hall of Records that I do," Francine said.

"Let's not go back there," Finias said. "How about my place, and I'll see if I can cook up something to whet our appetites."

"Mine is whet just thinking about it," Francine said.

"Keep talking like that, and we may not make it back to my room," Finias said.

"Is that so?" Francine said.

"Yes," Finias said.

"Then I suggest we hurry," Francine said.

And so they did. After unlocking his door, Finias scooped Francine into his arms and carried her, kissing as they went.

"You are not taking me to bed so soon, are you?" Francine said. "Maybe we should start in the kitchen."

"You mean on the table?" Finias said.

"No, silly, with lunch. I'm rather starved," Francine said.

"Actually, I was thinking that we could first just unwind for a bit. How about I pour you a glass of wine while I jump in the shower? I'm feeling a bit sticky having been stuck in that room all morning," Finias said.

"How about if we both relax for a bit with a glass of wine, then I join you in the shower?" Francine said.

"Marvelous idea," Finias said.

The two relaxed on the sofa for a time, enjoying their wine and talking mostly of past experiences. Finias shared his experience with his father growing up, working with wood and building structures, and Francine spoke of how it was growing up with her mum and dad. Both the challenges of them being away from home so much and the rewards of having loving parents. They both felt lucky in their own way and found the discussion to be therapeutic.

Having finished their wine, they moved to the shower and, though a bit awkward, managed to make love. Finias asked Francine to join him in a nap, but she declined, suggesting that she would return the favor of breakfast in bed by preparing lunch for the two.

"Because ours is a reciprocal relationship, right?" Finias said.

"Exactly," Francine said.

It seemed just seconds had gone by before Finias awoke and made his way to the kitchen to check on Francine. She was stirring something at the sink, looking away from him in nothing but an apron, so Finias paused to enjoy watching her. She was dancing a bit to a song in her head, and he thought she couldn't look lovelier or more content.

"Watcha making?" Finias said.

Francine, having been startled, let out a yelp and flipped brownie batter from her whisk all up the wall in front of her.

"Oh, you are in so much trouble," Francine said. "Why did you do that? I nearly wet myself."

Laughing, Finias said, "I didn't really mean to. I'm sorry."

Francine brought the bowl of brownie mix to Finias and asked, "Want a taste?"

"Of you? Anytime," Finias said.

Francine dipped a finger in the batter and, as she was offering it to Finias as a sample, instead smeared it across his face.

"That's for frightening me," Francine said.

Finias snatched the bowl from her hands as Francine turned to run, and smeared a handful of the mix across her backside. A full-on brownie mix fight ensued, and soon they were covered in gooey chocolate and pieces of walnut.

Francine removed her apron, and they embraced, kissing the mixture from their faces.

"I suppose we should jump in the shower again," Finias said.

"I have a better idea," Francine said. Grasping Finias's hand, she led him to the bedroom. "Seems like a waste not to enjoy some of this fine chocolate," she said.

Chapter 47

Finias and Francine joined the group as the last to arrive. The others were milling about, chatting and sipping coffee. Lindsey made her way to Francine and asked, "So, what did you two have for lunch?" she asked in a suggestive way.

"Brownie mix," Francine said.

"Brownie mix?" Lindsey said, looking puzzled.

"Twice," Francine said. "Actually, once in the shower and once with the brownie mix," Francine added with a mischievous smile.

"You are a wild little thing, aren't you?" Lindsey said. "And twice in an hour? You're going to wear yourself out."

"Actually, that happened only once in the shower; the brownie mix time was just playtime," Francine said, still smiling.

"Might I ask you ladies to join us?" Calderón said, having moved up between them. "There are brownies and coffee if you like." He gave Francine a playful smile as Lindsey swatted his arm.

"Oh, you, you heard us, didn't you?" said Lindsey.

"And you ladies can trust that it will go no further," Calderón said.

Francine was, of course, mortified, and she took her seat rather shyly, staring at her hands now folded in her lap.

Having taken his seat, Calderón said, "What say we get started?"

"It appears that our Miss Mary has possibly run into some difficulty as she has yet to return," Calderón said. "This is most unfortunate, of course, and it is my great hope that she will be joining us shortly. As for the business at hand, I believe we were discussing the matter of Marcon's ownership of a slip at the port and how it is we intend to determine its location."

"We have been tracking Marcon's container ship, but it is cleverly used. Our hope had been that we could simply follow this ship to its landing at Grand Port Harbor, but Marcon is too shrewd to bring his ship here. It seems to transport whatever it carries between ports in Singapore, Thailand, Istanbul, and China. The pickup of supply takes place at one or more of these locations, which is then transferred via container to any number of other ships. Thus, the importance of finding out the location of the docking slip previously owned by Marcon," Theodore said.

"You must understand, the Grand Port Harbor is several miles long. The level of activity is breathtaking, and it goes on twenty-four hours a day," Teri said. "It is no easy task to determine where it is that Marcon's shipments land. We need to find his slip number somehow."

"As I mentioned before, we are in the process of trying to get one of our own involved with operations at the port. It is a slow and trying process as we need to establish union affiliations, ingratiate ourselves by greasing the palms of the union heads and their representatives at the port, and the port authority itself, having oversight of who the union brings on board, of course, and they are very careful about who they hire, especially someone with no experience," Theodore said.

"I could give breaking into their system another go," Finias said.

"I thought about that, but it may be too risky," Theodore said. "If they were to trace the hack back to Briarwood, things would become very dangerous, very quickly, I believe."

"Actually, there would be no way for them to trace the hack to Briarwood," Finias said.

"How so?" Teri said.

"I use their own computers to break into secure files on their own network," Finias said.

"And how do you do that?" Theodore said.

"I teleport my mind, so to speak," Finias said. "I use a computer at this end to relay the image that I seek from their end, then transpose the commands I type into their computer system. From their end, they would detect the hack, but there would be no sign of an outside connection. The hack would seem to have come from nowhere."

"What in blazes are you talking about?" Theodore said.

"I know it sounds crazy, and I don't know how it works exactly, but it does," Finias said. "The closest thing I can think of is a form of telekinesis."

"Telekinesis?" Francine said.

"It's the ability to manipulate physical objects at another location," Teri answered.

"I've heard the term, but I've never heard of such a thing actually put to use," Calderón said.

"Neither have I," Theodore said. "A most gifted group we have here, it seems, Calderón."

"Indeed," Calderón said. "Might I suggest you give it another go then, Finias? And this time, try not to finish early."

Francine gave Finias a playful squeeze of his arm.

"It will be difficult, but I shall try," Finias said, giving Francine's knee a light squeeze in return.

A knock on the door turned their attention as Mary walked in.

"Good day," Mary said in her cheery manner as she moved to take a seat.

"Good day to you, Miss Mary. And what good news, I am hopeful, do you have for us?" Calderón said.

"Oh, it was a simple task, really," Mary said. "Finias was right, though his approach was wrong, about it being very much like riding a bike. You never seem to forget how."

"I take it the car has arrived safely then?" Calderón said.

"Of course," Mary said. "It was a bit of a mess, having been covered in ash from the fire that destroyed Lindsey's home. I'm so sorry, by the way. Anyway, I took the car to the wash and had it detailed inside and out, and I may have strayed off course a bit on my way back, feeling the need to find my old rhythm. But I did stop for coffee and fuel, so I'm ready to go when you are."

"Very well," Calderón said. "Before we break up this little show, might I suggest that you, Teri, continue to locate ownership records at the port in case our Finias here is unsuccessful in his attempts, and that you, Theodore, shift your focus to across the border in the hopes of finding the colonies and not the ants."

"You mean, target the manufacturers and the growers rather than distribution," Theodore said.

"Precisely," Calderón said.

"But if we don't take down the distribution network, we'll not be able to apprehend those responsible," Theodore said.

"Yes, that will be a loss," Calderón said. "But being that we are short on time, if what we believe about Thaime holds true, destroying the fields where the product is grown as well as the manufacturing facilities shuts down the distribution channels. Without supply, their network will erode and scatter, and Thaime will have a difficult time bringing them back together."

"If that is how you would like for me to act, then I shall," Theodore said.

"It is," Calderón said.

"Very good then," said Lindsey. "Anyone want to go for a ride?"

As they departed, Francine took Lindsey by the elbow and said, "I'm so embarrassed. I can't believe Calderón overheard us."

"Oh, don't worry. He is a rather evolved man. I'm sure he thought it quite fun," said Lindsey. "He has a great sense of humor."

"Calderón?" Francine said, surprised.

"Yes. Oh, I know he can be a bit formal, but that is mostly for show," said Lindsey. "He has this large painting over his bed that looks like a tan and wheat-colored smudge, so I said to him, 'I guess that painting symbolizes a sense of inner turmoil, loss, and confusion.'"

"What did he say?" Francine said.

"He said he thought some kids or something got into the paint, but that he bought it because the colors completed his room and brought all of his other crap together rather nicely."

They both laughed.

"Do you know he surfs?"

"What? Calderón? I can't imagine," Francine said.

"He took me to his beachfront estate the night of the meeting for a nightcap. He must have gone out early because when I woke, he had just come through the door with his surfboard. I, of course, was more than happy to help him out of his wetsuit," said Lindsey.

"After we'd showered, I stepped out of the bath area wearing nothing to where he was seated drinking coffee. As I walked toward him, he stared at me with an odd expression," said Lindsey. "I asked him if there was something wrong, my heart skipping a beat because, you know, I was naked and suddenly self-conscious, and he put his coffee down and said, 'An Italian painter named Carlotti defined beauty as the summation of the parts working together in such a way that nothing needed to be added, taken away, or altered.' He then stood and kissed me and said, 'And that beauty is you.'"

"Oh my God, that is so lovely," Francine said. "I think I'm going to cry."

"Oh, don't start or I'll cry again too," said Lindsey, hugging Francine.

"You are so lucky to have had your house blown up," Francine said, hugging Lindsey back.

"I know."

Chapter 48

"So Mary, how was it to get back in the saddle?" Finias asked as they followed behind Francine and Lindsey, who were huddled close together in a discussion about what, God only knew.

"Are you suggesting I was born before the automobile and thus know only riding?" Mary replied, arching an eyebrow.

"What? No, of course not. But, if you were, cars would have come along eventually, right?" Finias said in his usual clumsy way.

"Why do I even bother talking to you?" Mary said with a sigh.

"I don't know. Francine just thinks I'm an idiot," Finias said.

"Bright girl, though I suppose one wouldn't have to be so bright to recognize that about you," Mary said dryly.

"Thanks," Finias replied, resigned.

The four of them met in the Grand Entrance as Theodore and Teri had left to do what they do. Francine placed a call to Elzibeth to let her know she would be leaving for a while as they were going for a drive.

"Don't you need me to come with you?" Elzibeth asked.

"Not today, honey. We are just doing a little exploration to try and refresh Lindsey's memory," Francine said. "With any luck, hopefully tomorrow."

"Can I come anyway?" Elzibeth asked. "I won't get to ride in the car tomorrow, and I've never been."

"Oh, of course. I should have thought of that," Francine said. "We are in the Grand Entrance about to leave, so come quickly, okay."

Mary got in behind the wheel, and Lindsey settled into the passenger seat. Finias, Francine, and Elzibeth climbed in back, all three facing forward, with Elzibeth in between.

"So, Lindsey, I'll need you to be my tour guide on this little adventure, so please feel free to speak up at any time to let me know how to go about things," Mary said.

"Okay, so I know that when Perino, sorry, Marcon had his car pick me up, we traveled west from my home in Kensington to the shore road then north. So, when we cross under the arch into Brighton Beach, go left," said Lindsey.

Mary did as instructed.

"I remember staying on this road for some time, so it might be a while until I recognize anything," said Lindsey.

The five of them drove on in silence for several miles before Lindsey said, "Hey, there's Betty's Boot Barn. I had the driver stop on one trip, and I picked up the most adorable pair of thigh-high boots."

Lindsey had turned around in her seat, and she and Francine were now in an in-depth discussion about boots and various fashions when Finias said, "Would you two save this for later? Lindsey, you need to pay attention."

"Yes, sir," Francine said, saluting as Lindsey returned her eyes to the road.

After several miles, they passed under an enormous, wide, flat bridge supported by an expansive concrete arch spanning eight lanes.

"Wait," said Lindsey. "We need to be on that bridge going that way." Lindsey pointed to her right, which of course was meant to signal east.

"How do we get there?" Mary asked.

"I don't know," said Lindsey.

"There must be a frontage road running parallel to us," Finias said. "Take the next exit and turn left, and we'll see if we can circle back."

Mary did so, and after backtracking a few miles, she could see a turn lane up ahead leading to the bridge.

"Okay, so we stay on this for a while and look for a sign that says 10," said Lindsey. "I know because once after we crossed the bridge, I asked the driver how much longer, and he said we should be coming up on the 10 shortly."

"Just '10'?" Mary said. "Not highway 10, or overpass 10, or dirt road 10?"

"No, just a small yellow sign with the number 10," said Lindsey.

They continued on with everyone, including Elzibeth, staring intently through the windshield. After what seemed like miles of walnut orchards mixed among fields of soybeans and alfalfa, they did indeed come across a small yellow shield-shaped sign that simply said "10."

"Right here, turn right here," said Lindsey, waving her hands.

"The road only goes to the right," Mary said.

"Yes, I was excited," said Lindsey. "I meant right as in 'here it is.'"

"Hey Mary," Finias said from the back. "I think it's safe for us to take the plates off of the car. When you get a chance, pull over, and I'll jump out and remove them."

"Why do you need to do that?" Mary asked.

"I expect there will be guards at the gate, and I doubt too many cars travel this road. They may become suspicious, and I wouldn't want them to trace the plates back to Lindsey," Finias said.

"Well, there's my little engine that could," Francine said. "Did you use up all your brain power getting up that hill?"

"What do you mean?" Finias said.

"I removed the plates just before we crossed the bridge," Francine said. "But I'm proud of you for thinking that you came up with something all by your little self."

Francine and Elzibeth chuckled at this.

"And there was no need to stop, silly. You could have just used your gifts to move them to the trunk as I did," Francine said.

"I'm really starting to not like you very much," Finias said. "I mean, I still love you. I just don't like you."

"Oh, come here," Francine said.

Elzibeth scooted out from between them as Francine leaned in to give Finias a kiss and a hug.

"I'm sorry, that was mean. Forgive me?"

"I think tonight will be your turn on the couch," Finias said, pouting.

"Francine, did you really have that young stud sleep on the couch the other night?" said Lindsey.

"My plan was to have him join me later, but it backfired," Francine said.

"That's a shame," said Lindsey. "Finias, why didn't you just wait a bit, then sneak into bed with her?"

"I don't want to talk about this," Finias said.

The road veered to the north and began a steady climb of switchbacks until it flattened out for another half a mile, ending in a wide turnaround just prior to a massive iron gate. There were indeed guards, two sentries posted on either side. Inside the gate, and just off to each side of the road, sat two white jeeps, each with two additional guards.

"Uh oh," Mary said. "I'm going to have to pull up to the gate and use the turnaround. The road here is too narrow for me to maneuver this thing."

Mary brought the car up quickly to the gate, but even the turnaround was not wide enough for the length of the car. Mary had begun a three-point turn when a large hand pounded on her window.

"What do you think you're doing here?" a loud voice boomed. "Hey, open up. What do you think you're doing here, lady?"

The man was dressed head to toe in all black. Black shoes, black pants, black tee shirt, black jacket, and most notably, a black eye patch over his right eye.

Upon seeing him, Elzibeth dropped to the floor, doing her best to remain out of sight.

"It's okay, honey. Everything is going to be alright," Francine said, assuming that Elzibeth was simply frightened.

"No, that guy. The guy with the eye thing. He's the one I jabbed in the eye with my sucker stick," Elzibeth said.

"Oh my God, Mary, you've got to get us out of here," Francine shrieked.

Mary, with quiet calm and steely reserve, threw the car in reverse, spinning the wheel to the right as she did so, knocking the man to the ground. She slammed the beast into gear and smashed down on the gas, and the big car roared into action.

The gates opened, and the jeeps took off in hot pursuit. Mary kept the gas to the floor until they entered the switchbacks. The jeeps were gaining ground quickly on the big car, even as Mary took up both lanes, drifting sideways into each corner.

Shots rang out from behind, and a pinging noise could be heard off of the car's windows.

"It's okay. Perino, or Marcon, or whoever bought me this car made sure the glass is bulletproof, as is the car," said Lindsey. "Come to think of it, that probably should have been a sign, right?" Lindsey asked.

The others were too intent on not dying to pay much attention to anything other than survival at the moment and simply ignored her comment.

Mary continued to struggle to maintain control of the beast of a car and said aloud, "No wonder it handles like a bear on skates," as she slid the big car around another corner.

"Oh my God, he's pulling up next to us," Francine said. "He's going to try and run us off the road."

They each looked out the windows to see that "off the road" meant a thousand-foot drop from the cliff to jagged rocks below.

"Mary, please, do something," said Lindsey as the jeep to their left smashed into the car's side, nearly spinning them out.

Mary, not to be outdone, steered sharply left, smashing the pursuing jeep into the cliffside sending it spinning off and over the edge of the canyon.

"One down," Mary shouted, but the maneuver left the big car out of her control. As Mary tried in vain to correct the slide, the car slid uncontrollably to the right, and they were suddenly off the road and falling. Hands shot forward as if to protect themselves from the impending impact with the rocks below. As the car turned nose-down, Elzibeth, not having been buckled in, hit the ceiling. Francine, Mary, and Lindsey screamed in unison, with Finias following a moment later.

As quickly as the car left the road, it was moving through dimensions of time and space and found itself parked under the portico at the entrance to Briarwood with everyone still screaming.

"What just happened?" Francine said. "Oh my God, are we dead?"

"If we are, we've all died and ended up in a strange version of heaven," Finias said.

Elzibeth, now on the floor again, said, "Wow, that was awesome."

"That was no such thing," Francine said. "I nearly swallowed my tongue I was so afraid. Is everyone alright?"

There were stunned nods of agreement that yes, everyone was fine.

"Does anyone know what just happened?" said Lindsey.

"Sure, I thought if you didn't weigh much when I teleported with you, I thought I'd give the car a try," Elzibeth said.

"Elzibeth...I don't know what to say," Francine said. "You, you...teleported a car full of people?"

"Sure, I guessed that if I could do the car, you guys would just come along."

"Elzibeth," Finias said, picking her up from the floor and hugging her. "I think you've earned yourself an ice cream cone."

"An ice cream truck," Mary said.

"A whole frigging Baskin-Robbins," Francine said.

Chapter 49

"What do we do now?" Lindsey asked as they stood just outside of the Grand Entrance.

"I guess we go inside and tell Calderón what we've found," Finias said.

"Mary, do you think you could arrange for us to meet with Calderón? Maybe later for dinner so that we all have a chance to change our underpants after that lovely ride? Say in two hours," Francine said. "And ask if he would like to have Mum and Dad there as well."

"Two hours to change your underpants?" Finias teased.

"Oh, shut up," Francine replied.

"Sure," Mary said in answer to Francine. "It doesn't usually take me long to change from super driver to dinner reservations coordinator."

"Oh, please don't take it that way," Francine said. "It's just that you know how to get hold of Mum and Dad better than I, and you have a pleasant relationship with Calderón. And, can I say, you were amazing today."

Francine moved to her and gave her a hug.

"Thanks, I guess it wouldn't hurt to say goodbye to my old dusty office anyway," Mary said. "While I have Calderón on the phone, I'll remind him that he owes me a new one."

Mary went off to set their dinner arrangement with Calderón at 9:00. When she came back, she told the group that Theodore and Teri would be back to attend, but that Calderón wanted to have dinner brought into his quarters so as not to bother the other diners with their conversation.

They said their goodbyes and went to their individual quarters to change.

Before departing, Finias suggested to Francine that once she had changed, she join him in the Hall of Records and Library as it was still early and he would like to get a start on retracing his steps on the port's network. Francine agreed, and with a small kiss, they set off.

Finias took a quick shower and changed clothes, finding himself at the same computer terminal as before. Fond memories, he thought as he executed commands on the remote workstation.

For more than an hour, he searched folder after folder with no results. Francine came in a while later, looking fresh in a sleeveless lace maxi dress in blue and white floral with color-matched open-toe shoes.

"How many outfits did you buy?" Finias asked upon her arrival.

"Hello to you too, and none of your business," Francine said. "Having any luck?"

"No, it's frustrating looking through all these old folders," Finias said. "There must be thousands of them."

"Why don't you try looking in the new folders first?" Francine suggested. "Just sort them by date."

"Why the new folders?" Finias asked. "Marcon has owned this property for years."

"What if there has been a recent change in ownership?" Francine said. "What bigger splash, other than killing Marcon, could Thaime make than to take ownership of his mansion and then his prized port?"

Finias thought this reasonable, so he searched for the most recently created folders. He then searched each of the folders beginning with the newest for the keyword "Thaime" and received a hit on folder number five. Opening it, he discovered a sub-folder with the oddly given name of "Grim Reaper."

"Look at this, Francine," Finias said. "Thaime fancies himself to be the Grim Reaper."

"Pregmierar, Thaime Pregmierar," Francine said. "It's an anagram."

"What are you talking about?" Finias asked.

"It's an anagram. Thaime Pregmierar. Don't you see? T-H-A-I-M-E equals 'I am the.' His last name is Grim Reaper."

"I always thought it was a stupid name. I just expected it was Icelandic or something," Finias said.

"Oh, be quiet and just open the folder," Francine said.

Finias did. A deed to slip number 36 of the Grand Port Harbor did now, in fact, grant ownership and full usage rights to Thaime.

"How about that," Finias said. "Good show, Francine."

"Just a bit of luck and a little intuition," Francine said.

"Maybe I should hang around with you more often. Say for the rest of my life and see if some of that good luck rubs off," Finias said.

"Maybe you should," Francine said, then kissed him.

Finias and Francine stayed in the Hall of Records and Library until a quarter of the hour, looking up the shipping manifests for slip number 36. Marcon, or now Thaime, was expecting several containers to be dropped on Thursday, the 22nd, which was but a few days from now. The manifest suggested their load to be machine parts.

"That's an awful lot of machine parts, don't you think?" Francine said.

"Yes," Finias agreed. "It is."

Finias broke the mental connection he held at the other end and gathered his notes to leave. On the way out, they said their goodnights to the security guard.

"Any trouble finding your pencil tonight, miss?" he asked playfully.

"Haven't started looking yet, but the night is still young and full of promise," Francine said with a smile as she took Finias's hand.

The guard broke into a wide grin and said, "You two take care."

"You too," they both said, giggling a bit as they moved quickly away.

Chapter 50

All had arrived for the night's meeting, and after exchanging pleasantries, casual conversation drifted about. Eventually, the group took their seats at the table to eat. Tonight's dinner consisted of garlic and thyme butter-basted rib-eye steaks, a Roquefort soufflé, spring peas with new potatoes, herbs, and watercress, followed by a Faro salad with fennel and arugula.

"Eating light tonight, I see," Theodore said.

"My hope is that the food tonight will make me sleepy so that I may doze through the bad news which I am sure I am to hear, my dear Theodore," Calderón said.

Elzibeth was pleased to see that she had been served nothing green and took delight in her hot dogs and fries, along with her shake and a bowl of chocolate pudding.

"Shall we mix dinner with what happened today, or do you want to save that for later?" Mary asked.

"Good to see one of us is on her toes tonight," Calderón said. "I myself would prefer to indulge in this lovely meal, then retire early for the evening."

Lindsey gave Calderón a knowing look, and they exchanged smiles. This, of course, was noticed by Francine, who gave Finias's arm a squeeze as if to say, "Isn't that exciting?"

Calderón continued, "But I'm afraid that is not to be, so unless there are exceptions, I propose that we get straight to the matters at hand that you have so graciously come here to share."

"I suppose I should start," Lindsey said. "Being that I was the one who started all this nonsense."

"Don't be silly, dear," Calderón said. "This nonsense started long before you. You've simply become tangled up in it a bit more than the rest of us."

"Thank you," Lindsey said, flashing Calderón a smile. "You are such a dear. So, getting straight to it, we set off and were successful in finding the location of the mansion."

"But we got stuck at the turnaround at the gate, and one of the guards attacked my window," Mary said.

"It was the guy I poked in the eye with the stick of my sucker," Elzibeth said.

"Then we were flying down the road and sliding around corners going down this mountain," Finias said.

"Mary was driving lights out," Francine said. "She was slinging that big car around corners like you couldn't believe, but the jeeps were just too nimble and they caught us and tried to run us off the road."

"Jeeps?" Teri interrupted.

"Yes, two jeeps came out of the gate and chased us down," Mary said. "No matter what I tried, I just couldn't shake them in that big, heavy car."

"So then, one of them slammed his jeep into our side, so Mary smashed him into the cliff and spun him over the edge. But in doing so, she lost control, and we started falling into the canyon below," Lindsey said. "And just as we were about to smash into the rocks..."

"I brought the car back here," Elzibeth said.

Calderón, Theodore, and Teri had all stopped chewing, and despite not having swallowed, sat with their mouths agape.

"I think I would like a brandy," Teri said.

"Whiskey for me," Theodore said. "And make it a double if you don't mind."

"I as well," Calderón said.

"Please, allow me," Finias said. "Anybody else?"

All but Elzibeth said yes, and brandy, whiskey, and wine were served by Finias.

236

"That is some tale," Theodore said, taking a long pull from his glass. "Can you go over again the part as to how you ended up back here rather than smashed to pieces on the rocks?"

"Elzibeth teleported us back," Francine said. "Actually, she teleported the car. We were just along for the ride."

"I see," Theodore said, taking another drink, having, of course, not understood at all.

"This is most unusual," Teri said. "Elzibeth, you teleported a carload of people?"

"Yeah, like I told these guys, I figured if I could do the car, they would probably come along."

"I see. I think," Teri said, somewhat dumbfounded.

"It was no big deal," Elzibeth said. "I was mad at those guys anyway for trying to knock us off the road, so maybe that helped."

"So anyway, here we are," Lindsey said. "All safe and sound."

"And nobody was hurt?" Teri asked. "You are all unscathed?"

"I screamed so hard that I lost my voice, but it seems to have recovered," Francine said.

"Well, all good things must come to an end, am I right, Theodore?" Finias said.

Francine smacked him in the back of the head.

"Ouch, woman," Finias said, and everyone chuckled.

"So anyway, my underpants didn't survive, but yes, I believe we are all fine," Finias said.

There was some light laughter at this, then some more nervous drinking.

"And this mansion, you believe it can be found again?" Theodore asked.

"Certainly, but driving there will do us no good," Mary said. "The place looked heavily fortified."

"Elzibeth, do you think that if I were to outfit you with the camera we discussed, that you could teleport there and take a look around?"

"Sure. I know how to get to the yellow sign; all I have to do after that is follow the road up the mountain," Elzibeth said.

"You intend to send our daughter back there after what she has just been through?" Teri said.

"Why, yes," Theodore said.

"Don't worry, Mum, it's no big deal. I could do it tonight if you want," Elzibeth said.

"You'll do no such thing," Teri said.

"Your mother is right, Elzibeth," Theodore said. "You'll do no such thing tonight. The camera I have doesn't have night vision capabilities, so you'll have to do it tomorrow."

Teri let out a gasp of exasperation.

"I don't know what I am to do with you two," Teri said. "You are both impossible."

"Why would she need to go back?" Finias asked. "Elzibeth identified the guy with the eye patch as her attacker. He must be of the Order to have conjured up that awful black fog, meaning Thaime must be in control of the mansion."

"Yes, but the people in the jeep were shooting at us," Francine said. "Why use guns and chase us down in jeeps if they were of the Order?"

"They were shooting at you?" Teri asked, alarmed.

"Yes, but the car is bulletproof," Lindsey said.

"Well, that's alright then," Theodore said.

"No, it's far from alright," Teri said, then followed with, "idiot."

"It may be that one of the other syndicate bosses had used members of the Order along with his own gang of soldiers to take control of Marcon's assets," Theodore said. "We need to be sure that's not the case and it is indeed Thaime who is pressing for control. I think that tomorrow it will be in our best interest to at least have Elzibeth do a quick reconnaissance."

"I disagree," Teri said. "Now that we know Thaime has taken ownership of Marcon's slip at the Grand Port Harbor, I believe it safe to assume he has taken the mansion as well."

Finias was stunned by this revelation. "How did you know that Thaime took ownership of the slip? I myself discovered that just today," Finias said.

"I looked up the most recent ownership of slips along the port," Teri said. "It seemed a most logical place to start, being that Thaime was taking control of Marcon's other assets. Thaime was either clumsy in his attempts to hide his taking control of the slip or left it to be easily found by his competitors. He even named the folder Grim Reaper as a joke, I suppose."

Finias looked upset that Teri had upstaged him, so Francine gave him a hug and said, "Ahhh, you poor baby. Back to being a good-for-nothing."

"You are certainly comfortable playing the pick-on-Finias card, aren't you?" Finias said, pulling away.

"Oh, don't be a poop, Shoop," Francine said. "We are all working on this together. As for Thaime, did you know that his name is an anagram for 'I am the Grim Reaper'? He must have had his name changed because that is too ridiculous to believe."

"Yes, very much like Thaime to want to be seen as the baddest of the bad," Teri said.

"Theodore, might you provide us with an update on your ants?" Calderón said. "Or, colonies of."

"The area covered by the growers is staggering. The manufacturing facilities, if you can call them that, are mostly backwoods operations located in remote areas. They are large enough, and sophisticated enough, though, to produce massive quantities of drugs. I've come into satellite imagery from...shall we say...a friend in the government, along with GPS coordinates of the locations of large fields of both poppies and coca, as well as the manufacturing sites of the largest producers. And when I say large, I mean imagine thousands of acres of product. Some of the poppy fields can probably be seen from space."

"And do you have a plan for their eradication?" Calderón asked.

"As you know, I've just begun my research into this. I was fortunate to have government cooperation, though they are as interested in the destruction of these operations as we are. My contacts were very happy to have us intercede in areas across the border where they have no jurisdiction. The next step, which is currently in the works, is to assemble a small army of the Order to destroy the crops and work sites. My expectation is that these multiple operations will take place within the next few days."

"And what will become of the workers and the many soldiers posted as security?" Calderón asked.

"The soldiers' weapons will be rendered useless in such a way as not to cause harm to their person or persons. The workers themselves will be given small bags of gold, as they are but poor people seeking to make a living. They are not of the cartels, and it is our expectation that with enough money to live out their years, they will not return. We will ask them to be on their way, and the product already produced, along with all chemicals and means of manufacture, will be destroyed. As will all the agricultural product."

"What will keep the soldiers from forcing the workers back to start up new sites or going after their gold once your men are gone?" Finias asked.

"They will be temporarily blinded for a period of six weeks. With their firearms disabled and little ability to purchase others once the cartels fall apart it is my belief that our operation will be successful in thwarting their ability to re-establish. For a time anyway," Theodore said.

"You mentioned that these operations will take place in a matter of a few days," Finias said. "Marcon, or Thaime, I guess, is expecting a shipment of a number of containers at the port on the 22nd. If that is not too soon for you, maybe we can hit the port at the same time you have your men take down the production capabilities."

"And you suspect these containers to be carrying something other than legal goods?" Calderón asked.

"Seven forty-foot containers of machine parts according to the manifest. Seems like an awful lot, don't you think?"

"Yes, yes it does," Calderón said.

"Theodore, when will you know if the 22nd is a viable date?" Calderón asked.

"Later today or if not, by noon tomorrow," Theodore said.

"Finias, do you and Francine have a plan for the port?" Calderón asked.

"Simple, we go in and smack them in the mouth," Finias said.

"Now you're back to mister smack-em'-in-the-mouth," Francine said. "First, that's not a plan. And second, when have you ever smacked someone in the mouth?"

"I'm thinking right now might be a good time to start," Finias said.

"That's not funny. We need to come up with a viable plan," Francine said. "We will have something to you in the morning as well."

"Very good," Calderón said. "Unless there are other matters that I may have overlooked, I suggest everyone retire for the evening and get some rest. It looks like you all will soon be very busy."

"That means separate beds for you two," Lindsey said, looking at Finias and Francine.

"Lindsey," Francine said, surprised.

"Just sayin', Miss Brownie Mix."

Chapter 51

"Elzibeth, do you think you'll be alright tonight?" Francine asked as the three of them made their way to their rooms.

"What do you mean?" Elzibeth asked.

"I don't know. You just seemed a little upset at what happened at Lindsey's the other night," Francine said. "Do you think you might be upset about what happened today?"

"Maybe," Elzibeth said. "Parts of today were fun, and other parts were scary. If I get scared, I'll just go wake up Missy so you guys can be alone."

"Nonsense," Francine said. "Now you stop that kind of talk. I've told you that you are never alone as long as I'm near, okay?" Francine gave her a quick hug of her shoulders.

"Okay," Elzibeth said. "Should I come look for you at Shoop's place?"

"I don't think so," Francine said. "After today, I sort of want to be alone with my thoughts."

"You can be alone with your thoughts with me tonight," Finias said. "Trust me, you won't hear a peep from me as I'll be busying myself with other things."

This got Francine thinking as she remembered fondly their hurried little tryst and that Google thing before the evening meeting in Calderón's quarters.

"Check my room first, dear. If I'm not there, do not hesitate to come wake us up," Francine said.

"Do you guys think you'll be going to sleep right away?" Elzibeth asked.

"Yes," Francine said before Finias could say the wrong thing.

"Okay, we'll see," Elzibeth said. "I'm tired, so I'll probably just see you guys tomorrow."

They all said their goodnights, and Elzibeth went on her way.

"It's still early. Would you take a walk with me?" Finias asked.

"I don't know, it's been rather a rough day," Francine said, thinking again of becoming comfortable in bed with Finias.

"Please," Finias said, stopping to take her hands in his.

Francine looked somewhat surprised by this, and sensing it was somehow important to Finias, she obliged to go.

The night was bright with the full moon as the two set off. Rather than going to the plateau as Francine expected, Finias took her toward the land bridge, which was now visible.

"Why would the land bridge be visible at this hour?" Francine asked.

"Maybe Mary is going to sneak out and take the limo to a drag race," Finias said.

"I'm sure that driving that car is the last thing Mary wants to do," Francine said.

As they made their way along, they both noted the small twinkling lights that wound their way through the branches of the trees, simulating a starry night. It was warm, still being summer, and a slight breeze tickled the leaves of the trees, creating a pleasant hum as if playing their own melody. The sound and smell of the sea surrounded them, and they took their time walking in silence, holding hands and enjoying just being near.

In what seemed to Finias to be too short a time, they came to the arch announcing their entrance to Brighton Beach. Finias stopped under the arch and took Francine's hands into his.

"Francine, though we have only known each other for what some might consider to be a short time, I feel as if I've been waiting for you my whole life. Aside from being my best friend, you are my everything, and I can't imagine a day alive without you."

At this, Finias went down to one knee and, looking into Francine's eyes as the moon and stars beyond posed as her silhouette, said, "And you are the person who I want to spend the rest of my life with." He produced a ring of such beauty, clarity, and dimension that Francine was too stunned to speak.

"Will you do me the honor of being my wife?" Finias asked.

Finias stood, and Francine hugged him with all of her strength. Tears of what Finias hoped to be of joy trickled from her eyes, and they remained this way for some time as she cried.

"I was kind of hoping to hear the word 'yes,'" Finias said, after what he thought to be too long of a pause.

Francine laughed. "I don't know," she said. "It's not been my childhood dream to marry a knucklehead."

"Not even the world's giantest?" Finias said.

"World's giantest? Well, that's a different story," Francine said, while again hugging him. "Why, what woman wouldn't want to marry a man with the title of world's giantest knucklehead. And yes, of course, yes, yes, yes."

They kissed under the moonlight for some time and talked about how they met and the good times they had shared. They spoke of life and love and the promise of the future, and holding hands, they made their way across the bridge back toward Briarwood.

"Would it be impolite of me to ask where and how you came up with such a beautiful ring?" Francine asked. "You've not been out of my sight for days."

"Tonight, after we arrived at Calderón's, I spoke with him about the day's events and how fleeting life can be," Finias said. "Knowing the potential dangers we are about to face, Calderón excused himself and came back with this ring. It was his mother's and was passed onto him after his father died. He told me to please accept it and in typical Calderón fashion, told me not to waste time giving it to you, suggesting rather forcefully that tonight would be a good time."

"So it was Calderón who made the land bridge visible," Francine said. "And how did he know you wished to marry at all?"

"Yes, it was Calderón," Finias said. "And I don't know. It was as if he knew that when I brought up life being fleeting, that my intent in doing so was to suggest that I was worried that I may never have the chance to at least ask you."

"I'll be. Lindsey was right. He truly is an amazing man," Francine said under her breath.

They strolled along under the lights twinkling in the trees as they enjoyed the rhythm of the fluttering leaves and the feeling in their hearts.

"Finias, why is it that you love me?" Francine asked, hugging his arm in her usual way as they walked. "I've not been overly kind to you with all my teasing and arm socking."

"That's part of your indelible charm, my dear," Finias said. "Like when I said I feel as if I've been waiting for you my whole life. I meant that's how I feel while I wait for you to get ready to go someplace. Just part of you being you."

"Like you are going to die before I finish getting ready?"

"Yes."

"Come on, I'm being serious," Francine said. "I don't even find myself to be overly likable."

"I love you because, to me, there are no others worth all the teasing and socking," Finias said.

"That doesn't sound like much of an answer," Francine said.

"When I was a child, I was told a tale of a princess who was found by her father to be most disagreeable," Finias began. "Finding no way to tame her, he placed her on a mountaintop surrounded by hellfire and guarded by a dragon. The knucklehead who loved her scaled the mountain, slayed the dragon, and walked through the fires of hell to save her. Do you know why?"

"Because he was the 'giantest?'"

"Exactly," Finias said.

Francine socked him.

"Oweee…"

"Heroes don't say 'oweee,'" Francine pointed out.

"Beside the point. You see, he saved her because to him, and maybe only him, despite her being disagreeable, she was worth it," Finias said. "Simple as that. So, count yourself lucky to have found someone so inclined to being socked and teased and thinking in spite of that, you are worth it."

"I do," Francine said.

"I can't wait to hear those words," Finias said.

"Me too," Francine said.

"I have an idea," Finias said. "And please don't ask if it hurt my wee little brain."

Francine laughed and said, "No, not tonight."

"What say we go back to my suite to make our engagement official and find out if you are truly worth it?"

Francine reached out to embrace him and said, "How about finding out right now? We could enjoy the evening and each other right here?"

Francine went to one of the nearby benches lining the walk and patted the seat as a signal for Finias to sit.

"My, you are a most agreeable young woman, aren't you," Finias said.

"Sometimes," Francine said.

"I can't believe I had to entice you into a walk tonight with that Google thing," Finias said.

"Believe me, there is no stronger motivation," Francine said.

"Good to know. So, a seat you say? Yes, good idea. For a second, I thought we were going to try that shower thing again. Without the walls, I'm not sure I could manage," Finias said.

Francine laughed, and with that, Finias took a seat and Francine joined him as one for the first time as an engaged couple.

Chapter 52

Francine kissed Finias on the cheek and stepped out from under the covers to shower after the two had celebrated their engagement that morning.

"I think I'll give Elzibeth a call to make sure she is up and ready for her little tour of Marcon's mansion today," Finias called out over the sound of the shower.

"Okay," Francine said. "Let her know to come by around 8:00 so I might have time to give you a proper scrubbing if you are interested in joining me in the shower."

"Forget the call, it can wait," Finias said, having appeared beside Francine in the shower as if by magic.

"No, not now. Now go. Mum and Dad will be by shortly, and they will be expecting Elzibeth to be here. Call first, soapy you later," Francine said.

With that, Finias made the call and Elzibeth, in her most uncommon way, said that yes, she was dressed and was just waiting for Finias to call.

Upon his return from the seating area, Francine had stepped out of the shower and with only a towel around her head, moved to give Finias a kiss.

Teri and Theodore appeared seated at the table adjacent to the kissing couple, with Theodore shouting, "Oh my!" and Teri, to Francine's surprise, seemed to be admiring Finias's backside before she said, "Maybe you two should get dressed."

Finias and Francine, of course, gave a loud yelp at this intrusion and scattered to the bedroom, hiding whatever parts they could as they went.

When they returned, now fully dressed, the two slunk in and offered their apologies.

"So sorry about that," Finias said. "Maybe it would be best that in the future you came to the door rather than just popping in."

"Yes, certainly," Theodore said. "I believe that Teri and I both owe you an apology. Sometimes we forget that Francine is a grown woman. Fully grown from what I have seen. Thankfully, my retinas didn't burn after seeing my adult daughter in all of her...self."

Changing the subject, Teri said, "Will Elzibeth be along shortly? I would prefer to get this nonsense of her floating about Marcon's mansion behind us."

"Yes, I gave her a call just before the two of you surprised us," Finias said.

"Hey, Shoop," Elzibeth said over the intercom. Her picture now on the television.

"Hey, you," Finias said. "Just a minute."

Finias moved to the door and let her in.

"Hey, Mum, hey Dad," Elzibeth said, as hugs were exchanged.

Elzibeth, in typical fashion, had dressed for the occasion, wearing her bib overalls, white tee shirt underneath, and white tennis shoes.

"So, are you ready for this little event?" Theodore said. I know this is something most unusual for all of us actually, so if you are uncomfortable, even a little bit, or if you are concerned with proceeding you must let us know now.

"I guess it's a little scary to think about, so I'd really rather not. Could we just get it over with?" Elzibeth said.

"Honey, you know you don't have to do this," Teri said, giving Theodore a look. "But it seems your father has his mind made up that you do."

"No big deal," Elzibeth said. "Let's just do it."

And with that, Theodore produced a small camera-like device and placed it upon her head.

After he buckled her in and secured the device, he said, "Now remember not to stop. Just come back safely, and we will take a look at what you come up with."

"Okay," Elzibeth said.

And with that, she left.

Chapter 53

Elzibeth, having found the yellow shield-shaped sign with the number "10," began thoughtfully winding her way through the mountain switchbacks. She eventually came upon the place where she had rescued the car and its passengers from destruction. She let out a soft sigh.

"Man, that was close," she thought to herself.

She arrived at the gate and took a moment to capture Eye Patch and his gang standing sentry. She was pleased to see Eye Patch wearing a full-length cast on his left leg, presumably from when Mary backed the car into him while trying to maneuver the big vehicle out of the turnaround. "Serves you right for picking on a little kid," she said out loud for no one but herself to hear.

Remembering not to stop, she then made a tour of the grounds, beginning with a complete loop of the perimeter, then circling in closer to spot individually each of the thirty-something guards posted within.

Having been shown a picture of Thaime and having recognized his cruel down-turned shark-like smile, she came near to a man she thought to be him, lounging peacefully on a chaise by the pool. She had just zoomed in for a closer look when what she thought was a condor landed on her head and began pecking at the camera.

Elzibeth stopped, trying to shoo away what she found to be a pigeon, but the bird seemed not to be in a mood to leave.

"Go, come on, get," Elzibeth said, having paused in space while swatting at her head.

"What the?" She heard Thaime say.

"The girl. It's the girl. Take her," Thaime said, as he tried to extricate himself from his seat.

Fire rang out in random fashion from those having guns rather than gifts, and a round of fireballs exploded around what was supposed to be Elzibeth from the others, lighting up the sky.

Finding things to be a little too hot for the time being, Elzibeth decided the time was right for her to leave, and she popped back into the sitting area of Finias's suite.

"Oh my God, you're on fire, and there's a bird on your head," Teri said, moving quickly to put out a small flame at the back of Elzibeth's pants.

Her hair had been singed as well, and the smell of burning cloth and hair hung in the air. The bird flew off to the kitchen and began poking at a loaf of crusty bread.

"So, how did we make out dear?" Theodore said.

"Theodore? Who cares how she made out with your stupid camera? She was on fire for goodness sake," Teri said.

"Yes, but a small one. Not to worry, dear," Theodore said.

"It is my greatest hope that someday you will grow a brain," Teri said.

Finias and Francine, having been caught off guard as well, moved to see that Elzibeth was indeed okay.

"What on earth happened to you?" Francine said.

"A dumb bird landed on my head," Elzibeth said.

"And this caused you to stop, didn't it?" Finias said.

"Knucklehead and now master of the obvious. Lucky me," Francine said.

They all shot her a look but chose not to comment. Elzibeth, appearing not to notice, continued.

"Yeah, but just for a moment," Elzibeth said. "Then the guys with guns started shooting at me, and the other guys threw some pretty good fireballs. I guess that's how I caught fire."

"My poor baby, come here," Teri said, as she gave Elzibeth a hug and sat her on her lap.

"Here, let's get this stupid thing off your head," Teri said, removing the camera, which she threw at Theodore.

"There, take that ridiculous thing and go do with it what you will," Teri said. "I'll stay here with Elzibeth."

"I'll get you some juice," Finias said, more to be excused from the situation than to be polite.

Francine followed him to the kitchen.

"Finias, these little excursions are getting out of control. We need to move to put an end to this nonsense," Francine said.

"I agree. Tomorrow we move," Finias said.

Chapter 54

Lunch was arranged by Mary, and the eight of them took their seats around the now familiar, though oddly mismatched table. Francine, not wanting to interrupt the purpose of the meeting, had asked Finias if it would be okay if she left her ring behind.

"Of course," Finias said. "It would serve us well to wait for such an announcement."

Calderón sat at one end with Lindsey by his side, with Theodore and Teri at the other. Francine sat next to Finias in the middle to Calderón's left, with Mary and Elzibeth sitting opposite.

Calderón gave Finias a look as if to suggest why Francine was not wearing her ring. Finias just shrugged his shoulders, providing no answer.

"So Theodore, it appears that things are coming to a head rather quickly, are they not?" Calderón began.

"Yes indeed," Theodore said. "Elzibeth was able to secure footage of the mansion and its occupants this morning. If you will allow, I would like to show you what she found."

"Of course," Calderón said.

Theodore moved to the far wall and pressed a small button. A large white screen descended from the ceiling, and a projection unit arose from what the others had thought to be a sculpture of the Greek god Zeus. Theodore plugged in a thumb drive from his pocket and hit the play button on what would be the video feed from Elzibeth's head-mounted camera.

The video clearly showed the guards and jeeps standing watch at the entry, as it did others stationed at various points around the property. Suddenly, the camera paused, showing the face of Thaime as he lounged poolside. The image shook side to side, and the voice of Elzibeth was clear in her intention to shoo away something that was bothering her head. A volley of gunfire ensued at first, then a number of yellowish-orange globes appeared to fill the sky. Then, nothing as Elzibeth teleported back to Finias's suite.

"Dear Lord," Mary said first, then others followed with similar sayings.

"Elzibeth, I've been thought to be the daredevil here, but I am nothing in comparison to you," Mary said.

"I shouldn't have stopped, is all," Elzibeth said. "That dumb bird messed things up."

"Regardless," said Lindsey. "You are most amazing by any standard."

"I guess," Elzibeth said, though smiling a little.

"And you did all this just this morning?" said Lindsey. "I've barely begun my day."

Lindsey gave Calderón a knowing look, which he acknowledged by taking her hand in his. Francine took Finias's hand in hers under the table and leaned to give him a kiss on the cheek.

Having seen this, Theodore said, "I think that I have seen enough of that from the two of you this morning."

"Oh, leave them be," Teri said. "Things are about to get dicey here, and who knows how long it might be, if ever, before they get to do that again."

Teri's words held true to those around the table, and there were subtle nods of acceptance that indeed things were about to get dicey. Mary, for one, considered the situation rather exhilarating and suggested she would like to be a part of things.

"Mary my dear, you are not one given to this type of work," Calderón said. "I insist that you remain here in the protections of Briarwood."

"For what purpose, Headmaster? To continue to make meal reservations and to notify others of their guests? I think not,"

Mary said. "I will not stand idly by while others risk their lives for me."

"Very well," Calderón said. "I am but an old man wishing for things to remain as they are. But trying times are ahead, and I know that your help in such matters may be most welcome."

"Theodore, have you assembled the arsenal of men necessary to strike tomorrow's targets?" Calderón said. "Now that we know that Thaime is indeed poised to take over Marcon's forces in order to mount a great push toward disrupting police order, I am hopeful you have the army you need in order to sever his ties to the colonies of distribution of drugs which feed his appetite for power."

"Yes, I believe us to be ready," Theodore said.

With this came a knock at the door, and upon answering, Calderón let in two waiters with carts.

"Frankly, I've no appetite at the moment," Theodore said. "Though the food smells wondrous."

"Relax and enjoy, my good friend," Calderón said. "For today's meal may be your last."

Chapter 56

Lunch was expertly served by a pair of waiters, as was customary. Each of those seated received a mixture of heirloom tomato, bagna cauda, and lap cheong topped with crème fraîche and fine herbs. Elzibeth, for her part, was most pleased to see a simple grilled cheese sandwich with fries and a Coke.

The group ate mostly in silence with occasional nods to the delicate flavors of the food. Wine was served chilled, and the waiters departed at Calderón's request, suggesting that the dishes be cleared at a later time.

"A toast, my good friends," Calderón began. "To life, to love, to a return to simpler times."

"Yes, to simpler times," Theodore said.

"And to love," Teri said, giving Theodore a jab with her elbow.

"Yes, to love," Theodore said.

"I don't suppose this is necessary to say, but I wish all of you luck tomorrow," Calderón said, hoisting his glass.

"Finias, are you prepared for what it is that you plan to do to take apart Thaime's operations at the port?" Teri asked.

"Yes, but I'm afraid it will involve Elzibeth. And Mary, if you will be so kind as to lend a hand," Finias said.

"Of course," Mary said.

"What do you mean by this? Having Elzibeth involved?" Teri said.

"Marcon, or Thaime now, I guess, is expecting delivery of seven sea-going containers at the port early tomorrow morning. We will not know what is contained within those without Elzibeth's help," Finias said.

"And how will she help you in that regard?" Teri asked.

"I can see inside of stuff," Elzibeth said.

"You what?" Teri said.

Everyone turned to look at Elzibeth.

"Yeah, I didn't know I could until I couldn't find sis the other night when I was worried about what happened at Lindsey's. I knocked on her door, but when she didn't answer, I could see inside that she wasn't there, so I went to Shoop's place and saw that she was in bed," Elzibeth said.

"And you knew about this?" Teri said, looking to Finias.

"Not at first, but it became apparent. I asked her about it just before we went to scare the crap out of Lindsey," Finias said.

"The what?" Calderón said, somewhat taken aback.

"Oh, nothing," said Lindsey. "They just came pounding on my door suggesting they were Marcon."

"What in the devil's name has been going on around here?" Calderón said.

The four of them grew silent before Francine spoke.

"You see, there was some friction between Lindsey and myself at first. Her being as beautiful as she is, and my being unaware that she considered me so. We have made amends, of course," Francine said.

"Of course," Calderón said, giving Lindsey a sideways look.

"Lindsey, I must say, I'll not allow you to partake in the matters at hand tomorrow," Calderón said.

"Of course not, dear. I wouldn't expect you to," said Lindsey. "So, what time do we leave? And please don't say 7:00 a.m."

"No, not 7:00 a.m. 3:00 a.m.," Finias said. "Do you really wish to join us?"

"I hadn't considered the hour, but I suppose with the right company, I may well just be up anyway," said Lindsey. "Do you suppose you too will be…up?"

Calderón looked at her and said, "Yes, I suppose I will be. And I too think that I'll not let you out of my sight. So, what will this entail for us, might I ask?"

"We will have to fit in somewhat. I've taken the liberty of producing pictures of the port workers' uniforms. Mary, if you will be so kind as to produce and provide one for each of the five of us. Elzibeth, you can wear what you want as you will not be seen," Finias said.

"Certainly, I can't wait to be so helpful," Mary said, sarcastically. "Of course, it would be easier in a new, comfortable office."

"Yes, of course," Calderón said. "It is unlike me to forget such things. It shall be done before the dishes are cleared."

"I propose the ladies drop in just inside the slip's armed personnel, then they make friendly with the guards and workers while you and I cover Elzibeth as she goes about dumping the containers into the bay. Regardless of what she finds, we will take our cue from her. Once she has examined all seven, she is to teleport each of the containers into the bay and sink them irrespective of what they hold.

Elzibeth, you do what you do as quickly as possible. No need to teleport the containers too far, maybe a hundred feet or so. Remember not to stop, sweetheart, and check the contents of each container first.

Headmaster, if you will, I would ask that you destroy the three gantry cranes which service the dock.

Lindsey, you, Mary, and Francine will pretend to be new hires. Play the men up and use your particular assets to keep them busy.

I will be between containers providing cover for Elzibeth. Everyone clear?" Finias said.

"No, not at all," came the unanimous reply.

"So, then what? I'm to try and play nice to the guards in a dock worker's uniform?" said Lindsey. "What if I were to wear a skirt, high heels, and a wet white tank top?"

"No, you will not," Calderón said. "Believe me, my dear, with your looks, you could wear an onion sack and still be bewitching."

"Aren't you sweet," said Lindsey. "Would it be alright if I missed a button or two?"

"Use your charms as you wish, just not overly so, my dear," Calderón said.

"Teri and I will be leading the charge against the production of crops and the manufacturing facilities," Theodore said.

"I will lead the men to destroy the fields," Teri said.

"And I will lead the other units to unhand the guards, set the village folk free, then destroy their manufacturing capabilities," Theodore said.

"And Elzibeth, you are to quickly ascertain the contents of each container. If there are drugs, dump the container close to the slip so that when notified, the authorities can discover the contents. If not drugs, take them out to sea and dump them farther out to avoid their retrieval," Finias said.

"How will I know they are drugs?" Elzibeth said.

"I suspect, with the long trip of six weeks on the water, that they will be full. If they contain bags of stuff that looks like flour or maybe bags of pills blue in color, dump them. If in doubt, dump them near the slip and the port authorities can work it out later," Finias said.

"Okay," Elzibeth said, in her usual understated manner.

"Well, it looks like a rather late start, or an early morning," Calderón said. "Might I suggest we get to our quarters for some sleep? Barring anything unforeseen, I will expect all of you to be back here posthaste once the tasks we are to perform are finished."

"And how do you propose we spend what might be our last night on earth?" Finias said to Francine.

"Together," is all she said.

Chapter 57

At 2:45 a.m. the six of them met in the Grand Entrance. Teri and Theodore had left early to rally the troops. The mood was grim, possibly due to the task at hand, but more likely the hour in which it was to take place. The women greeted each other with welcomes and made suggestions on how to look their best in their drab olive-green pants and buttoned-up tan shirts. Elzibeth stood idly by, looking fresh and ready to go. Finias and Calderón shook hands, preferring not to say anything.

"Let's all wish Teri and Theodore Godspeed in their quest, and prepare ourselves for what may come," Calderón said. There were small shakes of their heads and a whisper of "Godspeed."

"So, let us be off," Calderón said. And with that, they went.

Thaime's newly owned section of the port was massive, over half a mile long and very busy. The tall gantry cranes attended to a ship so large it appeared to fill the entire slip. Bright lights lit up the terrain as workers moved to situate the newly arrived containers side by side, using hand signals and radios to convey their commands to the crane operators.

Lindsey, Francine, and Mary were hardly noticed as they moved about the busy dock. Not knowing what to do next, Francine suggested that she move to the north, Mary cover the entrance, and Lindsey move to the south. Both Finias and Calderón appeared dockside, now pretending to work to release the massive ropes which held the container ship at bay.

"Hey you," called one of the dock workers to Calderón. "Release that spring line." "And you," he said to Finias. "Let loose that forward line."

At this, the dock master gave the signal to the crew to begin pulling bags. Finias wasn't sure what any of that meant, but he saw other workers on board the great ship beginning to pull up large black bulbs used to cushion the ship from its landing against the slip.

As final preparations were completed, a fleet of tugboats began a choreographed dance to maneuver the huge ship to sea.

Elzibeth, unbeknownst to anyone, had begun her inspection of the containers. Sensing the moment to be critical, Calderón, knowing Elzibeth was close to moving the containers, suddenly blew out the circuit to the station-mounted floodlights used to illuminate the slip, plunging everything into darkness.

Finias, caught somewhat off-guard by this, looked out and could now just barely see the silhouette of the huge ship as it was escorted to sea by the fleet of tugs.

The grounds crew, also caught off-guard by the loss of light, left the newly arrived containers and headed for the main terminal, shouting, bumping, and feeling their way as they went to try and restore power to the lights. This gave Finias a reprieve from his anxiety, as their absence he knew would allow Elzibeth a bit more time to complete her task.

Lindsey, unnoticed, buttoned her top and stood still behind a forklift. Mary, standing near the guard shack with a guard who took the opportunity to bump into her in the dark and feel her breast, kneed the guard in his groin and took off toward the slip, hoping to find Elzibeth. She called out to Elzibeth to answer any questions she might have about whether to dump a particular container and, if so, where.

Elzibeth, not knowing exactly what she was looking for, had already dumped six of the newly arrived containers into the bay before she heard Mary's shouts. Two of the containers were full of bags of a white substance, which she scuttled just off the dock. Upon arriving at the seventh and last container, she was surprised to hear voices. She looked inside to see maybe sixty or seventy young women, most in their teens, looking scared and malnourished. The smell was foul, and two of the young women appeared to have perished and were set to one end. Elzibeth retched and left the container, moving into the blackness.

"Francine," she yelled at the top of her lungs. "Over here, this one has people in it."

All heard her cry and moved to where they thought her to be. Suddenly, a bright light appeared. It was Thaime, and he was angry. Seeing both Finias and Mary move to the last of the containers, he lofted what Francine thought to be a lightning bolt, and blasted Mary into the sea beyond.

"No," shouted Francine. Thaime had measured another bolt and was about to launch it toward Finias but Francines shout prepared him and he dodged away teleporting in behind Thaime as the bolt sent containers sprawling and dumping into the sea.

Sensing he was near, Thaime turned to confront Finias. "So, here we are. I'll tell you what, you give up the little girl and I'll allow you to live."

Finias laughed a shallow laugh and said, "Thaime, you know this is not going to end well for you. You are outnumbered here and though I know the authorities will do no good going after the likes of you, I will hunt you to the ends of the earth."

Both men stood wary of the others powers. Finias was an unknown to Thaime as he had no knowledge of his abilities and he could not discount the fact that someone, possibly this man had destroyed his home.

Both men stood ready to fire when Francine came up behind Finias and said, "prepare to die you low life backstabbing weasel."

Thaime took advantage of the time it took for Francine to berate him and he simply vanished.

"Took a bit too long with that." Couldn't you have just killed him or maybe have just run up and socked him in the arm?" Finias said.

"I'd sock you a good one, but I'm just glad you are alive. God, and Mary, she's...de." Francine began but was unable to finish the thought.

The five of them gathered near the guard shack, whose occupants, as well as the port crew, had been immobilized by Francine. They found themselves without words, so deep was the feeling of loss for their dear departed Mary.

Elzibeth said, "I know this is a lousy time to bring this up, but we need to get those people out of that container. I'm pretty sure by the smell they're dying in there."

"Yes, of course. Do you think you can teleport them to the local authorities? And if possible to open the doors and allow them to be found? And please, instruct the authorities that Briarwood has excellent medical facilities as well as room for all if they should be in need of shelter and that all would be welcome to stay if they so choose." Calderón said.

"Sure," was all she said, and she was gone.

"If I may suggest, the rest of you might want not to be near as I intend to put this slip out of business in the name of our dear lost Mary," Calderón said.

And with that, he grew to a size the likes of which none had seen and created an energy burst the size of a stadium, blowing the half-mile-long slip into dust and boiling ocean.

Chapter 58

The loss of Mary took everyone by surprise. Theodore and Teri, having returned from a mostly successful mission, also mourned the unfortunate loss of six of their fine soldiers.

Seven coffins, one empty, lined the entrance to Briarwood. All had said their goodbye's and there was nothing more to be said or done. A fleet of waiting cars stood ready, as each of the caskets, draped in the cloth of the Briarwood Crest, were moved to their final resting place.

Francine, after having consulted with both Calderón and Finias, had placed her ring in the empty casket of Mary hoping that she too would find love in another place and in another time.

The weeks ahead passed slowly, but time it would seem as always began to heal the wounds felt by all.

The news of the destruction of the port, along with the death of Marcon and the obliteration of cartel operations across the border were heralded as the beginning of the end of any desire of others to attempt to control all syndicate operations as had been the goal of Thaime and Marcon.

The young women, who's futures were meant by Thaime to be as horrible as their habitation in the containers, were brought to Briarwood's medical facility by the authorities, and were nursed back to health in a most successful and fanciful way and were offered the opportunity to either be joined again with their native families, or to become new members of the Briarwood family. All sixty-eight of them stayed.

Finias and Francine, along with Calderón and Lindsey, took a bit of time to go shopping in a northern city where rings were selected and private plans were made for a dual wedding.

Walking along under the northern city lights, Calderón stopped the four of them most unexpectedly in front of a real estate office he had scouted.

"You know, the two of you will need to find a place of your own now that you are to be wed," Calderón said.

"Why, we haven't had any discussions regarding that, but I suppose you are right," Francine said.

"Yes, I suppose he is," Finias said, looking at Francine.

"Lindsey had a most splendid idea regarding this," Calderón said. "She thought that it would be wise to post a member of the Order in Marcon's mansion so that others of that ilk would not be tempted to take it as their own trophy."

"And Calderón, wishing to reward you for your bravery and valiant efforts thought it nice to present the mansion to you as a wedding gift from all at Briarwood," said Lindsey.

Stunned, Finias and Francine exchanged anxious looks, then Finias said, "what better than a knuckle head and his lovely wife to protect such an asset. What do you think Francine?"

"It is such a generous offer. Of course we would be honored," Francine said. "But, what about Elzibeth?"

"With forty thousand square feet, I'm sure that we will be able to find space for her," Finias said.

"Really," Francine said. "You would be okay with her staying with us? At least when not in school at Briarwood?"

"Francine, it would not be home without her," Finias said. "And, it's not like you can't just pop in to visit her at Briarwood at any time in case you miss her."

"She may have no need to miss her at all," Calderón said. "That is, if you Francine would do myself and Briarwood the great honor of being my personal assistant in the absence of our dear departed Mary. That is until you decide it is time to have a little Elzibeth of your own."

"Mary Elzibeth Shoop has a nice ring to it I think if we ever should," Francine said. "And, Finias, if it is okay with you, I would like to say yes to both the home and the job."

"Okay. I guess that if you'll be gone all the time, I could always get that dog I spoke of," Finias said.

Finias turned and hugged Francine and said, "I'm just teasing. I've learned that if you are happy, then my happiness is guaranteed."

"My, you have trained him well," said Lindsey.

They laughed and Francine hugged both Lindsey and Calderón in thanks as did Finias.

Chapter 59

The day began with a slight warm breeze teasing the blades of grass upon the plateau. Elzibeth, in a smart white dress and matching shoes, walked down the aisle of the wedding area, tossing rose petals to either side of the seating as she moved to take her place under a large arch of intertwined brambles and wildflowers. Teri and Theodore were to conduct the ceremony, and the two of them stood at the center of the arch looking pleased.

Elzibeth moved to her mother's side and asked, "Mum, Missy told me that sometimes the brides cry at weddings. Why is that?"

"Well, dear, they are simply practicing for what's to come," Teri said.

Elzibeth appeared puzzled by this, but her attention was soon drawn to the two brides-to-be as they prepared to walk down the aisle.

Finias and Calderón waited under the arch as drums began to play a low melody out of sight, and a baritone voice started a rendition of "Por Ti Volare." Francine and Lindsey moved down the aisle together in matching white wedding dresses, both smiling brightly. To those in attendance, they appeared to shimmer slightly, radiating an essence of confidence and inner peace, knowing they were about to embark on a new journey called life with the ones they loved.

As the four stood, two on each side of the heart-shaped white cloth doused with red rose petals, Theodore and Teri took turns asking each couple to recite their vows as they were wed.

As each of the four had decided to write and recite their own vows, it was something of a surprise to Francine when Finias said at the end, "and to many more days of our efforts together being expended for the sake of bettering this world."

At this, cheers rang out from all on the plateau as doves and monarch butterflies were released into the gentle breeze. The two couples kissed, not for the last time.

Made in the USA
Columbia, SC
04 August 2024

e55b1253-0a10-49aa-801b-2d1907b0dd6fR01